NUCLEAR MISSILES TARGETED EARTH FROM SPACE

"The Man wants the Venture Star back at all costs, and we're an expendable part of the equation, pure and simple."

"That's fine with me," Hawkins said, smiling grimly, "just as long as I know the score up front."

Brognola let his gaze fall on each man in the War Room. Though he stayed safely behind each time he ordered these men to put their lives on the line, he felt closer to them than to anyone else in the world. Every time he sent them into action, he steeled himself to the reality that some of them might not return. Their skill and experience had seen them through more times than he could count.

This time, there was a better-than-average chance that they would all be lost, but he still had to send them.

"Gentlemen. Good luck."

Other titles in this series:

STONY MAN II
STONY MAN III
STONY MAN IV
STONY MAN V
STONY MAN VI
STONY MAN VII
STONY MAN VIII
#9 STRIKEPOINT
#10 SECRET ARSENAL
#11 TARGET AMERICA
#12 BLIND EAGLE
#13 WARHEAD
#14 DEADLY AGENT
#15 BLOOD DEBT
#16 DEEP ALERT
#17 VORTEX
#18 STINGER
#19 NUCLEAR NIGHTMARE
#20 TERMS OF SURVIVAL
#21 SATAN'S THRUST
#22 SUNFLASH
#23 THE PERISHING GAME
#24 BIRD OF PREY
#25 SKYLANCE
#26 FLASHBACK
#27 ASIAN STORM
#28 BLOOD STAR
#29 EYE OF THE RUBY
#30 VIRTUAL PERIL
#31 NIGHT OF THE JAGUAR
#32 LAW OF LAST RESORT
#33 PUNITIVE MEASURES
#34 REPRISAL
#35 MESSAGE TO AMERICA
#36 STRANGLEHOLD
#37 TRIPLE STRIKE
#38 ENEMY WITHIN
#39 BREACH OF TRUST
#40 BETRAYAL
#41 SILENT INVADER
#42 EDGE OF NIGHT
#43 ZERO HOUR
#44 THIRST FOR POWER

DON PENDLETON'S

MACK BOLAN®

STONY MAN®

STAR VENTURE

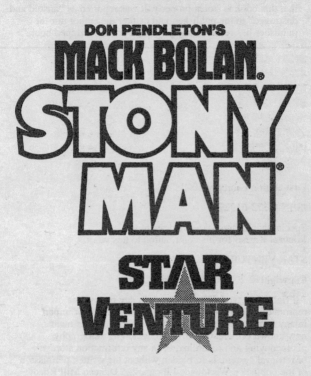

A GOLD EAGLE BOOK FROM

WORLDWIDE®

TORONTO • NEW YORK • LONDON
AMSTERDAM • PARIS • SYDNEY • HAMBURG
STOCKHOLM • ATHENS • TOKYO • MILAN
MADRID • WARSAW • BUDAPEST • AUCKLAND

First edition February 2000

ISBN 0-373-61929-4

Special thanks and acknowledgment to Michael Kasner for his contribution to this work.

STAR VENTURE

Printed in U.S.A.

STAR VENTURE

CHAPTER ONE

Palmdale, California

Carl Lyons's eyes swept the sunbaked tarmac of the Lockheed Martin aerospace complex one last time as he listened to the reports of the security teams on his earphone. The reflection of the China-blue California sky made his mirrored sunglasses look like flattened Christmas tree balls. It was another beautiful day in paradise, but Lyons wasn't buying it, not today. He was on the job.

When he received the final team report, he keyed his throat mike. "Control," he said, "this is Sierra Alpha. Security is go."

"Copy security go," the voice of Lockheed Launch Control Palmdale repeated in his earphone. "Venture Star is cleared for launch countdown."

Lyons could barely see the launch site east of the main building, but the vehicle on the pad, the Venture Star, was about to take exploration of space into a new era. It was fitting that this revolutionary vehicle was a product of the most advanced aerospace engineering facility on the planet, the famed Lockheed Martin Skunk Works.

Since the early days of World War II, Lockheed's design team had called itself the Skunk Works, and it was the stuff of aeronautical legend. America's first operational jet fighter, the F-80 Shooting Star, had been the first Black Project. Though it had been too late to see combat in World War II, the pioneering Shooting Star fought the first jet-to-jet dogfights in the Korean War, and its descendants went on to become mainstays of American air power for decades.

Following that early leap into the Jet Age, the Skunk Works kept the lead by creating spectacular aircraft. The F-104 Starfighter was the first fighter to break Mach unity going straight up. The infamous high-flying U-2 spy plane, the futuristic SR-71 Blackbird spy plane and the F-117 Stealth Fighter were all Lockheed products. Now that the cold war arms race had ended, at least for the moment, the Skunk Works was engaged in its first ever civilian White Project, and it was a spacecraft.

The Venture Star was a radical new design and the first of the second-generation space shuttles that would become the workhorses of America's renewed exploration of space. They would carry the materials into orbit to build the space station *Freedom* and resupply it once it became operational. They would also lift the components of the deep-space vehicles that would be built in orbit and would finally carry men to Mars. The old space shuttles had kept the dream of interplanetary flight alive, but the Venture Star would make it a reality.

The biggest advantage of this new space shuttle over the old Rockwell designs was that it was able to take off and land like any conventional aircraft. Any airport with a runway long enough could serve as a spaceport. No longer would space shuttles need the cumbersome external fuel tanks and solid-fuel boosters of the current vehicles. That had been made possible by the new linear Aerospike rocket engines that powered the Venture Star. Instead of burning the fuel inside a traditional rocket engine bell, the Aerospike engines burned the fuel externally with much greater efficiency.

Though the Venture Star was a civilian project, the security surrounding the craft's development had been as tight as for any of Lockheed's military Black Projects. Nonetheless, there had been problems with the program. Accidents had happened that would have been considered sabotage had they occurred in a military project. When Lockheed's own security force wasn't able to get a handle on the high-stakes problem, the President had asked Stony Man Farm to send in their security experts, Able Team, to give the Skunk Works a hand.

With the increased security, the accidents ceased and the Venture Star was presented to the public with great fanfare only a few months after its original debut date. The President himself attended the rollout ceremony, where he rededicated the nation to the peaceful exploration of space. Three weeks earlier, the first suborbital flight had gone off without a hitch, and now the new spacecraft was poised to make its first multiorbital flight. If this, too, was successful, the Venture Star would be turned over to NASA for further development, and the Farm would be able to call it another job well-done.

"I'll be glad when that damned thing finally gets turned over to NASA so we can be done with this gig and go home," Carl Lyons said as he turned to his teammate Hermann "Gadgets" Schwarz, standing beside him on the observation platform atop the Lockheed headquarters building.

"I'm in no hurry to wrap this up, Ironman," Schwarz replied. "This place is unbelievable, and I'm having a lot of fun."

"But you've been screwing around with all the tech weenies, not trying to keep some asshole from dropping a wrench on something that breaks easily. And, if that's not enough, now I've got to make sure that some wild-eyed fanatic doesn't try to sneak in and plant a bomb in it because he thinks space flight is the work of the devil."

As the security expert, Lyons had argued for transporting the Venture Star to the Groom Lake, Nevada, test site, the famed Area 51 of UFO lore, before conducting its test flights. The security at that remote base was the tightest in the world, but his suggestion had been overruled at the highest level in the name of PR. The Venture Star was a civilian project, and the American taxpayers had the right to see what their money was being spent on and they had come in droves.

Thousands of spectators were on hand, crowding the perimeter fence around the Palmdale facility as they did at Kennedy Space Flight Center for the shuttle launches. State and local police, as well as the Lockheed security force, were keeping an eye on them and, so far, no problems had been reported. That didn't make Lyons feel comfortable, though. He knew the wackos were out there, and he liked his enemies in the open so he could get a clear shot at them.

Lyons was sweeping the tarmac with his field glasses again when a code-four security alert came in over his earphone. A code five was an actual attack, so this had to be big. "We got one," he told Schwarz.

"Launch Control, this is Sierra Alpha," Lyons said, keying his mike. "Request a code-four launch hold. Over."

"Control, roger. Security launch hold in effect."

"What is it?" Schwarz asked.

"A code four," Lyons called over his shoulder as he headed for the stairs.

"Wait for me!"

THE DARK BLUE VAN with the yellow Lockheed Security logo on the side braked to a halt in front of the outside door to Lyons's office in the headquarters building. A four-man security squad jumped out, escorting a man with his hands bound behind his back with plastic restraints. The prisoner had been stripped to his T-shirt and undershorts and, not surprisingly, looked as if he'd been tossed around a bit.

"We caught him coming in behind the bird, sir," the squad leader reported to Lyons. "He was wearing a company jacket and was carrying a forged security pass."

"How close did he get to the bird?"

"Not close at all," the squad leader said. "We nailed him before he got any closer than a quarter of a mile."

Lyons keyed his mike. "Launch Control, this is Sierra Alpha. I'm releasing the code-four security hold."

"Control, roger."

"I'm a journalist," the prisoner protested loudly when Lyons turned to him, "and I claim freedom of the press. I demand that I be released immediately."

A slow smile broke over Lyons's face. "Well, Mr. Media Man, let me give you the facts of life they obviously didn't teach you in journalism school. For the record, you are in violation of the National Security Act and you are in deep shit."

"What are you talking about?" the man said. "I'm an accredited journalist, and I demand that I be allowed to talk to my editor and my lawyer."

"You aren't going anywhere or talking to anyone until I say so."

The man looked stunned. "You can't do that to me. I have rights!"

Lyons's smile grew wider. If there was anything in the world he loved, it was a smart-ass who thought he had covered all the bases and then did something really stupid.

"For your information," he said, "being in violation of the National Security Act means that I can do anything I want with you until I determine that you are no longer an active danger to this facility."

The Able Team leader shrugged. "For instance, I don't know that you're not wired with explosives and were trying to get in close enough to detonate them and destroy the Venture Star. Suicide terrorists are all the rage now."

"But I'm not a terrorist!" the man protested. "I'm a photojournalist and I just wanted to get a picture of the Aerospike engines!"

Lyons wasn't surprised to hear him say that. Everyone involved in the aerospace business wanted to get a look at the new rocket engines that propelled the Venture Star. They were as radical a leap forward as the first jet engine had been in its day. The only question was, who did this man expect to sell his photos to? He wouldn't be the first American citizen who had followed the big money into treason.

"Thanks for telling me that," Lyons said. "This conversation is being recorded, and you just bought yourself a long prison sentence. You'd have been better off trying to break into a nuclear-weapons storage facility. You'd get less time for it."

"But I'm a reporter," the man repeated. "You can't do this to me!"

Lyons got into the man's face. "I can 'do it to you,' as you put it, mister, and I'm going to, in spades. I suggest that you live with it and do everything you possibly can to cooperate with me if you ever want to see the light of day again."

Lyons turned to the guards. "Take him to the sick bay, have the medics give him a cavity search and run him through the MRI. Then, bring him to the interrogation center as soon as they're done."

The man was still yelling about his "rights" as he was dragged away.

Popping that smart-ass journalist had put Lyons in a much better mood. He hated jobs like this where he had to put in long hours without much to show for his efforts. It was true that he'd had a hand in getting the Venture Star rolled out safely, but he always measured his successes in terms of body count.

So far, this was his first score on this gig and, if he was lucky, it would be his last. Glancing at his watch, he saw that he had a little over an hour left, though, before he was home free.

Stony Man Farm, Virginia

AT A REMOTE FARMHOUSE in Virginia's Shenandoah Valley, David McCarter sat with the Stony

Man crew watching the countdown of the first orbital flight of the Venture Star. This was downtime for the Phoenix Force warriors, and, as McCarter often did, the ex-SAS commando was hanging out at the Farm in case there was something useful he could do in his time off.

On this day, though, little work was being done around the Farm. The entire Sensitive Operations Group staff was taking a break to watch the televised launch of the new spacecraft. Even the blacksuit security force had been cut to a minimum so the guards could watch the show from their barracks. Aaron Kurtzman and his computer crew had linked the War Room's big-screen monitors to both the NASA feed and the Lockheed Martin telecast for a ringside seat to the festivities.

Not since the Apollo moon-landing days had NASA put on such a dog-and-pony show for the viewing public, but a lot was riding on this new space shuttle. The old shuttles were still in service, but they were reaching the end of their expected life span and would have to be taken off-line soon. The continued exploration of space was centered around the space station *Freedom*, but its success depended upon this new vehicle being able to perform as advertised.

After the initial delays in the launching of the space station components when the Russians couldn't meet their deadlines, the program was finally back on track. The old shuttle fleet was being kept busy hauling both the U.S. and European components of the station into orbit, but the Venture Star fleet would replace them as soon as they finished their test flights.

Half an hour before the scheduled liftoff, a dark blue Lockheed van emblazoned with the Venture Star logo drove up to the launch platform. The three astronauts who would make the flight stepped out wearing orange pressure suits and carrying their helmets under their arms. They waved to the cameras and the crowds before taking the elevator up the gantry to the Venture Star's crew hatch.

The gleaming white spacecraft sitting in the sun was a completely new sight on a launch pad. It wasn't a traditional rocket, nor did it look like the old Rockwell shuttles America had grown so accustomed to seeing. This spaceship looked like something straight out of a science-fiction movie.

It was a long triangle, a lifting body it was called, 127 feet long. The nose was blunt, and the cockpit windows were flared into the smooth lines of the upper fuselage. The thickened wedge shape was broken only by two small vertical fins at the base and small swept wings on the sides. Like the old Rockwell shuttles, it sat on its tail for the launch, but it didn't have external fuel tanks or boosters of any kind attached to it. The Rockwell shuttles had always looked as if they had been made up out of bits and pieces left over from other rockets.

The Venture Star looked like a true spaceship. All that remained now was to see if it flew like one.

After a wait that felt like three hours but was only thirty minutes, the welcome words were heard.

"Begin ignition sequence," the voice of Launch Control intoned. "Five ... four ... three ... two ... one ... ignition."

The blue-white flame that shot from the blunt end of the Venture Star was so bright that it dazzled the eyes. "We have ignition!"

Unlike the space shuttle, the Venture Star didn't sit on the launch stand while billowing clouds of fire and coolant steam obscured the ground. Almost immediately after the Aerospike engines ignited in brilliant flame, the craft rose into the air. Like other conventional heavy launch vehicles, it moved slowly at first, but swiftly accelerated into the blue sky.

The traditional launch-control chant could be heard over the open mike. "Go! Go! Go! Go!"

"Look at that sucker go," Kurtzman said as the gleaming white spaceship streaked upward on a pillar of fire. This was how a spaceship was supposed to fly.

The telescopic lens of the TV cameras followed the plume of flame from the Aerospike engines until they shut down. When they winked out, the spacecraft was too high to see.

"Engine shut down at 1342," the command pilot radioed Launch Control. "We are go for orbit."

"Roger, Venture Star. You are clear for orbit."

Everyone in the room cheered like schoolkids at a championship game. The day-to-day business of

America's most secret clandestine operations force required that the Stony Man crew deal with the darkest side of human nature. It wasn't every day that they could witness something so purely good and beneficial for humankind as the rebirth of the exploration of the last frontier.

"Bloody good show!" McCarter grinned widely.

Though he was still a British subject, he took great pride in the accomplishments of his adopted country. It was always nice to be on the winning team. And, regardless of the rantings of the doom-and-gloom crowd, he felt that America was still man's best hope for the future. The Venture Star was just one more sign of that bright hope.

"Isn't it just." Kurtzman beamed.

CHAPTER TWO

Stony Man Farm, Virginia

With the successful launch of the Venture Star, the Stony Man crew relaxed and enjoyed what was left of the spread the cook had prepared for the launch party.

"I'll bet Carl is overjoyed that thing has finally gotten off the ground," McCarter said around bites of a sandwich. "Now he can hand the security over to NASA and go back to busting heads."

Though McCarter's Phoenix Force and Lyons's Able Team were two separate entities, they often joined forces. McCarter knew his counterpart well, and Carl Lyons had not been nicknamed Ironman for nothing. The former LAPD detective was a man of action. Static security work drove him crazy.

"You got that right," Aaron Kurtzman, the Farm's cyberspace wizard, said with a chuckle. "And I can tell you he's not the only one who's glad to see the end of this Skunk Works gig. He's had my guys reconfirming FBI and CIA background checks for months now, and it's been boring as hell. I'll be glad to go back to watching the threat board and figuring out where to send your guys next."

"Don't be in too big a hurry to find us any new business," McCarter cautioned. With Phoenix Force being Stony Man's main strike force, Kurtzman's assignments always meant going far away and getting down and dirty before the job was over. "The lads and I are enjoying this little holiday, and I think we've earned it."

"I'm surprised at you, David," Barbara Price said from the other end of the table. "I thought you liked to be out in the bush a hundred miles from nowhere."

Though she looked a bit out of place in an organization of warriors, Price was Stony Man's mission controller. Whenever the action teams were sent out, she was the one who made it all possible. It was an unusual job for a woman, but she wasn't just any woman. The blonde's fashion-model face and figure contained a steel-trap mind and determination that would put a mule to shame.

"Even the most dedicated bushman needs a touch of real civilization now and then," the ex-Briton replied.

"I'm not sure this really qualifies as being called civilization," Hal Brognola spoke up. "We're a little bit too rural around here for that title."

Brognola was the man behind Stony Man. The Justice Department honcho split his time between Washington and the Farm as he passed on the President's orders to this more than top secret organization. The Sensitive Operations Group was the President's secret muscle, and he called upon them whenever he needed something done that could never be allowed to see the light of day.

"Speaking of guys who don't like downtime," McCarter asked Price, "what's Striker doing?"

"Mack called in yesterday," she replied. "He had wanted to be here to watch the launch with us, but he got held up. His new ETA is noon tomorrow."

Though Mack Bolan wasn't officially a part of the Stony Man Farm operation, he was always welcome to join in on any of their missions. More often than not, when Phoenix Force was called into action, Mack Bolan was with the commandos.

"Good," McCarter said. "Maybe we'll have time to hoist a pint or two before you send us out again."

"The threat board looks clean," Kurtzman said, "so your chances are good and I might even join you."

"You' re always welcome."

Palmdale, California

EVEN THOUGH the Venture Star had lifted off successfully, Carl Lyons's job at the Skunk Works wasn't done yet. When the flight was over, NASA would assume control and Able Team could stand down. But until the spacecraft was safely back in its hangar, he was still responsible for its security. With the spacecraft in orbit at the moment, though, there was nothing he could do to guard it so he took a break.

Lyons, Hermann Schwarz and their third team member, Rosario Blancanales, met in the Lockheed employees' lounge to drink coffee and listen to the radio chatter between the spacecraft and the LBJ Space Flight Center. Shortly after launch, control of the flight had been turned over to the NASA complex in Houston, and the familiar sight and sounds of Mission Control once more filled the TV screens. Big-screen monitors mounted at both ends of the room displayed the spacecraft's orbital path over a view of Earth from space. It was almost as good a view as actually being up there.

Everyone in the lounge was in a terrific mood. Their hard work and long hours had paid off again. The atmosphere was similar to the glory days of the Apollo program when the United States had been neck and neck with the Russians in a race to the moon. The Russians weren't even in the running now, and America was back in space with the hottest thing that had ever flown. The good old US of A was on top again, and Able Team was proud to have been a part of it. Americans were always happiest when they were winning.

The Venture Star was in a low orbit, roughly 180 miles above Earth, so its orbits were passing quickly. The ship was scheduled to make ten orbits, but the total flight duration was going to be only a little over four hours. It would land back at Palmdale before the sun went down over the Lockheed Skunk Works.

"Houston, Venture Star." The voice on the loudspeaker was tense. "We have a problem."

Those four words exploded in the lounge like a grenade. In an instant, the raucous crowd went as silent as the dead. The last time those words had been heard, the astronauts of *Apollo 13* had almost lost their lives.

"Houston, go ahead."

"We are experiencing a problem with one of the APUs," the pilot reported. "After automatic shutdown, it came back on and it's running erratically. We can't shut it down."

The Auxiliary Power Units were powered up on launch and reentry to provide power for the aerodynamic control surfaces. Since the control surfaces were useless in the vacuum of space, they were shut down when the main engines were cut off. Since they were fueled by hydrazine, a very explosive fuel, having an APU operating when it shouldn't be could be dangerous.

"Houston—" the voice from space sounded very strained "—we are now showing a fire in the APU hold. Activating fire-suppression system now."

"Houston, roger," the voice of Mission Control was still calm. Panic was never useful in an emergency situation, so it wasn't allowed at Mission Control Center. "Suggest you also activate your backup scrubbers to preserve the CO_2 levels."

Before the Venture Star could answer, there was a burst of static, then silence.

"This is Mission Control Houston." The professionally calm voice finally cracked. "Our radar reports indicate that the Venture Star has exploded. We are tracking multiple returns at this time."

In the stunned silence, Lyons got up from the table and headed for the door.

"Where you going, Ironman?" Schwarz asked.

"I've got a prisoner to talk to."

Lyons didn't really think that the photographer had anything to do with whatever had happened to the Venture Star, but that didn't matter. A bright dream had just died, and he needed someone to take his frustration out on. Mr. Freedom of the Press You Can't Arrest Me would do nicely in that role.

"I'm coming with you," Schwarz said.

Stony Man Farm, Virginia

"OH GOD, not again." Barbara Price's voice expressed the anguish of everyone in the Farm's War Room. The Stony Man warriors weren't strangers to death and destruction, but usually it didn't come in this form. And it was always hard to watch a dream die.

Aaron Kurtzman instantly switched screens to follow the radar track of the debris of the spacecraft as it reentered Earth's atmosphere. From the plot he was seeing, it was headed for a watery grave in the depths of the Pacific Ocean. Much of it would burn up in the reentry, but hopefully enough would be left so the engineers would be able to find out what had gone wrong. At a time like this, the only thing that helped at all was to search for answers.

Brognola drained the last of his coffee without a word before turning to Price. "I'm going back to town," he said. "The President will want to talk about this. Get in contact with Lyons and find out if he has anything on his end."

"Will do," she replied. "And, Hal..."

"Yes?"

"Tell him that we're sorry."

"I will."

AS HAD HAPPENED after the *Challenger* disaster, the entire nation went into mourning. Even though there had been fewer astronauts lost this time, the grieving was deeper. Not only had American heroes been lost, but so had the dream of taking the next step in the greatest adventure of all time. Americans had a name for being an adventurous people, but they also had very short memories.

Once upon a time, Americans had pushed the boundaries in every endeavor that they encountered. First, they conquered their own continent, then they went on to explore the farthest reaches of the planet. From the most remote mountains to the depths of the seas, Americans had gone to see what was there. And, once the planet was explored, they had gone to the last frontier, space.

Now that America was the world's richest and

most powerful nation, it was as if the national thirst for adventure had been shut off with a switch.

Almost before the last of the wreckage had settled to the bottom of the ocean, the clamor from the antispace movement cranked up full bore. A prominent liberal representative from southern California took the floor in Congress and started condemning the space program in terms usually reserved for people like Saddam Hussein or the leaders of the drug cartels. When she started raging about the military industrial complex taking milk from babies' mouths to fuel the criminal enterprise of the space program, she was shouted into silence.

In a rare display of congressional good taste, the Speaker declared a period of mourning in the House of Representatives and banned all further speeches except those in honor of the fallen. The congresswoman from California was unanimously censured when she attempted to protest. And, when she refused to be quiet, the Speaker ordered the sergeant at arms to remove her from the chambers.

The tape of her being dragged out of the House chambers was played on the top of the CNN news all evening. After the third showing, a recall movement was announced in her home district in California.

THREE DAYS LATER, a presidential-style funeral was held in Washington, D.C., for the fallen astronauts. The Army's Old Guard solemnly marched down Pennsylvania Avenue escorting three black riderless horses and three caissons bearing empty caskets draped with Old Glory. Only one of the fallen had ever been in the military, but in the public eye, NASA service was seen as being worthy of the honors. The rest of the astronaut corps marched as an honor guard behind the last caisson.

Every congressman who could walk was in the reviewing stand with the President, the vice president, the Cabinet members and their wives along with the NASA brass. Foreign diplomats and special representatives from America's allies also showed their respect. No invitation, however, had been extended to the female representative from California. She was back in her home district fighting a rampant recall movement.

The three national TV networks, as well as CNN, preempted their regular programming to cover the funeral from start to finish. As always happened, some viewers called their local stations to protest the cancelation of their soap operas and ball games. But, for the most part, the nation took the day off to watch the honors given to the fallen. A national day of mourning had been proclaimed, and all fifty states followed suit. America came to a standstill to grieve.

Though it had been impossible to recover the astronauts' bodies for burial, a cenotaph had been erected in Arlington National Cemetery to remember them. After the rifle salutes had been fired and taps played, members of the astronaut corps placed a wreath at the base of the black stone and said their goodbyes.

On the day of the funeral, the U.S. Pacific fleet assembled over the middle of the debris field at the bottom of the Pacific and conducted another ceremony. Dozens of ships, both military and civilian from almost every nation with a navy, joined in the tribute to the fallen over their watery resting place.

When the ceremonies were over, the nation took a deep breath. Then the real debate began, as did the investigation. More than just national pride was at stake here. Five billion dollars had been spent on this project, and a lot of people wanted to know what had happened to their money.

SINCE THE DISASTER had taken place before NASA had assumed control of the Venture Star, much of the investigation was being conducted at the Lockheed Palmdale Skunk Works. Carl Lyons's photographer prisoner found himself in a situation that exceeded anything he could have ever imagined in his worst nightmare. Not since Lee Harvey Oswald had a suspect been in this kind of situation. But, this time, there would be no Jack Ruby to keep him from being questioned.

It didn't take long before Lyons and Schwarz satisfied themselves that the photographer had just been an opportunistic, self-serving idiot with an expensive camera. Detailed photos of the Aerospike engines would have been worth hundreds of thousands of dollars to a number of people and not all of them American publishers. He had seen an opportunity to make a fast buck and had taken it.

With the mood of the country being what it was, though, Lyons's assessment of the man wasn't good enough. Everyone from the state police to the FBI and the CIA were grilling the photographer in relays. He was all they had, and a grieving nation wanted answers. He would be released only when everyone concerned was convinced that he'd had absolutely nothing to do with the explosion, and that could take some time.

CHAPTER THREE

Stony Man Farm, Virginia

The President hadn't asked Stony Man Farm to get involved with the Venture Star investigation, but keeping Aaron Kurtzman out of it would have taken more than simply being ignored. The fact that he felt a little put out by being overlooked was only part of his motivation. Something, or someone, had injured his country, there was no way he wouldn't get involved.

Since there was no film of the disaster to examine and the instrumentation readouts indicated no errors, the only hope of finding out what went wrong lay with examining the wreckage. The problem was that, unlike the *Challenger* disaster or the explosion of Pan Am Flight 800, the pieces of the Venture Star hadn't impacted in shallow water. The watery grave of the spacecraft was miles deep and beyond recovery by even the most advanced deep-sea exploration vehicles. Also unlike the shuttle, the destruction of the Venture Star had taken place in orbit. The debris had gone through reentry, and only the biggest chunks of what had once been America's dream had survived. The smaller pieces had burned up on reentering the atmosphere like so many meteors.

Deep Blue II, one of the world's most sophisticated deep-water oceanographic research ships, happened to be in the Pacific and had been immediately dispatched to the crash site to sweep the area. It also happened that Kurtzman had a cyber-buddy on the ship's crew. Even though he was confined to a wheelchair and rarely left the Farm, Kurtzman had a worldwide network of contacts and good friends he'd met in cyberspace. More than once, they helped in more ways than they knew.

An e-mail put him in contact with his friend on the ship, and he quickly got a promise of a back channel to whatever information they came up with.

SINCE THERE WAS nothing Aaron Kurtzman could do until *Deep Blue II*'s submersible reported back, he had time on his hands. Since idle hands were the devil's playground, he knew that he really should do something useful. And getting caught up in the continuing national brouhaha and blame fixing over the Venture Star disaster wasn't the kind of thing that would yield positive results.

Space travel was dangerous. Period. The space shuttles were the most complicated machines that had ever been built, and every machine was subject to failure. The possibility of human error added even more danger. The amazing thing wasn't that the *Challenger* and the Venture Star had ended their careers in tragedy. What was truly amazing was that there had been so few space disasters over the years. For the number of missions flown, there had been very few deaths. If you counted it in miles traveled per number of deaths, space flight was still the safest way to travel short of walking. But, even though dozens of pedestrians got picked off the side of the road each and every year, they didn't have the entire nation watching when it happened.

Kurtzman knew, though, that rational thinking wasn't going to work on this topic, so he decided to go somewhere and exercise a little rationality on his own. When he called up his reading file, the first thing that popped up on his menu was a report of renewed volcanic activity in Southeast Asia.

The most recent steam venting from Mt. Pinatubo had the Philippines in an uproar again. The vulcanologists had been predicting the "big one" in the islands for several years now, but all the mountain had been able to produce was more steam and ash falls. Every time the mountain burped, thousands of Filipinos panicked. To keep an eye on that volcano, as well as on the others dotting the region, an international vulcanology project under the auspices of the United Nations had installed a series of seismic detectors in Southeast Asia.

The interesting part of the report was that a number of these detectors had gone off all at the same time, and not in conjunction with Mt. Pinatubo's hiccup. Even more interesting was that when these anomalies were plotted, the seismic alerts were almost in a straight line. Since nature abhorred a straight line, something was definitely wrong.

An alarm went off in Kurtzman's mind where he filed the seemingly trivial but actually useful information he inputted on a daily basis and remembered something he had read about the proposed Orient Express hypersonic airliner. The article had mentioned that the flights were going to play hell with Japan's earthquake-detection system because the hypersonic shock waves of the Mach 8 aircraft could mimic seismic disturbances and set off the automatic alarms. Since earthquakes didn't travel in a straight line, or even a slightly curved one, as in this case, something entirely different had to have caused those alerts.

He reached for the phone, then called up the Los Angeles County Disaster Center to talk to their earthquake team. They had some of the best seismic-event detectors in the United States, and the Venture Star had passed right over them en route to her first landing at Palmdale. If her hypersonic flight could produce earthquakelike ground tremors, they would have it on record.

When Kurtzman hung up the phone, he sat and stared at the screen for a few moments. The plot of the Asian seismic alerts made a line pointing directly into the Western desert of China where they faded out. More food for thought.

Calling up another menu, he started digging into

the history of the Lockheed Martin Venture Star and her crew.

AARON KURTZMAN WASN'T surprised when *Deep Blue II* reported back the next day that the wreckage resting on the Pacific floor probably wasn't that of the Venture Star. The debris field was huge. The space vehicle's pieces had scattered widely during reentry, but the vessel's radar had been able to plot it and had sent the submersible down to take photos.

What they found bore no resemblance to what the wreckage of the Venture Star should have looked like. Then, even considering that much of it would have burned up during reentry, there wasn't enough to make up the remains of a 129-ton spacecraft. Taking a hard copy of the report, he went hunting for Hal Brognola.

"Goddammit," Brognola growled as he read the report. "Now we're going to have to start the process all over. They went to the wrong place."

He turned to Kurtzman. "What the hell went wrong, Aaron? We plotted the impact from the radar tapes—why isn't it there?"

"Actually, it is," Kurtzman said. "The wreckage from the plots, I mean. And I'm not too surprised that it isn't the Venture Star."

"Would you care to explain that one?" Brognola asked. "If we didn't plot the fall of the Venture Star, what were the radars following and where did the shuttle go?"

"Well, I'm not really sure yet what crashed into the Pacific, but I expect that it will turn out to be a Chinese CZ-2E launch vehicle. And the Venture Star? I haven't found it yet, but I wouldn't be surprised if it's in China, western China to be exact."

Brognola looked tired. The Venture Star disaster had affected the entire nation, and even he hadn't been able to escape being touched by the tragedy. The fact that the Man was putting the spurs to everyone in government service to find the answers wasn't making it any easier. The last thing he needed right now was for the Stony Man team to start cracking up on him. "You'd better be able to explain that one, Aaron."

"Well," Kurtzman said, "my working hypothesis is that the Chinese hijacked our spacecraft and sent another rocket up and exploded it to throw us off the scent."

"Dammit, Aaron," Brognola exploded. "This isn't a space cadet comic book we're dealing with here. You can't hijack a damned space shuttle."

"You can if you do it before it takes off."

That stopped Brognola cold. "What do you mean?"

Kurtzman hit a key, and a photo of the Venture Star's crew flashed on the monitor. "Well, the Venture Star launched with a crew of three, and the copilot, James Chin, was a Chinese-American. Do you remember all the fanfare about his having been chosen when the original copilot died in a car wreck?"

Brognola nodded.

"In hindsight," Kurtzman continued, "that was a very convenient accident. And, if you also will remember, Venture Star launched with a female astronaut on board as the mission specialist, Selena Del Gato. On this flight, her mission was to monitor the performance of the Aerospike engines in deep space, and she's an accomplished aerospace engineer. The fact that her birth mother was a Chinese-American isn't well-known because her adoptive family is Hispanic and she speaks perfect Spanish."

When Brognola didn't comment, Kurtzman went on to his next point. "The command pilot is, was, as American as apple pie and hot dogs—that is to say his family is German and English. But, if he was to be disabled, the copilot was trained to fly the ship."

"So you're saying that two of the three crew members on that flight were Red Chinese agents?"

Kurtzman shrugged. "Stranger things have happened. You have to remember that even fourth-generation Chinese Americans maintain close ties to the Mother Country. Look at the hold the Triads have on so many of them."

"And you expect me to take this science-fiction story to the President?"

"Along with some cold hard facts, yes."

"What facts?"

Kurtzman flashed a map of the Pacific region up on the big-screen monitor. "This, for one."

"What is it?"

When Kurtzman hit a key, a series of red blips appeared on the map. "These are sites where seismic disturbances were recorded very soon after the Venture Star disaster. You will notice that they inscribe a slight arc terminating over the western desert of the People's Republic of China."

"Western China's in for another big earthquake, so what? It happens in that region all the time."

"These seismic reports weren't the result of tectonic movement," Kurtzman explained patiently. "The detectors were tripped off by the passing of a hypersonic shock wave. The kind of shock wave the Venture Star makes when it reenters the atmosphere at Mach 16."

"Can you prove that?"

"I already have. I checked with the L.A. County Disaster Center and confirmed that their seismic recorders went off the scale when the ship returned from her first test flight. The recordings they made match the ones from the Pacific sites almost to the exact wiggle."

"You're saying that Venture Star survived the explosion?"

"Like I said, I'm not sure that there ever was an explosion on board. Something blew up in space, yes. The question is what."

Brognola peeled back the paper wrapping from a roll of antacid tablets and flicked one into his mouth. Even though this Venture Star incident was well off the national-catastrophe scale, Stony Man wasn't officially involved, and neither was his stomach lining. As long as the President hadn't ordered him to get involved, he wasn't going to. Not until he had a better idea than the one Kurtzman was peddling.

"Aaron, I can't take this to the Oval Office. The Man will have me cleaning garbage cans in Antarctica if I try it. You're going to have to do better than that before I present it to him."

Kurtzman knew that he was right, but he also knew that it did sound like a science-fiction story. No one had ever hijacked a spacecraft before. But, as he also knew, there was a first time for everything. "Okay," he said. "I'll keep working on it."

"And keep it to yourself."

Cheyenne Mountain, Colorado

THE COLD WAR might have ended almost a decade earlier, but the North American Defense Command, buried two thousand feet under the solid granite of Cheyenne Mountain, Colorado, hadn't yet gone out of business. Anyone who thought that the game had ended when the Russians folded their cards simply wasn't playing with a full deck. If anything, the threat had gotten worse. At least the Russians had known how the game was played. Too many renegade nations that didn't play by the rules now owned missile-delivery systems and nuclear weapons to mount in their nose cones.

Not many of the Third World nuke club had launch vehicles capable of hitting the United States from their own countries, but that wasn't the only way to launch an attack. Even though their missiles were short ranged, they could be launched from the deck of a freighter offshore in international waters. As long as nukes were in the hands of wackos, the United States wasn't safe and NORAD still had a job.

One of NORAD's secondary missions was to keep track of all the space vehicles and associated junk that circled the planet. The Space Control Center, or Sky Watch, as it was called, wasn't as glamorous as the other assignments at the Cheyenne Mountain complex. Watching for missile launch signatures could get your adrenaline pumping, but counting space junk and communications satellites could get real old, real quick.

It was so boring that the high point of any Sky Watch shift was to be the first on the team to see that a piece of space junk's orbit had degraded enough that it was going to fall out of the sky. Then, the entire unit swung into action and tried to plot where the discarded rocket booster or dead satellite was going to hit before it did. So far, none of the debris had ever killed anyone on Earth, but there had been some close calls. A Russian satellite carrying a nuclear power cell had fallen in northern Canada. The debris of the American Skylab had come down in the middle of the Australian desert.

To help pass the long hours without going crazy from watching a radar plot that rarely changed, the Sky Watchers had come up with a harmless way to pass the time and still do their job. Someone decided that since most of the so-called UFOs showed up on radar, they should try to track them before they entered Earth's atmosphere. It was a harmless enough pursuit and since it was good practice using the long-range radars, the shift commanders let them do it.

The man on the number-one Sky Watch workstation that shift, Staff Sergeant Dale Bergman, was a fairly typical Air Force volunteer of the post-cold war era. With the Evil Empire gone, he had entered the military to learn a trade and get paid while he was doing it. He had intended to become an air-traffic controller, but the crunch came at the end of his first hitch. The FAA had been going through one of its periodic upheavals, and there had been no air traffic openings. In fact, the waiting list had been several hundred people long. Not liking the prospects of unemployment, Bergman signed on for another four years and was given what was considered a plum assignment, NORAD.

He was at the control console on his shift and, when it came time for him to do a routine check of the long-look radar complex, he aimed one of the main dishes into deep space. Unlike some of his Sky Watch teammates, he wasn't so certain that UFOs existed. But he knew that if they did, the long-range NORAD radars should be able to pick them up.

He was almost jolted out of his chair when a return showed up from where no satellite should have been. Looking at the range-to-target readout, he thought he was seeing something wrong when he read 2,532 miles. The highest satellites, even the classified military birds, were only at 2,200. For a moment, he thought that he had actually locked in on a UFO.

After watching the track for a few minutes, he saw that it was just another satellite in a stable polar orbit. What it was and who had put it there, he had no idea. Figuring it to be some kind of supersecret vehicle, he logged the track as required and filed it for someone else to figure out.

CHAPTER FOUR

Quinbaki, China

"Oh...I like the way it looks now," ex-Lockheed astronaut and mission specialist Selena Del Gato said in English. "Our spaceship is as sexy as hell in black."

Del Gato was herself dressed in a black flight suit with the red flag of the People's Republic of China emblazoned on both shoulders under the epaulets of a major in the newly formed PRC Space Force. Usually, a Chinese flight suit was a unisex garment, but she managed to make it look like a slinky cocktail gown. It wasn't as revealing, of course, but what it didn't show, it promised.

Her companion on the observation deck of the secret launch complex tunneled out of the mountain was her onetime crewmate on the Venture Star, copilot James Chin. He had gone a long ways at her urging, all the way to China, but he didn't agree with her this time. The triangular spacecraft that had once proudly worn the flag of the United States on a gleaming white finish didn't look the same in a coat of matte-black radar-absorbing paint.

Before, it had looked like a bright arrow aimed at the stars. The new finish gave it a sinister appearance, and the bloodred flag of the People's Republic of China on the tail fins looked decidedly out of place.

When the stolen spacecraft had been used to put the first of the four planned nuclear-missile launch platforms in orbit, it had still worn its original radar-visible finish. The pressure to get the platform launched hadn't allowed time for it to be changed. The Chinese general in charge of the operation had felt that the risk had been worth taking, and his gamble had paid off. Now that the first platform was fully operational, the ship had been taken off-line long enough for the radar-defeating coating to be applied for the rest of the missions.

Even more sinister than the new black finish, however, was the purpose the Venture Star was being put to at its new base. The satellites it was ferrying into space would create a ring of nuclear weapons aimed at Earth.

As Chin watched, another missile platform was being loaded into the Venture Star's cargo bay. The platforms were small because all they needed to do was relay firing commands from ground control to the missiles the platform carried. The six weapons arranged around the satellite's central structure looked stunted. Their nose cones were the same as other ballistic missiles, a blunt curve to withstand the heat of atmospheric reentry. But the weapons didn't have the long bodies full of fuel necessary to propel a conventional land- or sea-based missile.

Launching a missile from space to a target on Earth was much easier than launching it from the ground. From orbit, everything was downhill to Earth. All a space missile's engine needed to do was to slow it enough to break the orbit, and it would fall to Earth by gravity alone. Computer-controlled thrusters around the base of the warhead section would control its reentry so that it would hit the target.

This was the second of four such platforms the hijacked Venture Star would carry to a high orbit above Earth. Once they were all in place, China would be able to target any spot on the planet with complete invulnerability. Unlike in science-fiction movies, there were no space weapons or armed spacecraft to defend the planet. No space fighters armed with photon torpedoes or blaster weapons would lift off from Earth to do battle with the platforms. Once they were all in orbit, China would rule the world.

"Well, Jimmy—" Del Gato turned to him "—don't you think it looks sexy?"

"I don't know if I'd call it sexy," he answered. "But it's sure something."

She studied him for a long moment, her dark eyes sweeping his face. "You're not fun anymore, Jimmy. You need to loosen up and start enjoying this opportunity you've been given. Not many men get a chance to go down in history as the savior of their people."

"I guess not." He tried to smile, once more feeling the power of her sexuality.

Back in California, Chin had usually dated all-American blondes, but the fact that Del Gato was stunning in anyone's language hadn't escaped his notice. Until halfway through the Venture Star training program, he hadn't known that she was Chinese. With the style of makeup she wore and the Hispanic last name, he had just figured her to be another one of the mixed-race women California was so famous for. It was only when she had started recruiting him into the plan to steal the Venture Star that he had learned that she was Han, as the Chinese called themselves.

Chin was having serious second thoughts about having helped the Chinese hijack the spacecraft. At the time, it had seemed like the right thing to do, particularly since Del Gato had come as part of the deal. Now, seeing his ship painted black and being loaded with nuclear weapons that would be used to force the land of his birth into submission, he acknowledged the enormity of what he had done.

But, as someone had once said, the die had been cast and he was now a lieutenant colonel in the Chinese Space Force and the command pilot of the most advanced space vehicle in the known universe, now renamed the Star Dragon.

EX-LOCKHEED TEST PILOT and civilian astronaut Jimmy Chin wasn't having an easy time being the top astronaut at the Quinbaki space complex. He had gotten used to being called by his Chinese name, Chin Wu Lee. He had even gotten used to going without a Whopper hamburger with large fries or a Sara Lee cheesecake when the mood hit him, to say nothing of ice cream, tacos or a hundred other things that had been a part of his daily life in California. At least, though, he could get a soft drink here.

The main thing that was making his job difficult wasn't the diet; it was the cultural bias he encountered on a daily basis. In California, he had been Chinese. But in China, he was an American. It didn't matter that his bloodline was one hundred percent Chinese. He had been born in the United States, and nothing could change that. To make it worse, he only spoke Cantonese, his parents' language, and not the Mandarin dialect that was the official language of modern China. It wasn't a real problem on the job, since most of the scientists and technicians at the center spoke English, the international language of space travel. But, in social settings, he was made to feel as if he were mentally retarded.

Not that there was much social life at Quinbaki. The commander and mastermind behind the hijacking of the Venture Star, General Ye, didn't see any reason to allow his staff to take time off for socializing. They were working for the future of the

Mother Country, and they would put forth their best efforts every day or suffer.

Yet, even when he was understood clearly, Chin was having difficulty training the Chinese astronauts who were supposed to replace him and Del Gato in the Venture Star. They were competent military pilots, as far as that went. But the aircraft they had trained on were at least one generation behind most Western aircraft. Fly-by-wire was still new to them, and letting a computer make flight decisions for them was alien to their thinking. Transitioning them to the state-of-the-art flight-control system of the Venture Star was going slowly.

Had Chin known that he would be facing all of this, he might have been able to resist Del Gato's enticements and keep his honor. Instead, he had allowed himself, body and soul, to be captured by her. She, of course, was having none of those problems. Moon Daughter, as Selena Del Gato was now calling herself in Chinese, had instantly become more Chinese than the Great Wall.

GENERAL CHUI YE, the Quinbaki complex's commander, joined the two astronauts on the observation platform. After greeting Del Gato in Mandarin, he turned to Chin. "It's the star man from the Golden Mountain," he said in Cantonese.

Of all of the staff, Ye was the only one who would speak Cantonese to him before trying Mandarin first. It was as if the general were rubbing his nose in his linguistic shortcomings. "Good afternoon, General," Chin replied in the same language.

"You are ready to fly?"

"Yes, sir."

In the pause that followed, Chin asked the question he always asked each time he saw Ye. "What is the status of the American astronaut, Miller? Has he gotten any better?"

Disabling the Venture Star's command pilot, Kurt Miller, so he could take command of the ship still haunted him. It was true that Del Gato had actually administered the drug that had knocked him out, but Kurt had once been a friend. Del Gato had sworn to him that the drug was harmless, but Chin hadn't seen Miller since the medics had taken him away after landing.

The general's almost black eyes were completely unreadable. "He remains the same."

More and more, Chin was convinced that Miller had died or had been killed. That would be the most expedient solution to the problem he represented, and he had learned that Ye was a man of great expedience. As the grand architect of China's new space force, he would allow nothing to get in the way of the goals he had envisioned. As the Chinese people had spread over the earth, they would spread into space as soon as they could. The Celestial Empire would truly extend to the stars. Nothing and no one would be allowed to keep China from her destiny. Certainly not an American astronaut.

"When can I see him?" Chin asked as he always did.

"When the schedule permits."

"Do you know when that will be?"

Ye's eyes looked like those of a dragon, and Chin felt that they could look into his very soul. "There will be time for you to rejoin your comrade after your work is completed," he said without expression.

Chin almost wished he hadn't asked.

Stony Man Farm, Virginia

WHEN CARL LYONS WALKED into the Farm's Computer Room, it was apparent to one and all that he was in a foul mood. He was wearing his Ironman face and didn't look amused.

"How was sunny California?" Kurtzman greeted him.

"How the hell should I know?" Lyons shot back. "Ever since that damned spaceship blew up, I haven't been out of the Skunk Works building for more than five minutes."

"Why'd they cut you loose now?"

"I cut myself loose," he said. "The big boys took over, and the place is crawling with every kind of Fed you can think of. I swear I saw two guys from the Food and Drug Administration walking hand in hand with a straggler from the Marine Fisheries Bureau. The place turned into a zoo, and I got tired of fighting my way through the crowd. On top of that, it was a complete waste of time. We're no closer to finding out what happened than we were when we started."

Kurtzman pointed to the guest chair beside his workstation. "Have a seat and let me tell you what we've come up with."

"I hope you've got good news for a change."

"Well," Kurtzman said, "to start out, the Venture Star didn't blow up, it was hijacked."

Lyons stared at Kurtzman blankly. "You're kidding me."

"Nope. The only thing is, Hal isn't buying it yet."

"The Chinese?" Lyons asked.

Kurtzman nodded without asking how Lyons had come to that conclusion.

"What went down?"

After Kurtzman gave him the short version, Lyons shook his head. "I knew I didn't like that woman."

"Our Chinese American astronaut with the Hispanic name, Del Gato?"

"You got it," he replied. "She kept playing sex kitten with every man who came in sight, and I didn't see her as professional-astronaut material. It was a little too much, you know, like something out of a James Bond movie. But her background checked out, and I wasn't there to keep an eye on the flight crew."

Lyons shook his head. "How'd they pull it off?"

"To be honest, I don't know yet. All I know is

that they did explode something up there, probably one of their CZ-2E satellite-launch vehicles. And, in the confusion, the Venture Star broke orbit and was brought back down for a quick reentry. I have a track of its flight path into western China, to Xinjiang Uygur, but I don't have a photo of it on the ground to convince Hal that I'm right."

"Is there anything I can do to help?"

"We've got the China end of it pretty well covered, but how about really getting into Del Gato's background and seeing what you can develop? If we're right about her role in this, she has to have left some traces behind. I see a Triad connection somewhere and maybe some family pressure. That's the way the Chinese usually work it."

"I can handle that." Lyons's jaw was clinched. "Where's a terminal I can use?"

"You can take the one next to Hunt."

Cheyenne Mountain, Colorado

WHEN STAFF SERGEANT Dale Bergman went back on shift in NORAD's Sky Watch, he ran through his check of the eight thousand objects Space Command Center kept track of daily. Every little piece of space junk was where it was supposed to be, and nothing looked to be degrading enough to become a problem anytime soon for anyone on the ground. The sky wasn't going to fall on his watch.

That done, Bergman remembered that unknown satellite he had spotted on his previous shift.

Switching over to the deep-space radars, he plugged in the orbital data he had recorded and located it again right where it should have been. After watching it for a while, he logged the track. On a whim, he decided to sweep the rest of space at that altitude to see if it had any companions in that orbit.

Within fifteen minutes, he had located a second unknown object in the same geosynchronous orbit. This one was placed ninety degrees behind the first one he had spotted. The thought occurred to him that these mysterious birds might be some kind of recon satellite, and he decided to check to see if they were carrying nuclear power cells. High-orbit spy birds often carried nuke cells to boost power to the long-range sensors and cameras.

A few minutes later, the radiation readouts came back as being similar to what would be expected from nuclear warheads.

Bergman sat for a moment, staring at his screen. Keying his throat mike, he spoke to his shift commander. "Major, I have something on the screen I think you need to take a look at."

By the end of Bergman's shift, every senior officer in NORAD from the commander on down was clustered around the Sky Watch workstations. It hadn't taken long to confirm that the two deep-space satellites he had discovered were nuclear-missile launching platforms. From the radiation analysis, it was believed that each of the platforms carried at least four missiles yielding in excess of 1.5 megatons, or nearly one hundred times as large as the weapon that had been dropped over Hiroshima.

In warfare, the advantage was always with the force that could capture and hold the high ground. And space was the ultimate high ground. Not even the United States had a defense against space-launched missiles. Congress had seen to that when they cut the funds for the Star Wars program.

After printing out hard copies of the data, the NORAD commander hurried to the hot line to call the President.

CHAPTER FIVE

Stony Man Farm, Virginia

Aaron Kurtzman was thoroughly convinced that he had solved the mystery surrounding the disappearance of the Venture Star. The seismic data alone led to only one possible conclusion. He knew, however, that wasn't good enough for Hal Brognola. No matter how many times he had been right before, each incident had to be proved on its own merits. Unless, of course, Brognola was thinking the same way he was, then things got fast-tracked. Unfortunately, that wasn't the case this time.

A single satellite recon photo would have clinched his argument, but the Chinese knew all about spy satellites, having launched several of their own. There was no way that they were going to let an orbiting spy bird catch the Venture Star sitting out in the open. To do that, he was going to need an SR-71 run, but to get permission for that, he had to have Brognola on board. And to be able to convince Brognola to take him seriously, he had to build an ironclad case.

The biggest problem he faced was finding a motive beyond the ever present Chinese desire to dominate the Pacific region. It was well-known that they intended, at some time in the future, to be not only the dominant force in Asia, but also the only one. Usually, though, it was felt that they intended to reach that goal by becoming the Asian economic superpower. Old-fashioned military aggression wasn't going to cut it because the United States stood in the way. Any Chinese moves in that arena would be met by American retaliation.

China had made great strides in the economic struggle over the past decade. The peaceful takeover of Hong Kong had given them a giant leap forward by providing an established financial center to work from. Their closer economic ties to the United States had given them both a market for their goods and access to much needed capital and technical know-how. They were well on the way to conquering the world through the marketplace, and it didn't make sense for them to make a hostile move against the United States right now. The Chinese weren't a stupid people—far from it—and hijacking a spacecraft was tantamount to a declaration of war.

As Kurtzman well knew, the Chinese never made any move unless they had all the bases covered. All he had to do was keep gathering information until he could figure out the name of the game, and then he'd solve the puzzle.

WHEN THE NORAD alert came in, Kurtzman broke his train of thought to look at it. And, when he did, the picture instantly became clear.

"So that's what the bastards are using it for," he muttered to himself. "They're boosting missile platforms into orbit with our spaceship."

This brought the situation into fine focus, and now he didn't need the recon photos to prove his hijacking theory. He had the missing motive, and if Brognola didn't believe him now, he was in the wrong business.

Reaching out, he clicked on his intercom. "Hal, Aaron here. We need to talk. I've finally got this wrapped up, and I think you need to take a look at it right now."

BROGNOLA LISTENED intently while Kurtzman went over his data again, ending with NORAD's discovery of the two launch platforms in deep space. As improbable as it had sounded at first, the facts were now in place.

"Okay," Brognola said, rubbing the back of his neck after Kurtzman wrapped up his spiel. "Let's get everyone in the War Room and start working on this. And, Aaron..."

"Yes?"

"You were right again."

Kurtzman just smiled.

THE ATMOSPHERE in the War Room was tense. The hijacking of the Venture Star couldn't be allowed to pass without the United States taking action. No nation, least of all the world's only surviving superpower, could let something like that happen without responding. But taking military action against a China armed with space-launched missiles capable of striking anywhere in the world was a scenario for the opening salvo of WWIII.

If it came to war, the damage the Chinese land-based missiles could do to the West Coast would be bad enough. Adding the space-based warheads from the platforms made that scenario completely unwinnable.

After running through the background once again, Kurtzman turned the briefing over to Hunt Wethers. He displayed a recon-satellite photo of a mountain range rising out of the western desert of China.

"This is Quinbaki," he said, "and we feel this is where they're holding the Venture Star. This complex has been a high-security weapons-test area for years. You'll notice the typical Red Army–style defensive setup."

Red markers appeared on the photo, showing bunkers, radars, minefields, missile launchers and armored vehicle parks. In the middle of the defenses was a typical military cluster of buildings, fuel tanks, barracks and a long runway with aircraft parked in revetments.

"Over the past year or so, we've had indications that new construction has been going on, particularly around the bottom of this mountain. Whatever they've been doing, they've been careful to keep it low profile and we haven't had a clue. But, from what we have seen, they could have created an underground facility for a space vehicle like the Venture Star."

"And this is where the seismic alerts ended?"

"Almost to the kilometer."

Checking over the launch complex's defenses yet another time, Brognola asked, "Can we develop the targeting data needed to put a cruise missile in there?"

Kurtzman manipulated the computer mosaic he had created of the Chinese launch complex to show the southern exposure of the mountain where he thought the Venture Star was being hidden. "We can," he said. "But to do it right, I'll need an SR-71 pass to pick up the data I'm not getting from the satellites. I need a high oblique shot to complete the mapping."

"See here." He clicked on a laser pointer and swept it across the base of the mountain. "That's not really what the terrain looks like there. It's a computer simulation based on the overhead satellite view. To provide the terrain checkpoints for the missile's internal guidance system, I need a low-angle view of this area to provide the baseline data to refine the mosaic. If, that is, we're going to go for a surgical strike with minimal collateral damage. Right now, all I can do is get the missile within a five-hundred-yard CPE."

"CPE?"

"Circular Probable Error," Kurtzman explained. "Its impact point. Of course, going with a CPE that large means having to use a larger warhead to get the job done. Something in the forty-kiloton or larger range. If I can get the CPE down to five meters, we can go in with a 1.5-kiloton and not light up half of western China in the process."

Brognola made a few entries in his notebook computer.

"You know," Kurtzman said thoughtfully, "there may be a Stony Man solution to this that will save Uncle Sam a bundle and not create an international shit storm."

"What's that?"

"Well, if we could put Phoenix on the ground and send Jack Grimaldi along with them, they might be able to sneak in there and steal the Venture Star."

"It's been a while since I reviewed Grimaldi's rap sheet," Brognola said dryly, "but I wasn't aware that he had too many hours piloting spacecraft."

"I don't think he's ever set foot in one," Kurtzman said. "But that's not the point. The Venture Star almost flies herself with her onboard computer system. All he would need to do is light the fuse and hang on. If we can get him in the cockpit, he can fly her home.

"And—" Kurtzman shrugged "—even if it can't be flown out, they can always destroy it in place."

Brognola turned to McCarter, who had been

completely silent throughout this exchange. "David?"

"The Bear's right," he said. "We can at least destroy it so the bastards can't take it apart and build a fleet of the damned things. I'm not quite ready to start learning Mandarin yet."

He took a deep breath. "Since the alternative is a nuclear war, Phoenix might as well go out in style. Tell the Man that we'll go in and try to take care of this for him."

"How will you get out?"

McCarter smiled grimly. "Considering the defenses of that place, if we're going home, Jack's going to have to fly us in that spaceship. Nothing else is going to get in there to extract us."

"I'll give the Man your offer," Brognola said, "but we still need to keep working on the cruise-missile option. Aaron, give me the data on the SR-71 run you want made, and I'll pass it on. I assume that you want it done yesterday?"

Kurtzman grimaced. "Day before, actually. Considering the short turnaround time on the Venture Star, every day that passes brings them closer to the launch dates for the other platforms needed to cover the planet. Two more should do it."

Brognola didn't have to have that one spelled out for him. Once the missile platforms were in place, nowhere on Earth would be out of danger from the nuclear warheads they carried. The Chinese were already on the high ground, but they didn't have complete control of it yet and something had to be done before they did.

"As a matter of fact," Kurtzman continued, "I'm surprised they haven't launched them yet. The sooner they're up there, the sooner the war is won."

He paused. "Which brings up the issue of what we're going to do about the platforms. I'm afraid there's not much that Phoenix can do about them."

"There might be a way to deal with them, too," Wethers said. "The President will have to bring NASA in on it, though, and it will be more difficult to keep a lid on it."

Occasionally, Stony Man worked with the military on a mission and more rarely with the FBI, DEA or the CIA. But bringing in outsiders always carried the risk of breaching the security of the Farm and presidential actions.

"And that is?"

"If I remember correctly, the Brilliant Pebbles project developed a laser weapon that could be mounted in a space shuttle, carried into orbit and deployed against targets in deep space, like the platforms."

"What the hell is Brilliant Pebbles?" Brognola asked. With every half-assed military research project getting a fancy code name, a man needed to carry a lexicon to keep track of them.

"Star Wars," Weathers explained, "the canceled missile-defense project. They were working on several different kinds of defensive systems, but the best one was to have been a series of lasers. The one I'm thinking of would be perfect and there is reason to believe that it is still in existence."

"Get all this down on paper and I'll take it to the Man," Brognola said. "In the meantime, recall Phoenix and go into mission prep."

"They're already on their way in," McCarter said.

"And—" Brognola turned to Barbara Price "—get Katz back here, as well."

"I tracked him to southern France," she replied, "and left a message for him. He should be showing up here almost anytime now."

Brognola sighed. The problem with running an organization like this was that he couldn't lock all the players up in a room and drag them out only when he needed them. When they weren't on alert or on a mission, the Stony Man warriors did as they pleased. At least, though, they were good about calling in and letting the Farm know where they were.

"Just get him back here and put him to work with Aaron. We're going to need a good plan to have any kind of chance of pulling this off."

"We'll get on it," she promised.

ON THE FLIGHT BACK to Stony Man Farm, Hal Brognola had to fight to keep his anger under control. The hardest part of his job had always been keeping his personal emotions out of his decision-making process. Emotions had no place in the running of the Sensitive Operations Group. For Stony

Man to function as intended, every mission had to be decided purely on its own merits. That, at least, was the theory. In practice, though, it was impossible to maintain a cold mind, particularly at a time like this.

The President had sure as hell been emotional when Brognola had presented him with the information Aaron Kurtzman and his computer team had come up with about the fate of the Venture Star. In the days of sailing ships, it had been called piracy, and moving it into space didn't make it any less of a crime. The United States had always responded strongly to piracy. In fact, one of America's first ventures into international affairs had occurred in 1803 when an infant nation had struck hard at pirates preying on American shipping off the Barbary Coast of North Africa.

Unfortunately, this time America couldn't simply send the Navy in with sailing ships to take care of the problem. The old military axiom "Never fight a land war in China" had taken on greater meaning in the missile age. Now it ran "Never fight a war with China. Period."

Like it or not, the Chinese had just become a major nuclear power with the capability of striking any point on the planet. And, because of their cultural psychology, the deterrent of mutually assured destruction, which had finally caused the Russians to collapse, wasn't effective against them. The Chinese leadership didn't really care if a large part of the population disappeared in a mushroom cloud.

In fact, if it did, it might make them a more effective superpower. China had people to burn and threatening their lives wouldn't work. Were the President to confront the Chinese about this, they would laugh at him and invite him to surrender while he still could.

The cultural differences, however, also made the Chinese vulnerable in two critical areas. For one thing, they really believed that the United States' best days had passed. They looked at America's social problems and saw irreversible decay that was sapping the national will. Their history showed them that once that process started, there was no way to recover from it. From their perspective, the Americans had become weak and were going to stay that way.

In the scenario they had set up, the only outcome they could see being remotely possible was the surrender of the United States to the threat of their space weapons. That was what they would do were the positions reversed. A culture that was thousands of years old didn't understand that America's greatness was rooted in her ability to always do something new. They had also apparently forgotten that Americans rarely buckled under to threats.

Also, while the Chinese always laid their plans well, they were usually slow to react to something they hadn't planned for. They would have made plans for an American nuclear counterthreat, plans that probably entailed a sample nuclear strike on someplace like L.A., with the promise of more to come. They would have planned to tell the UN to shut up or die if the international body tried to get involved. And they might even have gone as far as to make plans for ruling a captive America. They wouldn't, however, have made plans to guard against a small but determined group of men dedicated to their work and ready to die to accomplish their mission.

The Chinese had always discounted the role of the individual in the shaping of history.

Brognola's face broke into a small smile, the first one he'd had since the Venture Star had disappeared. The President's okay for the Stony Man mission to attempt to recapture the Venture Star was only a part of the surprise package that was being put together for the Chinese.

While Phoenix Force was doing its thing on the ground, another small group of men would take Armageddon to outer space. The Chinese had stolen a march on America, but she wasn't out of the game yet, not by a long shot.

CHAPTER SIX

NASA Headquarters, Houston, Texas

In the wake of the destruction of the Venture Star, NASA Director William Kruger wasn't a man with a lot of time on his hands. Not since the dark days after the *Challenger* disaster had the future of NASA been so in doubt. As had happened back then, self-righteous finger-pointing was the order of the day. The fate of the space agency was being discussed everywhere from suburban dinner tables to the halls of Congress, and everyone had an opinion. The worst news, though, was coming out of Las Vegas, where the odds makers only gave NASA a one-in-four chance of surviving.

Kruger was living on coffee, doughnuts and vitamin pills, and sleeping on the couch in his office as he fought for his beloved agency's survival. But when the President called and told him to set up a meeting with some White House flunkies, he'd had no choice but to obey. NASA couldn't afford to anger the President and lose the support of the Oval Office.

The problem was that he had no idea what the meeting was supposed to be about. All he knew was that he had been told to expect a Mr. Hal Brognola who would explain the purpose of his visit. The last thing Kruger needed right now was to be uninformed, and he hadn't reached the position he held by being stupid enough to be blindsided. He immediately ordered his staff to run a background check on this Brognola and report back.

When they got back to him, though, their investigation didn't tell him much. Brognola turned out to be a midlevel Justice Department flunky who carried the tag of special assistant to the President. Special assistants around the White House were like fleas on dogs, too many to count. Nonetheless, his finely tuned bureaucratic senses told him that this wasn't going to be a routine visit.

Brognola was on time to the minute and turned out to be typically colorless, well-dressed but easily lost in the crowd. He could have come from any of a number of the alphabet-soup federal agencies. The three side boys with him, however, weren't midlevel Feds. They looked more like FBI or CIA muscle. The tall blond guy in the Secret Service–style mirrored sunglasses particularly looked as if he was bad news. Kruger didn't think he was going to enjoy this at all.

After the introductions had been made, Brognola got right to the point. ''First off, is this office secure?''

"Secure?" The director frowned. "I'm not sure what you mean."

"Do you have any active recording devices?" Hermann Schwarz asked. "And has the room been swept for bugs today?"

Kruger blinked. "Swept? No."

Opening his case, Schwarz brought out his multi-spectra bug sniffers and handed one to Carl Lyons. The two men carefully went over the room and everything in it.

"No active devices," Schwarz announced, watching his readouts as he spoke. "And no voice-activated."

"But—" he walked over to the phone bank on the director's desk "—we will want to neutralize this before we start."

"I have to have my phone," Kruger sputtered.

"Not for the next hour or so," Brognola said. "Nothing going on in your organization is as important as what we are going to discuss at this meeting. Your people can take care of anything that comes up."

After unplugging the phone, Lyons affixed a small device to the plate-glass window looking out over the Mission Control Center before closing the drapes.

"It's a countervibration device," he explained. "We don't need anyone aiming a directional mike at your window and picking up the vibrations off the glass when we speak."

"Do you mind telling me just what in the hell is

going on here?" Kruger's voice had a sharp edge. This charade out of a made-for-TV spy movie had gone on long enough. President or not, he had a lot on his plate that needed his attention.

Instead of answering, Brognola took a scrambler cellular phone out of his briefcase, dialed a number and held it up to his ear. "Brognola here, sir," he said. "I'm in the director's office now."

He handed the phone to Kruger. "It's the President."

The director was floored. He had talked to the President almost daily since the Venture Star disaster, but never with this level of security paranoia. "Mr. President, it's Bill Kruger."

The rest of the conversation was one-sided and when he handed the phone back, his face registered shock. "I've just been told to do anything you tell me to do without question. Who in the hell are you people, anyway?"

"We work for the President," Brognola said. "And I'm sorry, but that's all I can tell you at this juncture. Later, I might be able to tell you more, but that's all I can say right now."

Considering the instructions he had just been given, Kruger had to accept that.

"First off," Brognola said, "I need to inform you that the Venture Star wasn't destroyed. It was hijacked."

Kruger's hand reached for his phone to call security before he remembered that it had been disconnected.

"Don't leave your chair, mister," Lyons said as he undid the buttons of his suit jacket and moved it aside. "Just sit there and listen."

Seeing the threat, Kruger did as he was told.

"Secondly," Brognola continued as if nothing out of the ordinary had happened, "we're going to use the space shuttle *Atlantis* for a secret mission to destroy a series of nuclear-armed deep-space missile-launch platforms the Chinese have put in orbit. The current mission equipment that is being installed will be removed so we can load the necessary weaponry in *Atlantis*'s cargo bay."

"But that's in violation of the UN treaty on space exploration!" Kruger protested. "We can't take weapons into space!"

"The President has declared a national emergency, so he can do anything he feels he has to to protect the nation. And that includes disregarding a treaty."

"I know what the President told me," Kruger said, "but I want to hear this directly from his mouth. Anyone can sound like him over the phone, and I'm not doing a damned thing until I hear it from him personally."

"I can understand that," Brognola said calmly. "And, if it becomes necessary, that can be arranged. But I assure you that if a face-to-face meeting takes place, it will be to accept your resignation for reasons of ill health."

When Kruger pushed back his chair and started to get to his feet, Lyons whipped back the right side of his coat to reveal the .357 Colt Python nestled in the custom underarm rig he wore.

The director sat back down. "You can't threaten me in my own office," he snapped.

"Mr. Director," Blancanales said smoothly, "this isn't an empty threat, believe me. The President is dead serious, and so are we. The United States is facing the most dangerous threat since the Cuban Missile Crisis. But it's a space-based threat this time, and NASA is the only federal agency that can deal with it. And, unlike with the Cuban situation, the President cannot go on television this time and tell the people what is happening. If we can continue the briefing, I believe that we can make this clear and you will understand why it had to be done this way."

"And," Brognola cut in, "at the end of our briefing, if you still want to talk to the President, we will fly you to Washington. But, as I mentioned earlier, we will also take your second-in-command along so he can officially be informed of his promotion and given his instructions. One way or the other, NASA will comply with the President's wishes."

Kruger sat for a moment. "Can I call for a coffee service and a couple of doughnuts?" he asked. "I think I need a little pickup."

"I'll take care of that," Blancanales said smoothly, and headed for the door.

AT THE END of the briefing, Bill Kruger was no longer unhappy. He was enraged, but not at the four men the President had sent to his office. He was enraged at the unspeakable bastards who had dared to put his agency in jeopardy like this. He had devoted his life to NASA, and he would fight to the death against anyone who tried to destroy it. The fact that these same bastards were also threatening his country only added to his rage. Now he was really ready to fight.

"When do I bring the rest of my team in on this?" Kruger asked. "I understand the need for secrecy, but I cannot direct this mission by myself. I have to have the whole launch team on board."

"Not the whole team," Blancanales said as he reached into his briefcase. "This is a list of the men who have been cleared for this operation. And," he added, forestalling any questions, "if there are any others you feel are absolutely essential to make this work, they will be added. After, of course, they have been backgrounded."

Everyone who worked for NASA had been investigated all the way back to grade school, but Kruger knew better than to protest. "What's the timetable?" he asked.

Brognola looked him square in the eyes. "We should have launched yesterday."

The director shook his head. "I was afraid you were going to say something like that."

"WHY DO THESE space jockeys always have names like Buzz, Flash and Ace?" Hermann Schwarz asked rhetorically as he read over the rap sheets of the three military astronauts who had been chosen to fly the *Atlantis* mission. The President had decided that the crew had to come from the military officers in the astronaut corps to make it easier to maintain the necessary secrecy.

Major Roger "Flash" Bradley was the slated copilot for the mission. Major Douglas "Boomer" Boyd was the flight engineer. Only the commander, Colonel Gregory Cunningham, didn't have a typical flyer's moniker.

"Why do we call you Gadgets?" Carl Lyons answered. "It's the same thing."

"That's different," Schwarz said indignantly. "I got that nickname because I'm always screwing around with things."

"Maybe Flash here has a thing for photography or pyrotechnics."

"But what about Boomer?"

"Why don't you ask him?"

The three astronauts who walked into the briefing room at NASA headquarters looked like throwbacks to the golden days of the right stuff and the Apollo program. They all had the short haircuts, firm jaws and steely eyes that gave them that look made famous on countless fifties and sixties *Life* magazine covers. Even in nondescript civilian clothing, they could only be pilots, and the swagger marked them as hot rocks.

Blancanales was wearing an Air Force major general's uniform with the badge of the National

Security staff on his left breast pocket and enough ribbons to account for twenty years of service.

"I don't believe I've ever heard of you, General." Colonel Cunningham's eyes slid past the ribbon bar and insignia as he shook Blancanales's hand.

Blancanales smiled. "Well, Colonel, some of us don't see too much of the light of day in my line of work. I've been in Intelligence for most of my career."

"And," Cunningham continued, "if I might say, General, I find this all to be a little irregular. We've all been on several hush-hush missions, but never one set up like this. Normally, we get our mission briefings, even our classified ones, from NASA personnel."

"You're talking, I assume, about the Crystal Cloud and Center Point satellite launch and recovery missions?"

"Yes, sir."

Blancanales smiled. "Those were milk runs, Colonel, compared to what you and your crew will be doing this time."

"If I may ask, sir, just what are we going to be doing up there?"

"There are two Red Chinese deep-space nuclear-weapon launch platforms in high orbit, and your mission will be to destroy them."

The colonel's face went blank for a moment, and then he laughed. "With what? Every schoolkid knows that the shuttles aren't armed."

Blancanales caught the fact that the astronaut had failed to render the customary military courtesies that generals rated even in casual conversation. He had known that this wasn't going to be easy. These men weren't grunts who would take what came without question even if you threw them into a shit pile. They were the best and brightest of America's space program, and they were used to being treated like royalty. This time, though, they were going to be nothing more than glorified bus drivers.

"The UN space treaty has been suspended," Blancanales said. "And for this mission, the *Atlantis* will be carrying a multigigawatt laser in the cargo bay. These two men—" he gestured at Lyons and Schwarz "—will be on board as mission specialists to man the weapon."

For a moment, there was dead silence in the room. "Bullshit!" the colonel finally erupted.

Blancanales turned to the designated mission copilot, Major Bradley. "Major, are you qualified to fly as command pilot?"

"Wait a goddamned minute, General," Cunningham snapped. "Nobody's taking my ride away from me."

"Colonel," Blancanales snapped back, "I can ground you and I will if you don't sit down and shut the fuck up! Your mouth's writing checks your ass can't cash, mister. The President didn't send me down here to take any lip from a flyboy who isn't smart enough to keep his mouth shut in the middle of a mission briefing. If you don't like the job, no problem, you're dismissed. But if you say one single word to anyone about anything you've heard here so far, you'll be counting gooney birds on Wake Island until your retirement papers can be processed."

Blancanales drilled him with his eyes. "Is that abundantly clear?"

Cunningham swallowed hard. Being America's senior military astronaut, he was used to being treated like God, not some snot-nosed second lieutenant. Apparently, he'd stepped in it past his boot tops with this phantom general, and he'd better throttle back before he got his head handed to him on a plate. "I'm on board, sir,"

"I'll decide that after this briefing, Colonel."

Blancanales wasn't ready to let Cunningham off the hook yet. For this to work as planned, a couple of overinflated astronaut egos were going to have to be brought under control real fast. Particularly when they learned that their job was simply to get Lyons and Schwarz in position to use that laser.

"Now—" Blancanales swept his eyes past the three astronauts "—if there are no other questions, I would like to get on with this, gentlemen. The clock is running."

AT THE CONCLUSION of the briefing, the three astronauts were shocked and angry, and that was exactly where Rosario Blancanales wanted them to be. Under all the NASA Buck Rogers trappings, they were still military officers and their country was being threatened by an enemy power.

"What's the timetable for the mission, sir?" Cunningham asked.

"We start today," Blancanales replied. "You will be allowed one ten-minute phone call—monitored, of course—and then you will go into isolation and start rehearsing in the simulator. While that is going on, the *Atlantis* will be flown to Vandenberg, the weapon will be loaded and the other modifications made to the shuttle."

"General?" Major Bradley raised his hand.

"Yes, Major."

"If I might ask, sir. Where's this laser coming from? I'm an old Star Wars adviser, and I didn't think that any of the weapons we worked on had survived."

"It is from Star Wars," Blancanales admitted. "It's one of the Brilliant Pebbles test pieces."

"Damn!" Bradley smiled. "If I remember right, that's some popgun."

Blancanales consulted his notes. "Two hundred and twenty gigawatts, I believe."

"That ought to be big enough to do the job."

"We're counting on it," Blancanales replied.

CHAPTER SEVEN

Alamagordo, New Mexico,
Weapons Development Site

"That's it?" Hermann Schwarz frowned as the scientist pulled a dusty tarp off a piece of machinery in the secured warehouse on the back lot of the test site. This wasn't what he had expected a space weapon to look like at all. For one thing, the Brilliant Pebbles laser was only about twelve feet long and half that wide. Its barrel, if it could be called that, was short, stubby and didn't look like much of anything that could shoot.

"That's it." The weapons scientist laughed. "I know it doesn't look much like a science-fiction movie prop, but I can tell you that it works. We have a piece of thirty-six-inch-thick armor steel that has a series of three-inch holes drilled in it from a hundred miles away."

"We're going to be using it at a bit longer range than that," Schwarz said.

"I know," the scientist replied. "But that was as far away as we could get the target for our atmospheric tests. Remember, this is a line-of-sight weapon. If you can't see the target, you can't hit it. We also shot down target drones we could only see on radar at over twice that range. And you have to remember that this was supposed to be a space weapon, so it will work much better in a vacuum."

"I guess we'll have to take your word for it."

"Believe me, if you can get the beam on target, it'll do the job for you. Nothing has ever gone into space that this won't burn a hole in."

"When do we get to learn how to shoot it?" Schwarz asked.

"We have the simulator up and running," the scientist said. "And it's only by a quirk of fate that we have any of this stuff left. When the Star Wars program was closed down, we were supposed to have destroyed all the material associated with it along with the test weapons. It was a typical election-year congressional slash-and-burn operation.

"This particular laser, however—" the scientist put on an innocent look "—somehow never made it into the official destruction inventory, so it was overlooked as was the simulator that goes with it. Fortunately, it was also stored in a climate-controlled facility and is still fully functional."

"It's amazing how easy it is to overlook something in a large government operation like this, isn't it?" Schwarz asked.

"It is truly amazing," the scientist agreed.

"Let's get this thing rolled out," Lyons said. "The truck's waiting."

The scientist lost his fight with himself and asked the question that had been dogging him since getting the first phone call. "Is there any way you guys can tell me what you're going to use it for?"

Schwarz shook his head. "I wish we could," he said sincerely. "I really do. All I can say is keep a close eye on space developments over the next couple of days."

"But," Lyons said, "you'd better make damned sure that you keep any conclusions you form completely to yourself. Understand?"

"I understand," the scientist said, nodding. "Thanks."

"Thank you for having this available."

THE 18-WHEELER that would transport the laser to Vandenberg Air Force Base bore the markings of a fruit-and-vegetable company on the sides of the trailer. The doors of the cab announced that it was from a Stockton, California, shipping company. From the outside, it was completely indistinguishable from any of the hundreds of other trucks on the nation's freeways.

It had been Lyons's idea to use a civilian-marked truck rather than do with one of the white trucks that routinely moved nuclear weapons around the country. Until the Chinese spy ring that had set up this snatch had been destroyed, they could take no chances of its being spotted.

When the Able Team duo stepped out of the warehouse, Lyons briefly inspected the twenty-man

Delta Force unit that had been assigned to guard the shipment. They didn't expect to find any faults with either the men or their equipment. You didn't become a member of the nation's most elite military strike force by being a slacker. But the inspection was a tradition and the commandos expected it.

The infantry major commanding the unit was a typical Delta Force officer, which was to say he was very serious about his work. He also didn't know what was going on, but he didn't need to. He had his orders and they were specific. Nothing or no one was to be allowed to prevent the cargo from reaching Vandenberg Air Force Base, California.

"Okay, Major," Lyons said after looking over the last Delta Force commando, "have your men supervise the loading. We move out as soon as the package is on board."

"Yes, sir."

WHILE ABLE TEAM WAS retrieving the laser from the New Mexico test site, the *Atlantis* had been flown to Vandenberg Air Force Base on the southern California coast on the NASA Boeing 747-100 shuttle-transport jet. The shuttle had just come out of a postmission inspection and was immediately put into the vehicle-assembly building to be mated with its main fuel tank and the solid-fuel boosters. To do this job in the least possible time, Bill Kruger had sent two extra assembly crews with the shuttle to speed the work. By working three shifts, the *Atlantis* would be ready to launch in record time.

While the components were being assembled, the shuttle's cargo bay was quickly cleared of its originally scheduled cargo fitting and modified to accept the laser. Mounting the weapon wouldn't be difficult. The shuttle was designed to accept any number of different packages in the fifteen-by-sixty-foot bay. The fact that the shuttle's designers had never considered a laser weapon as a payload wouldn't be a problem. The remote manipulator controls would work on it as well as they did on other more peaceful cargo packages.

AS SOON AS the convoy from the Alamagordo test site arrived at Vandenberg, the payload handlers immediately took charge of the laser. While they installed it in *Atlantis*'s cargo bay, Carl Lyons and Hermann Schwarz started training on the simulator. Firing a laser was considerably simpler than firing an artillery piece, as there was no ammunition to be loaded after each shot. Unlike the science-fiction lasers, though, this weapon didn't shoot an unending beam of coherent light. This was a pulsed laser, and there was a pause to recharge between each release of energy.

Being concentrated light, the laser beam traveled at the speed of light, 186,000 miles per second. For all practical purposes, the two thousand miles between the *Atlantis*'s orbit and the Chinese missile platforms might as well have been two feet. When Lyons tripped the firing button, the beam would hit the target in less than one-hundredth of a second.

But at that distance, if Schwarz's aim was off by even as much as one-hundredth of an inch, the beam would miss by miles.

Therefore, the tricky part was learning to use the laser's specialized targeting radar. The radar inputted the laser's orbital position and movement, as well as that of the target. Were it not for the computers constantly solving the orbital equations as they changed, it would have been impossible to hit anything.

The pair worked on the simulator, breaking only for meals and short naps, until aiming the laser became almost automatic and their percentage of simulated hits was high. How it would work in practice they would have to wait and see.

Stony Man Farm, Virginia

DURING THIS TIME, Mack Bolan and the members of Phoenix Force had assembled and were going over the details of the assault plan. The insertion would be a standard HALO parachute jump—high altitude, low opening. That was still the fastest way to get on the ground without being seen, particularly when they used a radar-evading B-2 Stealth bomber as their transport. It was what they would have to face on the ground that presented the challenge. With the Chinese being very careful about what they allowed to be seen by the recon satellites, Phoenix Force would be jumping into the unknown.

"I know you want to go," Bolan told Yakov

Katzenelenbogen as they took a break, "but you are more valuable as a tactical adviser. If it hits the fan in China, we're going to need someone here who can help us get things sorted out quickly."

"Dammit, Mack," Katz protested, "I don't like your going in without an extraction plan. Even a single helicopter with midair refueling would do it."

"You know what the Man said. He's afraid that if we try to set something like that up, the Chinese will catch on and move the Venture Star. That's the bad thing about it. They can land it anywhere, and we'd have to start all over. Plus, with the defenses of that place, it wouldn't stand a chance."

"I just wish he'd authorize a cruise-missile strike and take the damned thing out the easy way."

Bolan smiled. "You're working for the wrong bunch of people, Katz. You know we never do it the easy way around here. You have to remember that the Venture Star cost the taxpayers five billion, that's with a *B,* and the Man doesn't have that kind of money laying around to spend on a replacement."

"I know," the Israeli said. "But that doesn't mean that I have to like it. If it's not fueled and ready to go when you guys show up, you're all going to be screwed."

Bolan's face set. "That's the name of the game. None of us are ever going to die in bed."

"But there are better places to die than the western desert of China."

"A few," Bolan agreed. "But there are worse ones, as well."

"You know what I mean."

"I know, old friend." Bolan laid his hand on Katz's shoulder. "But this is one of those times when we have to do it exactly the way the Man wants it done. "

"There are too damned many of those times lately." Katz shook his head.

"I know."

When Katz saw Barbara Price approach, he found something else to do.

"What's with Katz?" she asked Bolan. "He doesn't look very happy."

"It's nothing personal. He's been trying to talk me out of going on this one."

"Make me number two, then," she replied.

"I'd really rather not have to do this," he said honestly. "But there's too much riding on it, and it's not just national pride. If we can't put that thing out of action one way or the other, it's going to get really serious."

"Have you noticed," she said, abruptly changing topics, "that we all call the Venture Star a thing. Except for Katz and he calls it 'that damned thing.'"

Bolan smiled. "I guess we all need to give 'her' a break. It's not her fault she got hijacked."

"And the Stony Man teams are going to rescue her."

JACK GRIMALDI'S HEAD was spinning. The flight simulator was driving him crazy. As the Farm's ace pilot, it was automatically assumed that he could handle anything with wings, and maybe that was the problem. The Venture Star didn't really have wings. Usually, he could go in for a half an hour in the simulator for an aircraft he had never flown before and he could pick it up right away. He just couldn't get the hang of this damned thing, though.

A big part of the problem was that the spacecraft was the ultimate blind fly-by-wire machine, and the only way he could tell where he was going was to watch the instrument readouts. The other problem was what was called Newtonian Mechanics. In space, there was no air to work against control surfaces to stabilize the machine. A pilot maneuvered a shuttle in space by using small rockets called thrusters. They applied force to the airframe and moved it around by Newton's Third Law—for every action, there is an equal but opposite reaction.

If he fired the starboard nose thruster, the shuttle's nose went in the opposite direction, left. The problem was that once he was aimed in the proper direction, he had to apply the opposite thruster to stop the movement. But every time he tried to make even a simple correction, he overshot with both thruster burns.

"You're overcontrolling again." The voice of the NASA man in his earphone was driving him stark raving mad. But he knew that if he couldn't get this procedure down, he wouldn't make the mission. If he couldn't show the NASA weenies that he could fly the spacecraft, Phoenix Force would simply blow it in place, and they didn't need a pilot to do that.

"Pretend that you're flying the most sensitive plane you've ever flown," the NASA trainer advised. "And it doesn't have any automatic return on the controls, so you can't fly by feel. You have to go to the opposite control to cancel each move you make."

Grimaldi paused for a moment to collect himself before radioing back. "Okay. I'm ready to try it again."

At least the radio hookup allowed him to try to learn to fly the Venture Star at Stony Man Farm. That way, he could keep in touch with the rest of the team for the ground mission planning.

"You got it that time," the NASA controller said. "Now go for a three-and-a-half-degree pitch up change. Ready on three. One...two...three."

Grimaldi moved the thruster control stick back as he would on any earthbound aircraft. Watching the altitude direction indicator on the instrument panel, he followed the correction. At the exact right moment, he applied reverse thruster and the movement stopped.

"Not too bad," the trainer said. "You're only off a quarter of a degree. Now go for a half-degree portside yaw. On my command. One...two... three."

WHILE GRIMALDI SWEATED out the Venture Star simulator, Phoenix Force also went through a simulated training exercise. They didn't always run through a premission rehearsal, but assaulting the Quinbaki complex wasn't their usual mission. They usually didn't take on a target that large without outside fire support or at least backup of some kind to provide a diversion. But the nature of the mission left them completely on their own this time. Should they fail, submarine-launched cruise missiles would be their avengers. But they wouldn't be alive to enjoy seeing the secret launch complex go up in a mushroom cloud.

The simulation they went through was a product of Aaron Kurtzman, Akira Tokaido and John Kissinger getting their heads together. The three of them combined all of the data that had been gathered on the Chinese site and designed the simulation to reflect the worst-case assumptions about the defenses and enemy forces Phoenix Force could expect to face. There was no point in rehearsing against less than they would have to face on the ground.

The three trainers programmed the mission as a multiplayer computer war game, and they played the Chinese while the Phoenix Force commandos each played his own role. By the end of the third run, the commandos were penetrating the perimeter and making it to the launch site without stirring up too much trouble along the way. The simulation ended when they reached the Venture Star, because no one knew what they would find when they reached it.

To round things out, however, Calvin James, Gary Manning, Rafael Encizo and T. J. Hawkins reviewed their demolition procedures and made a mental list of places in the Venture Star that would most benefit from several pounds of plastic explosive. One way or the other, the Chinese wouldn't be allowed to keep America's new spaceship.

CHAPTER EIGHT

Vandenberg Air Force Base, California

Now that Carl Lyons and Hermann Schwarz were in premission isolation with the *Atlantis*'s military astronauts, Rosario Blancanales found himself out of a job. His need to masquerade as an Air Force major general was over, and that left him at loose ends. He had never liked to have time on his hands, and he felt left out of the two ongoing Stony Man operations. His comrades-in-arms were putting it on the line while he was sitting idle in his hotel room.

Suddenly, he remembered a loose end that hadn't been addressed and grabbed the phone. "Katz," he said when the Farm's tactical adviser came on the line. "Unless you or Barbara have something real important for me to do in the next couple of days, I'm going to stay in California. There's something down here I want to look into."

"What's that?" Katzenelenbogen asked.

"Well, in all the rush to chase down our missing spaceship, there's a little something that we completely overlooked."

"And that is?"

"If you'll remember," Blancanales said, "we seem to have a Chinese spy ring operating in this country that talks people into stealing spaceships. We need to put a hammer on those guys so this doesn't happen again."

"Damn," Katz said, "I completely forgot that end of it. We've been so busy trying to get these two missions off the ground that we completely overlooked that."

"Since I'm here anyway," Blancanales said, "I thought I'd start working on it. I need all the background you have on the Venture Star's Chinese American crew and a cover so I can get help from the local authorities."

"Hunt will research the background for you, and then I'll see if Hal will authorize your using the Justice Department cover again. That's well established, and you won't have to lose any time getting started."

Since Able Team mostly operated inside the United States, Brognola had them on the federal roster as special agents of the Justice Department and had given them bona fide paperwork to back it up. Since Justice cut a wide swath in law-enforcement circles, no one wanted to mess with them when they flashed their ID cards.

"Great," Blancanales replied. "How about putting Hunt on the line."

Stony Man Farm, Virginia

HUNT WETHERS HAD ALREADY compiled all the background information on the Venture Star's crew. He had the original background workup that had been done when they joined Lockheed, the supplemental material NASA had required and the back-door information Lyons had been working on before he and Schwarz escorted the laser to Vandenberg.

That was all delivered to Blancanales along with letters of authorization signed off by everyone who mattered, from the President on down. In the national consciousness, the Venture Star disaster was still a reality, and everyone was eager to assist in solving the mystery.

After reading over the material in his hotel room, Blancanales decided to start by investigating Selena Del Gato. Of the two Chinese American crew members, she was the one who was most likely to have been the weakest link. For one thing, she was female and, political correctness aside, women were more easily turned than men. Secondly, she had a bit of a checkered past. Regardless of her engineering skills, had she not been a woman, she probably wouldn't have made the cut for the Venture Star program.

Unlike the Skunk Works's earlier secret projects, the development of the Venture Star had been as much a political exercise as it had been applied aerospace engineering. This craft was to usher in a new age of space travel and, to keep the necessary funding flowing, it had been developed in the glare of a media blitz rarely seen outside of a presidential election. In an effort to mollify the liberal congressional critics of space expenditures, the crew selection had been a carefully orchestrated PR celebration of American cultural diversity.

The original crew had consisted of a white command pilot, a black copilot and Selena Del Gato, a Hispanic female mission specialist. It was a something-for-everyone crew with Del Gato serving as a two-for-one minority appointment. The fact that she was a double minority went a long way to cover up a background that would have caused a man to be eliminated in the first round of the selection process. Since she wasn't flight rated, though, she could have never pulled off a space hijacking on her own. It was only after the original copilot had been fatally injured in a hit-and-run car crash two months before the launch that James Chin of the backup crew had replaced him.

That accident put two people on board with family ties to the old country. And, if Wethers's information was correct, Del Gato had been sleeping with Jimmy Chin during crew training, which could be the critical link. If she had been recruited by the Chinese, using her sexual favors to turn Chin was the oldest story in the book. It would also be difficult to uncover because, like the Venture Star, both of them were no longer in the United States.

BLANCANALES'S FIRST STOP in his one-man investigation was the Palmdale Skunk Works. Using his

Justice Department credentials, he had no trouble getting the Venture Star project managers and Lockheed Martin's personnel director in the secure conference room on short notice.

"Gentlemen," he began, "the information I am about to give you is classified top secret, need-to-know. It will not go beyond this room, and you will be expected to sign a security agreement before you leave."

"If you'll bother to check," a deputy manager said with a smirk, "you'll find that we all have current signed security disclosure forms in our files. We're pretty well accustomed to working with top secret material around here."

Seeing that this was getting out of hand before he had even started, Blancanales took a page out of Lyons's play book. "Name?" he asked.

The man looked confused. "My name?"

Blancanales locked eyes with him. "Did I stutter, mister? I want your name and company badge number."

"Wait a minute, I don't know who in the hell—"

Blancanales calmly took out his cellular phone and punched in the number for the Skunk Works security office. "This is Rivera in the secure conference room. I want a custody team in here ASAP."

The man immediately took stock of the developing situation. "I'm sorry," he said. "I just wanted—"

Blancanales wasn't about to let him off the hook.

"You just wanted to show everyone here what a big man you are by taking a lowly federal flunky down a couple of notches. If you were authorized to look at my file, mister, you'd see that I have the authority to do things to you that you didn't know could be done without a federal court order."

When a knock sounded at the door, Blancanales opened it to admit four uniformed Lockheed security cops.

"If you leave now," Blancanales told the man, "you'll get to keep your job. Give me any more lip, even one word, and you'll be going through an extensive debriefing. I don't think you'll care for it because it will be part of your termination process here at Lockheed Martin. And, of course, you'll never work on any government-funded operation again. Do you read me, mister?"

The man nodded.

"Keep him isolated until I'm done here," Blancanales told the security team leader. "I'll debrief him then."

"Yes, sir."

After the deputy manager was escorted out, Blancanales turned back to the others. Needless to say, he now had the undivided attention of everyone in the room.

"Now, where was I? Oh yes, I was talking about need-to-know. No person outside this room has a need to know what I am about to tell you. Should I find that anyone has learned about it, each one of you will undergo a debriefing. Is that understood?"

When everyone nodded, Blancanales continued. "To start off, the Venture Star wasn't destroyed—it was hijacked."

Pandemonium broke out, and when questions were shouted to him, Blancanales raised a hand. "I can't tell you where it is at this point, but a team is en route right now to try to recover it. I'm here to make sure that something like that doesn't ever happen again, and I need your help."

From that point on, he had their fullest cooperation.

BLANCANALES'S VISIT to the Skunk Works had confirmed one thing—James Chin and Selena Del Gato had been getting it on hot and heavy throughout their training time. Prior to Chin joining the crew, however, Del Gato had been sleeping with Bill Garvy, the original copilot. It was apparent now that he hadn't wanted to betray his country, and unfortunately for him, he hadn't survived his refusal. Garvy's experience showed that the old adage about the fury of a woman scorned was still alive and well. She had been scorned, and her fury had gotten him killed.

While Garvy wouldn't be able to tell Blancanales what he knew, there was a chance that his family and friends might be able to help. No matter what security agreements a man signed, he almost always talked to someone about what he was doing for a living. Particularly if he was a man who was having woman troubles on the job.

NOT SURPRISINGLY, Garvy's best friend turned out to be one of the other Lockheed test pilots. The fraternity of those who buckled themselves into experimental aircraft as part of a day at the office was a small, close-knit group. A person who was a test pilot would find it difficult to be close to men who thought that the monthly sales figures were real exciting.

Blancanales found Rick Newton in a cubicle in the flight-test office of the Skunk Works. Blancanales's ID worked to drag Newton away from his computer and into an empty office. He didn't go into a long explanation to the pilot about exactly what he was investigating. Newton would make the connection on his own later.

After checking to make sure that the man knew Garvy, he launched into his questions. "Were you aware that Bill Garvy and Selena Del Gato were an item?"

"Yes, if you mean were they screwing each other's brains out," the pilot replied. "You'd have to have been blind not to see that. I told him she was bad news, but he wouldn't listen to me."

"What do you mean?"

"She was entirely too intense to be a good pilot's shack job. She demanded too much of his time. When he wasn't on the job here, he was with her."

"Do you know where they went on dates?"

Newton shrugged. "I can't really say. As far as I know, they spent a lot of time at his place, screwing, eating takeout and watching movies."

"Was it by any chance Chinese food?"

Newton had it on the tip of his tongue to ask what in the hell that had to do with anything, but he refrained. "Damned if I know." he said. "I guess it could have been."

"Did he ever mention going out for Chinese food, going to Chinese art exhibits, Chinese films, that sort of thing?"

"Not that I can remember." The pilot frowned. "But one time he did come in to work with a bad head saying something about Chinese whiskey. I don't know if he went out for it, though."

"Did he ever say anything to you about having problems with Del Gato? You know, Friday-night, happy-hour-at-the-bar kind of talk?"

"Not really," Newton said. "But that was probably because he knew I didn't have much use for her. I made the mistake of telling him that she was a 'cultural diversity' quota on the crew, and that pissed him off. Being black, he didn't like to hear things like that. It made him doubt why he had been chosen himself."

"So I take it you won't be able to help me with her background or her friends."

"Except for the guys she was sleeping with, she didn't have any friends around here, and I know zilch about her before she got here."

"Look," Blancanales said, "I'm going to give you my card. If you remember anything else, give me a call."

"Sure thing," the pilot replied. "But, if you

don't mind my asking, what in the hell is the Justice Department doing involved with this? The damned thing blew up in space."

Blancanales smiled. "Let's just say that damned near every Fed in the country is working on this one. I just happened to be in California and got reassigned to do some follow-up work on this. And I guess I don't have to tell you to keep this interview to yourself."

"No sweat."

"One more thing," Blancanales said. "Has the company emptied out the crew's lockers yet?"

The pilot laughed. "The FBI did that the day after the explosion."

"Thanks, I'll check with them."

SINCE THE HIT-AND-RUN accident that had ended Bill Garvy's life had taken place on a nearby state highway, it would have been investigated as a vehicular homicide. Blancanales' next stop was the local district office of the California Highway Patrol at Lancaster. His Justice Department ID card got him instant cooperation, and as he had expected, the wreckage of Garvy's silver Acura sports coupe was still in the impound yard behind the building.

The highway patrol had done a forensic workup on the case, but had not gotten anywhere with the investigation. Blancanales wasn't at all surprised to hear that. If the crash had been set up to kill the astronaut, it would have been done by professionals, and pros didn't let highway cops trip them up.

"We matched the paint marks left behind to an '87 Chevy Blazer color, southwest bronze," the investigating officer explained. "But that's as far as we got. We just don't have the resources to run down every '87 Blazer registered in California and check it out."

Blancanales didn't bother telling the officer that the Blazer that had left the paint behind had more than likely been turned into scrap metal an hour after the crash.

"What about the Acura's contents?"

"The family claimed Garvy's personal items."

"How about the trash, the junk in the glove box and under the seats?"

"If there was anything there, it should still be there. We didn't do a forensic sweep of the interior, since it wasn't really a crime scene."

"Do you mind if I take a look inside?"

"Help yourself."

The Acura's driver's-side door had been driven in almost to the transmission tunnel by the impact. The airbags had deployed, but it would have taken a bit more than a nylon bag full of nitrogen to protect the driver this time. He would have needed a tank to protect him from the heavy-duty brush bar that had done this damage.

Blancanales had to borrow some tools from the CHP mechanics to remove the crumpled driver's seat so he could look under it. The passenger's-side seat was easier, and under the left front corner he found a crumpled paper napkin that had been spotted with blood sprayed by the impact. Opening it up, he saw the imprint of a Chinese dragon flanked by Chinese characters on either side. A phone number, partially obscured with blood, was printed below the dragon. The prefix indicated that it was in Greater L.A.

This find was almost too good to be true, but sometimes things just fell in place. Blancanales knew, though, that it could just as well be a dead end.

CHAPTER NINE

Highland, California

After leaving the CHP impound yard, Rosario Blancanales headed for Selena Del Gato's apartment in nearby Highland. From the information he had, she had no family beyond a mother living in Florida. The elder Mrs. Del Gato was in deep mourning over what she believed was the loss of her adopted daughter and hadn't yet made arrangements for the apartment to be cleared out. It was a long shot that there'd be much to find there, but he had to check it out before moving on.

After letting himself in with his lock pick, Blancanales stopped inside the door in surprise. From her personality profile, he had expected Del Gato's apartment to be barely lived in. But the place looked as if an interior decorator had been given a blank check and told to furnish it down to the baseboards for a Realtor's open house. As he quickly went from room to room, he saw that everything an occupant would need from toothpicks to bath towels was present.

What was missing, however, was any sign that Selena Del Gato had ever lived there.

There were a few clothes in the closets and dresser, but they were freshly laundered and neatly put away again as if for a display. Several books were on the shelves and a few magazines on the coffee table, but they, too, looked as if they were decorator items. There were even some canned and boxed foods on the kitchen shelves and mineral water in the refrigerator. What was missing was the half tube of toothpaste, the open box of breakfast cereal, the unpaid bill, the burned-out light in the desk lamp, the trash under the sink, the usual signs of human occupation.

There was no way to tell that anyone, much less a missing-and-presumed-dead astronaut, had ever lived there.

The thought crossed his mind that Del Gato might have been an obsessive-compulsive personality type who had lived as if she were on display in a store window. But something like that would have been picked up in the psych tests, and she'd never have made it into the astronaut corps. Considering what he knew of her real fate, it was clear that a cleanup team had been sent in to remove all traces of her life. For that to have been done meant that there had been something in the apartment worth removing at the risk of creating suspicions about why it had been done.

Knowing what he was up against, Blancanales decided to search the apartment anyway. At a casual glance, whoever had cleaned this place up was good, but he might have not been all that good. Taking off his coat, Blancanales headed for the bedroom and adjoining bath.

Two hours later, Del Gato's apartment looked like the scene of a high-speed, multiple-vehicle collision at a garbage-truck convention. Unfortunately, though, his effort hadn't accomplished much. He had found a hairpin jammed between the mattress and the bed frame and that was it. Every inch of the carpet had been vacuumed, including under every piece of furniture. Every drawer and closet shelf had been dusted, as had the kitchen cabinets.

On the way out, he stopped to put on his coat and noticed the phone books neatly lined up beside the answering machine. Hoping against hope, he played the message-received tape and found it completely blank, as was the announcement tape for the machine. Another strikeout.

He was turning away when he noticed that the cover of the Pasadena phone book was in less than pristine condition. It showed a bit of normal wear and tear, which could mean that it might not have been replaced.

Tucking the phone book under his arm, he let himself out and headed for his car. With that kind of cleanup having been done, he knew there was no point in canvassing the adjoining apartments. No one would have seen or heard anything, and he might alert whoever was behind this that he was looking for traces of Del Gato.

WHEN BLANCANALES CHECKED in with the Farm to report his progress, or lack thereof, and get any updates, Akira Tokaido didn't have much for him. Kurtzman had tasked him with doing the workup on Del Gato's contacts, but everywhere he looked, he was running into a stone wall.

"I've been trying all the usual stuff on her," Tokaido told Blancanales, "but nothing's jumping out at me. Her bank account doesn't show anything more than her Lockheed paychecks, so she wasn't being paid off. I ran her credit cards and struck out there, too. From what I've seen from her bank records, she did mostly cash transactions."

"I'm not surprised," Blancanales said. "If she was the one who honchoed this operation, she would have left her paperwork trail as clean as she did her apartment."

"The one thing I keep coming up with," Tokaido said, "is a cell phone number. She always called it from her own cell phone, never from her home phone. Interestingly enough, when I checked, I found the cell phone she used wasn't recovered from her crew locker at Lockheed. Maybe she didn't want anyone finding a scrambler system or something like that had been installed in it."

"What's the number?" Blancanales asked.

"I checked it out," Tokaido replied, "and it's another cell phone, registry unknown. I even tried calling it, but got no answer."

"Give it to me anyway."

Stony Man Farm, Virginia

WHEN BLANCANALES HUNG UP, Tokaido was frustrated that he wasn't keeping up his end of the stick and decided to get really down and dirty. He wasn't blessed with the inspired flashes of pure cyberintellect that fueled Aaron Kurtzman nor even with the doggedly determined research of Hunt Wethers, but he did have his methods. He was good at working the loose edges of a problem even when it didn't look promising.

From everything he had learned so far, Selena Del Gato's background was bulletproof. All the way back to grade school, nothing criminal or subversive blackened her record as an overachiever fighting her way to the top of a male-dominated profession. But, as he knew so well, that was only an appearance. No one could go through life in modern America without leaving traces. Particularly someone like her who had lived a rather public life in California.

Since the obvious trails had been carefully erased, he would go off-road with a vengeance. And he would start with the one characteristic about her that almost everyone had mentioned—her overactive sex life. The political-correctness movement of the nineties had made a woman's sexual activities an off-limits topic as far as official concern went. A man could lose his job for telling a so-called sexist joke, but a woman could work her way through a pro football team on her lunch breaks and not raise an eyebrow, officially that was. That didn't mean, however, that no one had noticed what she was doing. Notes had sure been taken in her case.

Being an ardent student of female psychology, Tokaido was confident that Del Gato's randy behavior predated her involvement with the Venture Star project. To be as successful as she had apparently been at using her assets, a woman needed to start perfecting her art early in life, at least by high school and certainly by her college years. A cruise through Del Gato's academic career might turn up some interesting recollections, particularly from her old teachers and professors. She might have practiced her skills on her classmates, but she would have reserved her best work for those who could do something for her in exchange.

He was cruising through Del Gato's undergraduate course transcripts when he saw that she had taken a course in Chinese art and culture from a Dr. Lin Chu. That stood out because back then she had still been playing the Hispanic card, having parlayed it into a minority-preference admission to Cal Tech.

She had taken the course during her junior year, and flipping through the entries, he saw it was the only time she had shown any kind of academic interest in China. It could be just a blip in her engineering studies, a course she had taken on a whim because everything else she wanted to take that term was full. But it could also be when she was first approached by the Chinese. Whichever one it was, it needed to be checked out further.

Her professor for that course was easy to locate. He had almost a quarter page in the who's who of aerospace engineering and was the recipient of numerous awards for his contributions to Defense Department and NASA projects. He had come to the States from Hong Kong in the early seventies and had been hired by the Rocketdyne Division of Rockwell to work on the design team for the main engines of the space shuttle. For reasons unmentioned, he left Rockwell in the early eighties to join the aerospace-engineering faculty at Cal Tech. The Chinese culture course he taught there was just a sideline.

Checking Del Gato's transcript more closely, Tokaido saw that she had taken several of Dr. Lin's aerospace-engineering courses. He also saw that he had written letters of recommendation for her to get into grad school to continue her engineering studies. Considering her grades, it wasn't unusual for him to have done that. But, if you had suspicions, it could be a sign of something else.

At least Blancanales now had a loose end he could start looking at.

California

WORKING SOLO as he was, there was no way for Rosario Blancanales to put together an elaborate plan to work the lead he had from the paper napkin he'd recovered from Bill Garvy's car. The Happy Dragon restaurant was in Santa Clarita, but, beyond that, he knew nothing about the establishment or the people who ran it. He realized that it was a long shot, but he also knew that he had to look into it.

The problem was that he couldn't infiltrate it alone or even keep it under surveillance without getting another agency involved, and he needed an excuse that wouldn't involve the Venture Star investigation. If anything was to leak out connecting the two, word might get back to China and jeopardize the Phoenix Force and *Atlantis* missions. The old standby of dragging in the DEA for a drug investigation was overworked. Everybody and their dog was working the drug-interdiction drill these days, and a professional spy ring would know better than to get involved with that.

A good ploy, though, might be to get the Immigration and Naturalization Service to give him a hand. Illegal Chinese immigration was on the rise and not just from the mainland and Hong Kong. With the unabated financial turmoil in Southeast Asia, the offshore Chinese, as they were called, had been hit hard. Ethnic Chinese from Singapore, Indonesia and other countries in the Pacific Rim were looking for a place to start over again. As always, the United States was the destination of choice.

The INS wasn't known to be the best federal agency for an intelligence-gathering operation. But the cover story would fly with them no questions asked and leave him free to develop other leads.

What they were going to be, though, he didn't have the slightest clue. This was one of those cases where a single man, working completely alone, could have turned Del Gato and set up the hijacking. And, if that turned out to have been the case, there would be no need for a spy ring of any kind, no secret codes, no radio transmissions or secret bank accounts.

BRINGING THE INS on board turned out to be a piece of cake. Blancanales showed up at their regional office, flashed his Justice Department ID card and found a receptive audience. Popping illegal Latin Americans was getting to be a real old story with them. Nine out of every ten they caught and deported were back in California before the month was out. Bagging illegal Chinese would mean that they would be deported across the Pacific, and it would take them longer to make it back.

After making a couple of phone calls to authorize the operation, the INS put together a twenty-four-hour surveillance team and started doing the background workup on the restaurant's owners and employees. Blancanales didn't want to get his hopes up that anything would come out of this. But, like the Del Gato apartment search, this was something that needed to be done.

After leaving his cellular phone number with the INS team leader, Blancanales went back to his hotel to check in with Stony Man again.

Stony Man Farm, Virginia

WHEN HAL BROGNOLA RETURNED to Stony Man Farm from Washington, he found Jack Grimaldi and Phoenix Force ready and awaiting their move-out orders.

"You're still go for the first leg to Diego Garcia Island as scheduled," he told them at the final briefing. "But you'll have to hold there until we give you a go to continue. The President wants the *Atlantis* to launch first and get into orbit before you take off. He's afraid that if you make your strike first, the Chinese might retaliate by launching a space missile at us."

"You mean if we fail, they might launch," Katzenelenbogen said dryly.

"That, too," Brognola admitted.

"That sounds to me like the Man doesn't have a lot of confidence in us," T. J. Hawkins said.

"He wouldn't be sending you people in if he didn't think you could do the job," Brognola said, defending his boss. "But you have to realize that those damned missiles put this operation in a different category than most of your missions."

"You've got that right," Hawkins replied. "Usually, we don't drop into the middle of a desert and have to make our way through half of the Chinese army to do our job. I'm surprised he's sending us in at all."

"He wants the Venture Star back at all costs,"

Jack Grimaldi said, "and we're an expendable part of the equation, pure and simple."

"That's fine with me," Hawkins said, smiling grimly. "Just as long as I know the score up front."

"Spoken like a true Ranger." Calvin James laughed.

Brognola let his eyes fall on each man in the War Room. Though he stayed safely behind each time he ordered these men out to put their lives on the line, he felt closer to them than to anyone else in the world. Every time he sent them into action, he steeled himself to the reality that some of them might not return. Their skill and experience had seen them through more times than he could count. This time, there was a better than average chance that they would all be lost, but he still had to send them.

"Gentlemen, if there's nothing else, your ETA to catch your ride at Andrews is still good. I have to be in Houston when the *Atlantis* takes off, but I'll be in touch as soon as you land at Diego. Good luck."

Katzenelenbogen stayed behind as the Phoenix Force warriors dispersed. "We just got word that the USS *Seawolf* is on station in the South China Sea with a belly full of nuclear-armed cruise missiles," he told Brognola. "I sent them the revised targeting data, so they're ready to launch on command."

Brognola shook his head. "I wish I could order

the cruise missiles in right now and cancel this operation."

"That makes a bunch of us," Katz agreed, "but, that's not the game plan this time."

"It rarely is."

CHAPTER TEN

Vandenberg Air Force Base, California

No TV cameras were set up at the Vandenberg Air Force Base launch facility to record Carl Lyons and Hermann Schwarz's walk down the boarding gantry with the three NASA astronauts. They wouldn't be able to relive this historic event from the comfort of their living rooms later, and no one else would ever see them proudly wearing their orange space-suits. This was one space adventure that wouldn't make the record books except as a brief mention of a classified shuttle test flight. Even then, no mention would be made of the two Able Team mission specialists along for the ride.

Needless to say, no media in any form was on hand to record the event. No announcement had been made of the flight, and all inquiries as to why a space shuttle was sitting on the launch pad were being ignored. For once, a publicity-hungry NASA was acting more like the CIA. Even so, anyone outside the air base's perimeter who bothered to look could see the *Atlantis* on the launch tower. It was impossible to camouflage.

Along with the usual white-suited NASA technician escort, this time the astronauts were also accompanied by a squad of Delta Force commandos. The elite troops were in full battle dress and body armor, their weapons locked and loaded, and they were ready to fire on anyone who tried to get in the way.

Along with the armed guards on the gantry, another two hundred ground troops were deployed along Vandenberg's perimeter, and a dozen Apache attack helicopters circled directly over the launch complex. A little farther out, a pair of AC-130E Specter gunships also flew circles in the sky while an AWACS high overhead monitored all air traffic in the region. Outside of the air base, state and local police were out in force along with several vans of Delta Force ready-reaction teams poised to go into action.

The President had authorized live-fire rules of engagement, and while neither the troops nor the police knew what was going on, they were ready for anything. No one would be allowed to stop the *Atlantis* from lifting off on schedule.

IT WAS AN HOUR and a half before scheduled launch time when the crew boarded and strapped themselves into their acceleration couches. For those long minutes, the Able Team mission specialists had exactly nothing to do except sit in their reclined seats and listen to the communications between the cockpit crew and Launch Control. Part of the extraordinary security surrounding this flight was that all radio and telephone communications were being scrambled to prevent unauthorized interception. There would be no teenagers with multiband receivers listening in on the prelaunch chatter as had happened in the past.

"We are showing a voltage fluctuation in the number-three APU," Vandenberg Launch Control radioed to NASA headquarters in Houston. Though Vandenberg was controlling the launch itself, Mission Control Center was overseeing every aspect of the flight, and any launch hold had to be cleared through them.

"Disregard." Houston overrode them. The auxiliary power units were located in the tail of the spacecraft and came into play only on launch and reentry when they were powered up to control the aerodynamic control surfaces. The *Atlantis* had triple redundancy in that system and having one APU acting up wouldn't prevent her from making a successful launch.

Step by step, the lengthy launch checklist was counted off and finally, Able Team heard the welcome words in their headsets. "*Atlantis*, Control. H-two pressurization is okay. You are go for launch, over."

"Copy go for launch." Command Pilot Greg Cunningham sounded as if he were doing nothing more important than ordering pizza and a beer.

"Oh, Jesus," Schwarz said softly when he heard, and felt, the fuel pumps kick in.

"*Atlantis,* Control. You have onboard-computer ignition sequence."

"Roger."

"Five...four..." The controller counted down. "We have main-engine start."

The main engines ignited, and the shuttle vibrated from over six million pounds of thrust as the 4.4-million-ton spaceship came alive. Schwarz hunkered down in his seat and tried hard to pretend that he was somewhere else, anywhere else.

"Two...one...zero. SRB ignition. Liftoff!"

When the two solid-fuel boosters kicked in 2.64 seconds later, it was too late for Schwarz to do anything except go along for the ride.

Stony Man Farm, Virginia

THE STONY MAN Computer Room looked like an annex to Houston Mission Control. Kurtzman had linked his mainframe to the NASA machines and was displaying the familiar views of the Vandenberg launch tower and the orbital display on his big-screen monitors. Everyone who wasn't busy doing something important was crowded in to watch Lyons and Schwarz blast into space.

Upon hearing "Liftoff!" the Computer Room broke out in cheers. This time, Stony Man was personally involved and the cheers were sincere if a bit uncertain. To say that this mission was breaking new ground was a gross understatement.

"*Atlantis,* Control," the voice of Vandenberg Launch Control said over the loudspeaker. "You have cleared the launch tower and all engines look good."

"Roger," Cunningham replied.

Barbara Price's eyes followed the plume of fire as the shuttle climbed into the California sky. In all of her time as the Farm's mission controller, this was the most outrageous operation they had ever undertaken. Success or failure of a Stony Man mission always carried dramatic consequences, but taking it into space gave it an entirely new dimension.

The Farm crew was used to being a vital part of every Stony Man operation. Not only did they gather the premission intelligence and handle the logistics and transport, but they also stayed in touch when the teams went into action. Through the network of satellite communications and cyberconnections, they could send warnings and updates and provide backup. It was true that in every operation there came the time when the Farm crew could no longer aid the teams in any way. They had to just sit and wait out the results like the rest of the world.

This time, though, there was nothing they could do at all except wait.

IN MISSION CONTROL CENTER, Hal Brognola sat next to NASA Director Bill Kruger at the central control console and watched the shuttle go into the postliftoff roll maneuver that would orient the shuttle for her high-polar-orbit insertion. She would make one orbit to check out her special cargo before making the second engine burn that would boost her up to the orbit where she would deploy the laser.

"What's the media take on the launch?" Brognola asked the communications technician who was monitoring the radio and TV coverage of the launch. Even though the mission hadn't been announced, it was difficult to conceal a 184-foot-long rocket sitting on the launch pad and impossible to hide the launch. A local TV station had parked a mobile van well outside the fence at Vandenberg and had filmed the liftoff. Their feed was being rebroadcast on the networks.

"Just the usual garbage," the technician replied. "The antinuke freaks and the anti-NASA wackos have banded together to protest what they are calling a 'veil of secrecy' surrounding the mission and they're getting full coverage on the networks. They're saying that the military is doing something harmful to either the environment or to women and children. They haven't decided which."

He looked up at Brognola and grinned. "Even though they haven't the slightest idea what's going on, they're certain that it's a crime against humanity and Mother Earth because we launched without telling them what we were doing and inviting them to watch."

"The idiots," Director Kruger growled. "If they

knew what this launch was really about, they'd be screaming for us to save them and demanding congressional hearings into why we don't have a military presence in space.'' He shook his head. ''You can't win with those people.''

''Which is why I just ignore them,'' Brognola said. ''Living in a democracy like ours means that every moron in the country gets their allotted fifteen minutes of media exposure. This is just another few minutes for this bunch.''

''That's easy for you to say,'' Kruger shot back. ''You didn't just go through several weeks of grilling about the Venture Star disaster. It's a damned good thing that I didn't know what really happened to her back then or I'd have told the stupid bastards.''

''You must have a death wish.'' Brognola grinned. ''That would have only gotten you lynched as a scapegoat.''

''It would have been worth it just to see the panic on their stupid faces when they heard about Chinese missile platforms threatening their smug little lives.''

''You might get to see that yet,'' Brognola replied. ''This is by no means a done deal. There's any number of things that can go wrong and sink this operation. If the ground team isn't successful in China, we'll be back to square one so fast it'll make your head spin. And, if that laser doesn't work as well as it's supposed to, we might be starting World War III.''

"Don't remind me," Kruger said. "I've got enough to worry about as it is."

"I'll gladly trade jobs with you."

"Not on your life."

Space

IN HIS ACCELERATION COUCH, Hermann Schwarz was trying hard not to think of all the things that could go wrong as the *Atlantis* accelerated free from Earth's gravity. The images from the *Challenger* disaster were too well established in the national psyche for anyone to take a laid-back attitude about a space-shuttle launch. On top of that, the thundering roar and vibration of the engines combined with the G force felt as if they would strip the flesh from his bones and spread it around the cabin like red jam.

At 120 seconds into the flight, the two solid-fuel boosters burned the last of their fuel and fell silent. The pilot throttled the main engines back to sixty-five percent and went into a small dive to jettison the burned-out boosters. They would parachute into the ocean to be recovered, refueled and reused on some future flight.

As soon as the SRBs had separated, the pilot throttled back up to one hundred percent as the main engines continued burning the contents of the external fuel tank. When it went empty, the pilot again went into a release maneuver to send it on its trip back to Earth where it would crash into the Pacific.

It was six minutes into the flight, and the *Atlantis* was traveling at Mach 15. Escape velocity was Mach 25, but for this mission all they needed to achieve was an orbital speed of seventeen thousand miles per hour. That wasn't enough to break free of Earth's gravity, but it was fast enough to balance their speed against the pull of gravity and put them in a polar orbit 250 miles above the planet.

The Chinese missile platforms were over two thousand miles farther from Earth, but the distance wasn't an obstacle to the Brilliant Pebbles laser. Back when the most powerful lasers had been measured in only a few thousand, not several billion, watts, a laser beam had been bounced off the moon, 234,000 miles from Earth. As anyone who has ever seen a star in the night sky knew, light traveled through space almost unimpeded.

THE ANNOUNCEMENT in Houston's Mission Control Center that the *Atlantis* was in orbit was almost anticlimactic. The wonder of space flight had become so routine that even a mission like this didn't create much excitement among the professionals.

Brognola glanced at his watch before turning to look for Bill Kruger. The NASA director was checking the orbital figures against the mission profile. "I'm going to leave this in your capable hands now," he told him. "I have to get back to get the second part of this operation in the air."

Kruger was dying to ask what Brognola's shadowy organization was going to do about the Venture Star, but he knew better. When this was over, he intended to find out, but right now he had some Chinese missile platforms to kill.

Space

WHEN THE ROAR and vibration of the engines abruptly cut off, Schwarz felt a little disoriented. The shuttle wasn't completely silent, but it was no longer shaking, rumbling and roaring.

"Okay, gentlemen," Cunningham announced from the cockpit. "We're now officially in space. I'm going to ask you to stay buckled in for a few more minutes while I roll this thing over and put our belly to Earth."

The Able Team commandos could hear the hiss of the reaction-control thrusters as they burned to roll the shuttle around its main fore-aft axis. There was no feeling of motion as the big ship rolled, but the light from the two windows in the top of the rear of the cabin changed as the sunlight flooded in.

"Okay," Cunningham said. "Now we're what you would call right-side up, and you can get out of your seats. Remember what they told you at Vandenberg—use the handholds and the boots to keep you on the deck. If you break free and find yourself floating around, don't panic. One of us will glue you back down to something."

Schwarz and Lyons undid their seat harnesses and watched the loose ends of the belts float away. "Damn," Schwarz said. "This is just like in the movies."

When he tried to push himself out of his seat, he also started to float toward the ceiling of the shuttle. "Hey, guys!" he called out. "How do I get my feet on the floor so these boots will work?"

Boomer Boyd, the flight engineer, reached over, grabbed Schwarz's leg and tugged on it, sending him back down to the deck. "Remember to keep at least one of your feet on the deck at all times."

"Right."

"Feel free to look around, but keep out of the way until we can get configured for the postorbital burn."

"I thought we were in orbit," Lyons said.

"We're in what's called a low elliptical orbit, about 180 miles up. But we need to go up to a 250-mile circular orbit before we start shooting that cannon of yours."

While Lyons and Schwarz tried to keep out of the way, Flash Bradley and Boomer Boyd made their way back to the aft crew station. There, the crew opened the cargo-bay doors and swung them out to each side of the ship, exposing the special cargo.

When that was done, Bradley, the copilot, got out of his flight coveralls and started putting on his space suit. "Where're you going?" Lyons asked.

"Outside," Bradley said. "I drew the short

straw, so I get to go back to the cargo bay and get your toy ready to play with. It was bolted down in back so it wouldn't get banged around on liftoff. I have to free the locks and connect the power pack before you guys can see if it's going to work up here."

"It'd better," Lyons said. "Or there's going to be a lot of people pissed at us."

"Don't sweat the small stuff. Maybe it'll just blow up, and we won't have to worry about it."

"That would be too easy."

CHAPTER ELEVEN

Pasadena, California

Dr. Lin Chu stood at the window of his office at Cal Tech and looked out over the campus. It was the middle of summer term, but the school was as busy as ever. Hundreds of students scurried to and from their classes or strolled with their friends without a care in the world beyond the term's final exams and the weekend's party. It was almost sad that all those young Americans were about to wake up and find that their brave new world had suddenly disappeared, taking their future with it.

Lin was of two minds about the fact that his time in the United States was coming to an end. In a way, he had enjoyed living with the enemy for so many years. The last ten or so on the Pasadena campus had been particularly satisfying to him. His position at the university had been very rewarding, both professionally and personally.

As an aerospace-engineering professor, he'd had access to America's most advanced technology anytime he wanted it. Every time the Chinese engineers working with the stolen technology had a problem, he had been able to get the solution quickly. No matter how sensitive or classified the information might have been, a phone call or an e-mail from the Cal Tech engineering department was all it took for him to get an answer to almost any question. In matters of security, America's best scientists and engineers were fools.

The technical elite were also fools when it came to politics. Like most of the general public, they were abysmally ignorant of international affairs. Most of them could hardly find China on a map, and not one in a thousand knew anything substantial about the China of the nineties. Every so often, they might see something about China on CNN, usually concerning another American company going into business in the Mother Country, and believe that constituted knowledge. They knew nothing of China's long struggle to take her rightful place in the modern world.

And a struggle it had been. A century earlier, China had been a place of great history, but that history had all belonged to another age. As a Western observer during that time had said, China was a place where they had learned to eat rice with two sticks and carry two buckets of excrement with one. That had been the extent of China's technology.

After slow and not too successful attempts at westernizing, Mao had forced China to take a great leap forward with the help of Russian technological advisers. It had been a valiant attempt to bring the

Mother Country into the modern age, but for the greatest part, it had failed. Most of the blame for that lay in the poor choice in modeling Russian technology when it was a distant second to the West's.

Out of that failure had been born the Beijing Technical Intelligence Bureau, an organization dedicated to making China self-sufficient in the technologies and industries that would make her a real world power. Lin had been recruited by the bureau when he was in graduate school in Hong Kong and, after agent training, had been sent to the United States to practice his profession. As much as he had learned to enjoy American life, there had also been times when he had cursed those who had sent him to live among these clever barbarians. For a man of his education and learning, living in the United States had been a tour in hell.

The American mind was a wondrous thing of great strengths and even greater weaknesses. It was infinitely changeable and subject to the slightest whim like the mind of an undisciplined child. In Lin's observations, most Americans never grew up and remained mindless, self-centered, pleasure-seeking children all of their lives. The crime and addiction rates alone were proof of that. Nowhere else on Earth did people work so hard to destroy themselves as did the Americans. And the untold millions that were wasted trying to salvage these brutal adult children was of itself criminal.

Out of this cultural chaos, however, had come a

constant stream of sheer creative genius that was unprecedented in human history. Many important scientific and technological advances of the twentieth century were totally, or in great part, the result of the inventiveness of American science and industry. It was difficult to look at the modern world and not see the stamp of the United States of America on so many items in it.

People often spoke of the inventiveness of the Japanese and, to a lesser extent, of the South Koreans and Singaporeans. It was true that they had carved out a place for themselves in the postwar technological marketplace. But it had all been done by copying the work of the Yankees. Even the vaunted Japanese industry was merely an exercise in refining and producing American products. The last thing the Japanese had invented on their own was the samurai sword, and even it was a copy of an ancient Chinese weapon.

Lin's mission in the United States had been to see that China benefited from this never ending river of American brilliance. And while he had been extremely successful at sending both high-tech ideas and hardware back to China, the crowning achievement of his mission had been recruiting Selena Del Gato. The part she had played in the capture of the Venture Star would go down in history.

Lin had recognized Del Gato's potential long before she had been chosen to join the astronaut corps. He had seen it when she had taken his Chinese culture class as an undergraduate. At first, he had hesitated about approaching her because she was a woman. His superiors in the Technical Intelligence Bureau didn't trust female agents, as they were believed to be too easily swayed by their emotions. In this case, though, emotion had been the key to recruiting this remarkable woman.

Lin never ceased to marvel at the depths of Del Gato's mind and her iron discipline. Hijacking a spacecraft hadn't been an easy task. Undoubtedly she would go down as one of history's greatest women and certainly the greatest female agent of all time. She was certainly the most intensely sensual woman he had ever known. But, unlike all the other women he had ever been with, she had never approached sex from an emotional standpoint. In fact, the only emotion he had ever seen her express was her intense longing to find a homeland, a place she could call her own. She had finally found that place in the People's Republic of China.

Having been adopted into a Mexican-American family and raised with a Latino name had always weighed heavily upon her. She had been adopted as a baby, and her adoptive family had hid her real heritage from her. But, even as a child, she had known that she really didn't belong to the people who called themselves her family. Her skin, hair and eyes were dark and her mother had always crimped her straight hair and had her wear Mexican-style makeup, but her face and stature weren't those of a Hispanic.

She had been a junior in high school when her

father died and she learned from a relative that she had been adopted. From there, she quickly learned the secret of her birth and confronted her mother with this information. Rather than help her daughter get in touch with her heritage, though, Mrs. Del Gato refused to speak of Selena's birth mother or of the circumstances of her adoption.

Del Gato had yearned to drop the Hispanic fiction and become officially a Chinese-American. But, by this time, she had seen the openly approved discrimination against Asian-Americans in California that was laughingly called affirmative action. She had seen many brilliant young Asian Americans turned down by the state's top universities while far less talented Latinos and blacks had been eagerly accepted. While she detested the lie she was living, she took advantage of it to gain a minority slot admission to the school of engineering at the California Institute of Technology.

It was there that she first met other Asian American students and started learning about their cultures. After that, it had been a short trip to Lin's class on Chinese culture and his recruitment of her. He simply showed her that she was a daughter of the Mother Country and its brilliant many-thousand-year history. Finally finding her true home, she became his best agent.

LIN KNEW THAT it wouldn't be long now before America, and the entire world, woke up to the fact that the space over their heads belonged to the People's Republic of China. He was afraid how the Americans would respond when the knowledge of the space platforms became known. He felt that if the decisions that would need to be made were left to the government, all would be well. The American politicians would be able to understand the situation they faced and would make the sensible decisions that would keep the missiles from flying. But what the excitable American public would do about the threat was another matter entirely. They would react as children, and therein lay the danger.

It would start with protests, boycotts and marches, but would soon escalate into riots and the destruction of Chinese property in America. That was one thing Beijing couldn't allow to happen, and they would be forced to impose order on the United States. He, too, realized the need for order, but he was afraid that the typically heavy-handed Beijing rule would break the American spirit and stifle their engineering and scientific genius.

Somehow, he had to convince the ruling clique in Beijing that freedom of thought in scientific endeavors was critical to their long-range plans. The American inventive genius was critical to create the technology China would need in the twenty-first century. It was too bad that he couldn't stay behind and help guide it.

Lin knew that he was scheduled to leave, but he didn't know exactly when that would be. That decision was in the hands of the Beijing bureau's leadership. Looking around his office in the engineering department, he realized how much of this he would miss. Whatever position he would be given in China, he wouldn't have anything like the facilities he had enjoyed here.

His extraction plan wasn't elaborate. He would simply step across the border into Mexico and disappear. But that meant that he had to leave his office, his lab and his house intact as if he had just stepped out to go to the corner grocery. Sooner or later, someone would investigate his disappearance and there could be no traces.

Stony Man Farm, Virginia

WITH THE DEPARTURE of Phoenix Force, Barbara Price was finding herself a mission controller without anything to do on this mission. The technology level was beyond her expertise to do more than just observe. Even the Phoenix Force raid on the Quinbaki launch complex was out of her hands. Once the commandos made their parachute drop, they would succeed or fail completely on their own, and there was nothing she could do to help. She could, however, work with Akira Tokaido in support of Rosario Blancanales's California inquiry. She knew that his search was a long shot, but every base had to at least be looked at if not covered.

"Has Rosario come up with anything more?" she asked Tokaido.

"Not much," he replied. "He's signed on the INS to help investigate the restaurant for possible immigration violations, but that's about it. He just doesn't have anything else to work with. But I've been working on a long shot that's starting to get interesting,''

''What's that?''

''Well, considering the intense Chinese connection to this...''

Price repressed a smile at his choice of words. The ''connection'' couldn't be any more intense unless the entire People's Liberation Army marched down the Santa Monica Freeway waving red banners.

''I found an anomaly in Del Gato's college transcripts, and followed it up. I found a Cal Tech professor I think we need to take a close look at.''

He reached across his workstation and took a printout from his cluttered Out box. ''He's a Hong Kong import, a Dr. Lin Chu. He's a well-known aerospace engineer who had a lot to do with Del Gato getting into graduate school there, and he sponsored her Ph.D. thesis. I was getting ready to send this to Rosario, but maybe you should take a look at it, too.''

Pulling up a chair, Price sat down to cruise through Tokaido's information on the man. If Dr. Lin Chu was a Communist spy who had masterminded the hijacking of the Venture Star, he was the best spy she had ever seen.

He had been thoroughly backgrounded before being hired on at Cal Tech, and he had come up completely clean. His family had been declared clean, as well. At least as clean as any Hong Kong trading family could be. But it was very unlikely that any American inquiry would uncover any Triad associations they might have had. Triad connections never appeared on paper, and as long as you weren't arrested, they never came to official notice.

The only blip she noted in Lin's background was that it was a little too clean, particularly in the political arena. He hadn't spoken out for democracy after the Tianenmen Square incident, he hadn't written editorials about the need to open up trade with China, he didn't make even small contributions to either political party and was registered as an independent voter.

In a state where minority academicians often made headlines on any number of issues, he was completely absent from taking sides on any controversy, social or political. It was as if he had so devoted his life to engineering that he had no time for anything else, period. Except, of course, for his personal interest in Chinese art and culture, which could be seen as an exercise in cultural diversity.

Price was well aware that the monomaniacal personality abounded in the halls of academia. Professors who didn't know what time of day it was, much less the day of the week, if someone didn't tell them, were legend. The absentminded professor was a long-established cliché. But, except for his cleaner-than-clean background, Lin didn't fit the profile of a man who didn't know exactly what he was doing at all times.

He also had a couple of other eccentricities that marked him. He had a bank account, but he didn't write checks. He had no credit cards, not even an ATM card. He didn't have a cellular phone or an answering machine. He did have a state-of-the-art computer with all the Internet access and specialized programming anyone could use. His office computer was linked to his home machine, and they both gave him access to the Cal Tech engineering lab networks. He was cyberwired to the hilt, but he didn't even have a phone card. That struck her as a bit odd.

Tokaido had been trying to hack his way into Lin's computer, but he was coming up against first-rate encryption security. Price knew that if the rest of Able Team was working with Blancanales, it might be a different operation. Gadgets Schwarz would find a way to hack into the professor's computer and install a program that would search out all his secrets, or Carl Lyons would simply break into his office and steal the thing. Barring that, though, Blancanales would have to do it the old-fashioned way—pound the pavement and ask questions.

"This is a good hit," Price told Tokaido. "I think you're on to something here. If Lin was Del Gato's recruiter, the chances are good that she wasn't the only one he reached out to. I'd like you to look into the rest of his ex-students, particularly his Asian-American master's degree and Ph.D. people. Check them against his Chinese-culture class and see if he did letters of reference for them, as well. Then find out where they are now and what they're doing."

"No problem," Tokaido said.

WHEN TOKAIDO LOOKED into Lin's ex-students, he hit a gold mine. There were, of course, the aerospace engineers, but there were also computer engineering, robotics and other high-tech superstars. What was surprising, but shouldn't have been, were the people who were now big players in international trade. Without checking further, he knew that they would all be in the high-tech hardware end of the trading spectrum and focused on the Pacific Rim. And, interestingly enough, all of Lin's other protégés were male. Apparently, Selena Del Gato was the only woman who had ever caught Lin's eye.

Printing out a list of these men, their connection to Lin and their current occupations, he took it to Barbara Price. "If we assume that Dr. Lin is a spy master," he said. "I think I've just found out how he's running his spy ring."

"Damn," she said after scanning the list. "This would have to come up when Carl and Gadgets are busy in outer space. Get this to Rosario ASAP, and I'll see if I can arrange some backup for him. He's not going to be able to look into this by himself. It's too dangerous."

CHAPTER TWELVE

Diego Garcia Island

When the C-141 Starlifter carrying Jack Grimaldi, Mack Bolan and Phoenix Force from Andrews Air Force Base touched down on Diego Garcia, the jet transport taxied into an open hangar before shutting down its engines. Since the United States was no longer the only nation with a space-based reconnaissance capability, if they wanted to stay hidden, they had to keep out of sight from prying eyes, especially space eyes.

"Man," T. J. Hawkins said as he looked around the dimly lit hangar that was reserved for special operations. "I'm beginning to think that I live in this damned place."

He focused on the matte-black shape of the B-2 stealth bomber lurking in the corner. "And I know I've seen that ugly bastard before. I wonder if they've improved the latrine facilities in the PPP yet."

The Pressurized Personnel Pod the Phoenix Force commandos would ride in to their drop zone fit into the bomb bay of the stealth bomber. It was close quarters at best for seven men, but it was the only way to fly into a target without being seen.

"I doubt it," Calvin James said. "After all, that plane was designed to drop bombs, not paratroopers. You ought to be glad that someone designed that Triple P. Remember our last ride in a B-2? Rough."

"Okay, people," McCarter said, "let's get the gear off the Starlifter and start getting squared away. We have to be ready to launch whenever Hal calls."

"One thing I'd really like to see someone invent is a anti-jet lag pill," Gary Manning groused.

"Maybe I can give you a few pointers on sleeping in planes, my man," Hawkins said. "I always get my best sleep in the air."

"Can I learn how to drool on my chin like you do?" James grinned. "You've really got that part down."

"Let's get our fingers out, people," McCarter barked. "We have work to do."

Hawkins shook his head. "He's acting like it's the end of the world again, so I guess we'd better get busy and off-load this crap."

"Maybe the guy who came up with the Triple P can invent a mission equipment caddy to follow us around."

"No such luck."

THOUGH THE LAYOVER at Diego Garcia was supposed to be for sleep and mission preparation, the commandos didn't get much rest. After checking over their personal gear and mission equipment, they sat down to go over the latest information about the target that had been faxed to them from Stony Man Farm.

The secret base where the Venture Star was believed to be hidden wasn't completely unknown to American intelligence, and it wasn't the only launch complex the Chinese operated. The Xichang Satellite Launch Center in Szechwan Province in southern China was their primary, and very public, space-flight center. That was where they launched commercial satellites with their CZ-2E Long March rocket for a number of international customers. Since this multimillion-dollar business was a very open affair, they hadn't expected the stolen spacecraft to show up there.

Their target was a known secret-weapons test site in the southwestern corner of the Gobi Desert known as the Quinbaki complex. This was about as desolate a location as could be found on the face of the earth. In earlier times, it had been on China's westernmost border and was the beginning of the ancient Silk Road to the Middle East. It had also been the outpost blocking the primary barbarian invasion route into Imperial China. More than one invading horde had been turned back from this strong point, and now Phoenix Force would try their luck.

The region was completely off-limits to outsiders, and that included most of the Chinese military. Only a select group of scientists, their support personnel and the security forces that guarded them ever visited this barren site—and the pair of American astronauts who had delivered a stolen spacecraft to them.

WHILE BOLAN AND Phoenix Force were taking care of their hardware, Jack Grimaldi had his nose in the books, going over the Venture Star launch procedures one more time. Compared to preflighting something like an SR-71 for takeoff, the Venture Star's prelaunch checklist was a piece of cake. Even though the spacecraft was a hundred times more complicated than the Blackbird, the difference was the cutting-edge computer system that was built into it. Microchips were much faster than pilots, and they never made mistakes.

Nonetheless, the standard countdown checklist Grimaldi had been given was a thirty-minute-long process where every switch and every instrument was checked once by the computer and then double checked by the human pilot or copilot. The problem was that it wasn't very likely that the Chinese would cooperate and give him and McCarter a half an hour to run through it in peace and quiet. He'd be lucky if he had even five minutes to kick the tires and light the fires.

When that problem had been explained, Lockheed and NASA had come up with a bare-bones prelaunch checklist that ran a bit under five minutes. Most of the checks had been taken away from the crew and given over to the onboard computer. Grimaldi had no problem with that, because he knew the machine could do it faster than he could. Even so, there was still more than enough for him to do to get the ship ready to launch.

At Grimaldi's insistence, Lockheed had also come up with a last-resort, emergency-launch program that was completely computer driven. To run it, all he had to do was shove a program disc into the computer, punch the button and hang on. It was dangerous, both to the crew and the ship, but it would launch them in sixty seconds and that met the need. Even if something went wrong with the automatic launch and the ship was destroyed, it wouldn't be a disaster. The Chinese wouldn't be able to use it again, and that was the goal of the mission.

In that scenario, Bolan, Phoenix Force and Grimaldi were expendable.

Stony Man Farm, Virginia

WHEN HAL BROGNOLA arrived back at the Farm, he immediately jumped into the ground-based part of the mission. With the *Atlantis* in orbit, it was time for the China drop.

Aaron Kurtzman had gotten the SR-71 overflights he had wanted, and they were paying off. The Blackbird was still the queen of high-tech manned recon. In over thirty years of keeping a sharp eye on America's enemies, not a single SR-71 had been lost to enemy action. Once more, they were showing that they could go anyplace, anytime, bar nothing and see what was down there.

The problem with space satellites was that any person with an Army-surplus radar set and basic orbital math skills could figure out when they were going to pass overhead. All you had to do to hide from even the Keyhole series spy birds was to keep your head down while it was in the sky. As soon as it went down over the horizon, a person could go back to doing what he or she had been doing before it had shown up. The SR-71s supporting the Stony Man team's mission were two of the three Blackbirds that had been taken out of storage and completely refurbished after the Gulf War to do the work that the spy satellites couldn't.

The new incarnation of the spy plane wasn't any faster than it had been back in the days of the Vietnam War, but it was harder to find in the sky. Part of the refurbishment program had been the application of a stealthy paint job that had been originally formulated for the B-2. The coating had had to be reformulated to withstand the heat of the SR-71's Mach 3.5 flight, but that hadn't been difficult. Where the SR-71s had been difficult to spot before with ground radars, now they were almost impossible.

The sensors and cameras on board the new Blackbirds were better than the old ones by a wide margin. The original recon package had been designed back in the sixties, and technology had come a long way since then. Along with the six-inch resolution cameras, she could be fitted with digital imaging, infrared and MAD systems. Anything a spy satellite could see, the Blackbird could pick up.

The best part of the refit, though, was the real-time transmission capability the SR-71s now had. As soon as the spy plane saw something interesting, it was transmitted to a satellite and from there sent to any of a number of ground stations all over the world. One of those recipients of the data was the Computer Room at Stony Man Farm.

The Blackbirds hadn't picked up any sign of the Venture Star yet, but they were sending good data on the target area and updating it every five minutes. By rotating the two planes in and out of the area for refueling, they would continue to watch throughout the mission.

After looking over the data, Brognola turned to Barbara Price. "Tell them it's a go. I want them in the air as soon as possible."

WHEN THE B-2 STEALTH BOMBER carrying the Stony Man team cradled in her belly crossed the Chinese border at subsonic speeds thirty-six thousand feet over Pakistan, Kurtzman was still monitoring the recon feed from the SR-71s. The Keyhole satellites had gone down below the horizon half an hour earlier, and if the Chinese were going to make their move, this was the time to do it.

"There it is!" he almost shouted. "They've got the Venture Star on a launch platform."

Hal Brognola looked over Kurtzman's left shoulder while Katz took the right. The sensor readouts the Blackbird was transmitting couldn't have been of anything other than the missing American spacecraft.

"What's the chance that they're going to launch it any time soon?" Katz asked. "Like in the next hour or so?"

"Oh, Jesus," Brognola moaned.

"There's no way to tell," Kurtzman replied. "They have a Keyhole blackout for another ten hours."

"Is that a fuel truck pulling up to it?" Katz asked when he spotted a truck approaching the launch pad.

"It looks more like a cargo hauler to me," Kurtzman replied. "They might still be in the mission loading process."

"What's the team's ETA?" Brognola asked.

Kurtzman clicked to change screens. "They should be reaching the DZ in eight minutes."

THE B-2 STEALTH BOMBER had dropped down to twenty-eight thousand feet as it approached the IP, initial point. Because of the Chinese air defenses in the area, it was flying a bomb-run profile and the IP was where it would turn onto its final heading for the drop zone. As part of the approach, the copilot turned on the B-2's targeting radar. It would scan the drop zone and verify that it was correct.

"Phoenix One," the pilot called over the intercom, "we have an anomaly on the DZ."

"What's wrong?" McCarter called back.

"The radar is showing what looks like a vehicle convoy has parked a klick away."

"Can you send the data back here so I can look at it?"

"Roger. We'll go into an orbit while you take a look at it."

Bolan and McCarter studied the image on the radar screen in the Personnel Pod. Like the man had said, more than a dozen vehicles were parked on the sand about three-quarters of a mile from their planned drop zone. Though they could see the trucks, they couldn't see how many troops were with them.

"What do you think, Striker?" McCarter asked. "You want to go to the secondary DZ?"

Bolan studied the scan. From the plot, it looked as if the trucks were all headed away from Quinbaki, and they might have just stopped to change a tire, or something like that, before moving out again. In any case, there was almost no chance that the Chinese would detect them coming down from that distance. If they had to divert to the secondary DZ, it would add almost two hours to the walk into the target, and that would be pushing dawn.

"Let's go for the primary," Bolan decided.

"This is Phoenix One," McCarter called up to the cockpit. "Go for the primary."

"Roger," the pilot called back over the intercom. "DZ coming up in five mikes."

"Copy," Hawkins replied. "DZ in five mikes."

As team's jump master for this drop, the ex-Ranger's job was to make sure that everyone was buckled up properly before he jumped. It also meant that he would be the last one to exit the aircraft and would have to play catchup for twenty-five thousand feet.

"Time to go to oxygen, guys," he said over the com link. "Check in when you're hooked up."

Doing a HALO jump from twenty-eight thousand feet made oxygen a necessity. In the cold air, heated suits would have been nice, as well, but they had decided not to jump with the extra weight. Their equipment bags for this drop were heavier than usual as it was. Extra ammunition and the explosives needed for the demolition option accounted for most of the additional weight.

When his teammates had donned their masks and checked in, Hawkins called up to the cockpit that they were ready.

"DZ in two mikes," the copilot called back.

"Roger, two," Hawkins replied.

Sixty seconds before the DZ, the copilot selected the switch to manually open the bomb-bay doors. On a real bomb run, the doors would automatically cycle open just far enough for the weapons load to be released and then they immediately snapped shut again. Open bomb-bay doors created a major radar return. But, for a personnel drop, the doors had to remain open longer and the additional risk of detection had to be taken.

"Bomb bay open," the copilot reported. "DZ in three-zero. Good luck."

"Roger, standing by."

At zero seconds, the pod hatch popped open and the green light came on. McCarter was the first to step out into the below-zero night air at twenty-eight thousand feet over the Gobi Desert. At ten-second intervals, the others followed him.

"We're being painted by a SAM radar." The copilot warned the Stony Man team a Chinese air-defense radar had just picked them up.

At the height they were flying, the stealthy B-2 gave back a radar return the size that a seagull would have given. Having the bomb-bay doors open increased that return by a factor of four or five, but it would still show up smaller than a single-engined fighter would have. Even so, every second they were on the screen was one second closer to a Chinese SAM missile launch. Even with a full onboard ECM suite designed specifically to confuse SAMs, neither pilot wanted to try his luck.

As Hawkins prepared to jump, he clicked in the intercom. "Last man out in zero-three. Thanks for the ride, guys."

"Pod clear," the copilot called out. "Bomb bay closing."

"Roger," the pilot acknowledged as he shoved

the B-2 into a hard left-hand bank to try to escape the radar. A minute later, he executed a sharp right turn and leveled off on his new course.

"We lost them," the copilot called out.

"Let's get the hell out of here before they find us again." The pilot started to climb back to thirty-six thousand feet. "I don't feel like playing cat and mouse with a SAM missile tonight."

"You got that right, partner."

CHAPTER THIRTEEN

Space

The burn of the *Atlantis*'s two six-thousand-pound-thrust engines lasted only a few minutes, but it was enough to boost her up to a 250-mile-high orbit. Before Colonel Greg Cunningham shut down, he used the positioning thrusters to roll the shuttle around her central axis so her open cargo bay faced away from Earth, toward the deep space that hid the Chinese missile platforms.

"Okay, guys," he called back over the intercom, "we're on station. It's time for you to do your thing."

The Able Team duo unstrapped themselves from their seats and made their way back to the aft workstation. In weightlessness, one didn't need to sit in a chair to work, but standing wasn't easy, either. It took a few minutes for Hermann Schwarz to get the hang of wearing the microgravity boots. They had suction cups on the bottom to hold him in place, so he had to find a comfortable position for his feet, plant the boots and then leave them there. While they limited his mobility, they did keep him right side up.

With Schwarz at the right-hand workstation at the targeting radar screen and Carl Lyons on the laser firing controls to his left, they could finally see if this wild venture among the stars was really going to work.

The laser had been mounted on a powered turntable that provided changes in both traverse and elevation. The standard controls for the shuttle's RMS—Remote Manipulator System—arm had been modified to run the turntable and aim the weapon. This way, the shuttle didn't have to be moved around to get the laser on target. All the pilot needed to do was to position the shuttle so Schwarz had a clear field of fire, and then maintain that station.

"Give me a couple more degrees nose down," Schwarz called up to the flight deck.

"Down?" the pilot called back.

"Toward the earth," Schwarz said. Astronauts were used to hearing changes of direction stated in terms of pitch, roll and yaw, but he didn't have the time to try to remember which one was which. Up and down still had meaning to him and the space jockeys would just have to live with it.

"Okay," he called up to Cunningham again. "That should do it." From here on out, he would use the RMS joystick to move the powered turntable to aim the laser at the radar target as if he were playing a video game. Since that was something any thirteen-year-old could do in his sleep, he should be able to figure it out.

He was still getting used to the idea that the laser beam would actually fire across almost two thousand miles of space and not vary from its aiming point by even a millimeter. But without the effects of gravity pulling on a projectile, there was no ballistics to compute.

It was still critical, though, that he be dead-on target before firing. At a range of two thousand miles, being even a fraction of an inch off of the target would put the beam miles off. Also, he couldn't take many practice shots to check his aim. The power cell that provided the energy to fire the laser was good for only five shots. After that, the real astronauts would have to make an EVA into the cargo bay and change the exhausted power cell for a new one. The time required for doing that was two and one-half hours, which was entirely too long.

No one knew how long it would take the Chinese to prepare their space missiles for launch, but it was generally felt that it would be no more than half an hour. If they detected that their launch platforms were under attack, they might launch in retaliation, and the target for the warheads would be the United States of America.

The laser and its mount were heavy, but compared to the total weight of the *Atlantis,* it wasn't much. In a zero-gravity situation, the weight that was being moved wasn't a factor, but its mass still was. Traversing the laser to aim it caused a minute opposite movement in the space shuttle itself.

On the flight deck, Cunningham was watching his position readouts and caught the slight movement of the shuttle in reaction to Schwarz's traversing the weapon to aim it. Automatically, he reached out for the thruster controls and fed in the correction needed to bring the ship back to where it had been before Schwarz had moved the laser.

"Dammit!" Schwarz yelled to the cockpit. "Keep this thing still. I can't get a lock on the target if you keep moving around."

In their premission briefings at Vandenberg, the astronauts had tried to give the two Able Team recruits a quick lesson in Newtonian mechanics, but obviously it hadn't taken. Groundhogs didn't instinctively understand it the way space pilots had been trained to. Rather than try again to enlighten his novice mission specialist turned gunner, Cunningham let it pass.

"That should do it," Schwarz finally told Lyons. "Arm the laser."

Lyons hit the switch to send the electrical power to the synthetic crystal at the heart of the weapon. Though the earliest lasers had used natural crystals such as rubies to bend the light into a coherent beam, synthetic crystals that could be grown to precise dimensions had proved to be more efficient. This weapon had one of the largest crystals that had ever been made and, in lasers, size equaled power.

"It's armed."

"Hold while I confirm the aim," Schwarz said.

A moment later, he said, "Okay, I'm still on target. Fire!"

The sudden burst of light in the cargo hold came through the two windows by the aft crew station and lit up the inside of the shuttle. Since the interior of the cabin was white, it was like being inside a giant flashbulb.

When Schwarz could see clearly again, he checked his radar and saw that the target blip hadn't changed. "Damn! We missed!"

On the flight deck, Cunningham waited while Schwarz realigned the laser to correct his aim. Again, he saw that the shuttle had picked up a small drift from the laser's movement, but didn't correct it.

When Lyons fired the laser the second time, there was dead silence from the aft crew station.

"Okay," Schwarz said. "That's the second bolo. We've got to get serious about this shit, or we're going to be up here all month."

"Cunningham," he called up to the flight deck, "this damned shuttle keeps moving under me and I can't hold the laser on target. Do you have any suggestions?"

"Do you know what a deflection shot is?" the pilot called back.

"Vaguely," Schwarz replied. "It's something you flyboys do to each other in dogfights, right?"

"Right," Cunningham said, chuckling. "We aim ahead of the enemy aircraft and expect him to fly into the path of the fire. Do you think you can do that back there? Maybe aim at the edge of the target and walk the beam across it with the movement of the shuttle?"

Schwarz thought for a moment. "Okay, let me see if I have this right. Every time I move the laser, the ship goes in the opposite direction just a little bit, right?"

"That's it."

"Okay," Schwarz said. "I'll line it up this time on the far edge rather than dead center so the shuttle's movement will draw the beam in. Do you think that'll work?"

"It's worth a try."

When Schwarz was done, he closed his eyes before calling out. "Do it again, Carl."

When Schwarz opened his eyes, he saw that the radar target had vanished.

"Hot damn!" Lyons called out. "You got it, Gadgets!"

"But it took three shots," Schwarz replied. "I've got to do better on the next one."

Cheyenne Mountain, Colorado

"THE SHUTTLE IS in firing position," newly promoted Master Sergeant Dale Bergman reported from his console in the NORAD Sky Watch center. The other Sky Watchers were at their consoles, sweeping deep space with the Long Look radars, but since he had discovered the bogeys, he had been given the honor of being at the master console.

In the past few days, the NORAD Space Command Center had gone from having almost been ignored to being the most popular place in all of the Cheyenne Mountain complex. The NORAD commander, Major General Peterson, and his entire staff were on hand, as well as visiting VIPs from almost every high-level U.S. military command. If the *Atlantis* mission didn't take out the threat hanging over them, the nation could be at war before they knew it.

"The first target has disappeared from the screen," Bergman said calmly.

A cheer broke out, and even the most senior officers high-fived and slapped one another on the back like high-school football players.

The feeling of relief was thick enough to package and mail home. It was as if every person in the room had just been told that he or she had just won the lottery, which in a way they had. Every one of them knew that if the Chinese launched a nuclear strike from space, the NORAD complex would be at the top of the target list. The facility had been built to withstand near misses from medium-sized nuclear weapons, but the pinpoint accuracy of space-based missiles made that protection a moot point.

"*Atlantis* is maneuvering into position to engage the second target," Bergman reported.

Space

THE INSTANT that the second Chinese missile platform came over the radar horizon, Schwarz was on it. This time, he took several extra minutes to make minute adjustments to the weapon. He had only two shots left on the first power pack and didn't want to miss again.

"Okay." He turned to Lyons. "One more time."

When the radar target blinked out on the first shot, Schwarz let out a war whoop. "Okay, boss," he called up to the flight deck, "I killed it. Can we go home now?"

Cheyenne Mountain, Colorado

WHEN BERGMAN REPORTED the destruction of the second platform, the Sky Watch section and all their guests, official and otherwise, again broke out in wild cheers. The mutual congratulations when the first one had been blasted to bits had only been a warm-up for this celebration.

Bergman pushed his chair back from his console and stood. The sudden release of tension had made him weak, and he almost fell back into his chair. Even though the room was air-conditioned to a perfect seventy-two degrees, his coverall uniform was soaked through with sweat.

"Good work, Sergeant Bergman." The NORAD commander had stepped up to offer his personal congratulations.

"The astronauts did all the work, sir," the sergeant replied.

"But you're the man who spotted those damned things, Sergeant," the general said seriously. "Don't forget that. If you hadn't found them, we'd still be sitting around here with our thumbs up our butts thinking that we were on top of the world."

Bergman knew that any one of the Sky Watch crew would have found the Chinese missile platforms sooner or later, but he didn't mind being given the credit. It had already gotten him a promotion and the promise of any assignment in the Air Force he wanted as soon as this was over.

"I'm thinking of having your UFO search techniques instituted as a permanent part of the Space Command Center mission. If they did it to us once, someone might try it again. And—" the general smiled "—who knows, it might be the aliens instead of the Chinese next time."

"I'll be glad to write up the program, sir."

"You can start after you take a thirty-day leave. You've earned a little R and R."

"I appreciate that, sir."

"You've earned it, son."

Stony Man Farm, Virginia

STONY MAN'S WAR ROOM was linked to NORAD, and the big-screen monitor showed the same screen Master Sergeant Bergman was looking at. The cheering when the last missile platform blinked out of existence was every bit as enthusiastic as NORAD's had been. The Farm wasn't a primary target like Cheyenne Mountain, but those were their boys up there.

Hal Brognola felt as if a great weight had been taken from the middle of his chest. Stony Man missions were difficult enough without having to worry about one of them going wrong and triggering a nuclear attack from space. Even though he knew that the President was on-line with the NORAD Cheyenne Mountain Command Center, he would call him anyway and confirm that the danger was over.

Now that the *Atlantis* had been successful, he could focus on the other part of the mission. It was ironic that the greatest danger had been eliminated without really risking the men involved. Now men were being sent into a great risk to keep the danger from being repeated.

Above China

AS THE FIRST MAN OUT of the B-2 stealth bomber, David McCarter was leading the HALO drop. The nav-aid on his wrist was locked on to the center of the drop zone through a GPS satellite link, so all he had to do was follow it down to the ground. With the parked convoy the B-2 had spotted so close to the DZ, the team had to hit it right on the mark. His teammates were strung out behind him in a tight diamond formation so they could keep track of one another in the dark.

At the rear point of the HALO diamond, T. J. Hawkins referred to his own nav-aid as they fell through the sky while keeping an eye on the altimeter, as well. At the twelve-thousand-foot mark, he got on the com link to remind them to get off of the oxygen and stow the masks for landing.

Jack Grimaldi didn't have as much time on a parachute harness as the rest of the Stony Man team, but the pilot had always enjoyed falling spread-eagled through the sky. This was real flying. The rush of air past his helmeted ears and the muted hiss of the com-link earphone were the only sounds he heard as he plunged earthward at 120 miles per hour. He would have liked to stay up for hours, but every parachute jump had to end.

To insure that the jumpers landed as closely together as possible, they all had to pop their chutes at the same time. At nine hundred feet, Hawkins clicked in his com link to alert them and count down. "Deploy on my three count—three... two...one...pull!"

Seven black canopies opened within a few seconds of one another. They were jumping with their bat-wing steerable chutes, and they easily joined up in a line playing follow-the-leader behind McCarter for the last few hundred feet.

This was always the worst part of a paradrop for Grimaldi. Even though he was wearing his night-vision goggles and had a clear view of the ground, it always came up too fast for him. He hit with a heavy thud, knocking the air out of him, and rolled to the side to break his fall.

"Check in," Hawkins called over the com link. The last duty of a jump master was to make sure that everyone had arrived in one piece.

When everyone reported a safe landing, McCarter took over again. "Okay, lads," he said. "You all know what to do. Let's do it."

Manning broke out his satellite link radio to let the Farm know that they were on the ground and operational.

CHAPTER FOURTEEN

California

As Rosario Blancanales perused his California investigation, he couldn't escape being very aware that his comrades-in-arms were once more putting their lives on the line, both in space and on the ground. It was frustrating not to be able to do anything to help them, but he'd drawn the short straw this time. All he could do was to try to insure that an incident like this never happened again. It was doubly frustrating, though, not to be making more progress than he was.

He had quite a few people working for him, but he wasn't getting much out of them. The INS agents were doing a remarkably good job, but the Happy Dragon restaurant was coming up clean. The owner was a third-generation Chinese American citizen, and his employees, right down to the newest dishwashers, were all citizens or green-card-carrying legal immigrants. He was playing the game all the way, so it was unlikely that he was involved.

While it would have been nice to have had the answers fall into place that easily, he'd known that the Happy Dragon had been a long shot. He wasn't surprised that it hadn't panned out. The problem was that the restaurant had been his only clue, and now he had nothing.

When the call came from the Farm, Blancanales was ecstatic to get some promising leads. "How do you think I should work this?" he asked Barbara Price after she filled him in on Dr. Lin Chu.

He didn't feel at all shy about asking her advice on how to approach this lead. She and Katz were two of the sharpest operational minds he'd ever worked with. And while Katz specialized in the tactical end of things, Price had an instinctive grasp of how to put the people pieces of the puzzle together so they could be exploited.

"If we're right about Lin," she said, "my bet is that he's been doing more than just turning the occasional grad student into a Red Chinese agent. There was no way he could have known that Del Gato would become an astronaut and be chosen for the Venture Star crew. That was just a bit of good luck that he was able to exploit, so his mission has to have been broader than that. My guess is that he's been siphoning off high-tech ideas and hardware for some time now. I think working that end of it will pan out."

"Considering the access he's had both at Rockwell and Cal Tech, that makes sense," Blancanales said. "And it won't be the first time we've had the

Chinese back-dooring tech intel through the old-boy network. You'd think the American engineers would have figured it out by now.''

Postwar industrial espionage was more threatening to the security of the United States than the cold war military spying had ever been. And now that Russian industry had fallen into a political black hole, if the Chinese wanted to bring their technology up to world-class standards, the United States and Japan were the only two models left to copy.

Congress had taken several steps in the past few years to restrict the level of technology that could be legally exported to China, but the legal transfer was only a small part of what the Chinese were getting. They were buying much of what they wanted on both the international open and black markets, and not everyone was concerned about what they were going to do with their purchases. Even so, many of the things that were vital for the development of high-tech weaponry could only be found in the United States.

''I'll get right on this,'' he told her, ''and get back to you as soon as I turn up anything.''

''Keep us posted.''

''And,'' he asked, ''how are Gadgets and Lyons doing?''

''They've successfully handled their end of things,'' she said. ''It went off without a hitch. Phoenix is in the air for the second phase, so we're focused on that right now.''

''I understand.''

NORMALLY, Blancanales would be working in tandem with Lyons and Schwarz and, as was their custom, they'd do it their way. Barbara Price had offered to find him outside backup, but he'd asked her to hold them in reserve. He needed to move fast and couldn't afford the time to break in people who didn't know how Stony Man operations worked.

The first thing he did was to have Akira Tokaido run through the police computers to try to find rap sheets on Lin's ex-students. It was a long shot, but it was a base that had to be covered. He was a little surprised when Tokaido came back with an industrial-espionage rap on one of them, a Richard Beneudo.

Engineers usually lived staid lives, and criminal activity wasn't their forte. But one could say that industrial espionage would be the crime of choice for engineers and scientists who were out to make a fast buck. The charge against Beneudo wasn't a case of selling secrets to a foreign power. Instead, he'd been careless in front of a security camera and had been caught putting company computer disks into his briefcase and heading out the door with them at the close of business.

The company, a software firm, had filed charges on Beneudo to protect themselves, but in the end had elected not to prosecute and merely fired him. But a Cal Tech graduate rarely had to look for work for too long. Blancanales quickly found him working for an electronics import-export operation in San Diego.

A quick check showed that this company, Pacific Rim Exports, did most of their business with China and Latin America, particularly Mexico. Better yet, they had a record with the U.S. Commerce Department of several irregularities in import-export licenses. Cross-checking Pacific Rim Exports with other federal agencies turned up a report indicating that it was suspected of being a front company for the Mexican Mafia. Nothing had been firmed up, but the investigation had turned up the name of a Carlos Montoya.

Blancanales was familiar with Carlos Montoya, who had long been considered a linchpin of the Mexican Mafia's drug operations. But he had always managed to keep from taking a fall, partly because he was also a powerful legitimate businessman with connections to Mexico's ruling political party.

Blancanales was surprised that this had led to a Mexican Mafia connection rather than a Chinese Tong as he had expected. Considering how well Del Gato had played the Hispanic card, maybe he should have expected it. Even though he now had a lead, Blancanales was beginning to see that this was going to be considerably more complicated than he had first thought. If this Montoya connection checked out, it would be the first time he had ever seen a Hispanic-Chinese alliance.

Usually, the Chinese were paranoid about letting outsiders into their operations. The mainland and Hong Kong gangs were even leery about getting too close to American-born Chinese. To see a mainland Chinese operation linked to a Mexican drug lord was historic. But, in the realities of the late nineties, though, it made sense. The Chinese had the product, the Mexicans had the distribution network and the money to buy. And, if the Mexicans were offering smuggled U.S. high-tech hardware, it would be a perfect match.

Now that he had a target, it was time for Blancanales to see if he could get inside.

Quinbaki Launch Complex, China

THE MAN RESPONSIBLE for the success of the secret space program at the Quinbaki secret test site, General Ye, stood in the observation deck overlooking the launch area. Though the spacecraft being moved out to the launch pad hadn't been built in China, seeing it being readied to boost the third missile platform into space gave Ye a great sense of pride. Though he was a dedicated communist, he considered himself to be a man of culture. In China, that title meant something rather different than it did in the West. Ye's education in classical Chinese art and music would be expected in a man of culture, as would be his in-depth knowledge of his people's history.

What would stun a Westerner, however, was the general's heartfelt belief that the Chinese were the only true civilization on Earth and that it was their destiny to rule over all of the lesser races. To a

Westerner, rampant ethnocentrism wasn't a sign of a cultured man, but it had been a driving force in Chinese civilization since their earliest days.

Several times in China's history, barbarians with superior military technology had overrun the Celestial Empire. Each time this happened, though, China survived by subverting the invaders with their superior culture and slowly absorbing them. Traditionally, it had taken only three generations to defeat each invader. The last time China had encountered militarily superior barbarians, however, the experience had almost destroyed her. The Western gunpowder and gunboat technology of the late nineteenth century had completely overwhelmed China's traditional culture and swept it away.

Recovering from the disastrous impact with the West had been a long struggle, and the process had destroyed much that had made China unique. The empire disintegrated, and with it the traditional administrative system that had ruled China for thousands of years, the rule of the mandarins. In the place of the old mandarin system, China had tried several Western-style systems of government, but they had all been flawed. Communism finally proved to be the solution to ruling the world's most populous nation.

While Communism was a product of the West, as well, it had been a perfect fit with Chinese culture. The support the Russian Communists had given China had also been critical to China's successful recovery of her position in the world. Even though the Soviet Union had collapsed, the Chinese version of communism showed no signs of withering. In fact, it was stronger than ever and was now on the verge of making the age-old dream of Asian domination a reality.

Ye's pride in having been the architect whose work would make the Chinese the rulers of the world was the driving force in his life. But, as befitted a civilized man, Ye was publicly humble about his accomplishments. His descendants would honor him for a thousand years as he honored his ancestors who had worked to put him where he was today, commanding the destiny of the Mother Country.

He was also aware that the strides he had made had only been possible because of the information and material that had been stolen from the United States. A steady stream of data and material had been captured by the agents of the Technical Intelligence Bureau over a span of years. The flight of the Venture Star to Quinbaki had merely been the most important item, not the first by any means.

Though Ye was grateful for the ship the two American astronauts had delivered to him, he wasn't unaware of the problems they had also brought. As he had expected, both of them had turned out to be less than perfect. But they were doing China a great service, and he could put up with their imperfections for now.

The Cantonese Chin was particularly troubling. He was a man who had lost his soul along with his honor, and such men were dangerous. A man who had sold out his country once could be expected to do it again, and he could never be completely trusted. But Ye was pragmatic and knew that he had no choice but to continue using him for now, as the woman wasn't a rated pilot. One of the Han spacemen the Americans were training would fly as the command pilot on the fourth launch, but Chin's services would still be needed for some time.

Ye was even more disappointed in the woman, though. It was true that without her Chin wouldn't have become a traitor to his country. It was also true that her sexual energy was extraordinary to say the least. But, at this point in his life, Ye preferred subtlety in a female agent. It was true that he had a use for her right now, both in and out of bed. Once the last missile platform was in orbit and Chin was no longer needed to fly, her usefulness to him would be at an end.

Ye knew that Chin expected to be the one who would be exterminated, and the astronaut would be very surprised to learn that he would survive. The woman would live, as well, but she would be in an officers' brothel where she belonged. There she would be taught a woman's position in Chinese society and maybe even a little subtlety before her beauty faded. When that was gone, she would need subtlety to survive.

JIMMY CHIN WENT to the crew suit-up room before Selena Del Gato or the Chinese mission specialists to have a moment by himself as he donned his space suit. In a way, he was glad that this would be his last flight as the command pilot of the Venture Star. He knew that meant his career as the first Chinese astronaut would be over. But the way this had turned out, he really didn't care.

Not for the first time since coming to China, he silently cursed his birth. If he weren't Chinese-American, he wouldn't have had a father who was addicted to gambling or an uncle who was in one of California's biggest Triads. If it weren't for that, he might still be in California working for Lockheed. He also cursed himself for not knowing enough about the country of his ancestors to understand what he would be facing when he went "home."

He had no idea what his life in China would be now that his career in the Chinese Space Force hadn't worked out. Surely, though, the government wouldn't let a man of his talents go to waste. There were several ways that he could still be useful to them. If nothing else, he could continue working in the training program, turning out new astronauts. At least that was what he kept telling himself.

But, if what he had seen at the Quinbaki complex so far was characteristic of Chinese officialdom, he knew he couldn't count on that happening. This was a top-heavy system with the underlings considered to be completely replaceable. There was no place for a talented individual in the Chinese way of doing things. Like everything else about his new home, he hadn't known that aspect of what he was getting himself in for. But he knew that he was stuck with it.

There was no way that he could ever go back to the U.S.; that was completely out of the question. For one thing, once all of the missile platforms were in orbit, the United States might not even exist as a nation anymore. And, even if he could return, he would go from being a presumed dead hero to the most hated man in American history. Hanging would be the very best he could expect, being beaten to death on live TV would be more like what would happen to him.

He was leaving the Quinbaki complex, but Selena Del Gato would be staying on because she had a built-in advantage he didn't. Even though she was also a hated half-breed, "devil," as the Chinese called anyone who wasn't of pure Han blood, she was female. He wasn't sure if he believed the rumors that she was sleeping with Ye, but he didn't put it past her. She was an intelligent woman and a talented engineer; he had to give her that. But he also knew that she had made an art form of sexual politics.

His spirited recommendation was one of the main reasons she had been selected to be on the Venture Star's crew. The recommendation had been more the result of a three-month affair, which had left him emotionally crippled and physically exhausted, than it had been of her abilities as an engineer. The relationship abruptly ended when she was selected over several other equally qualified candidates to be part of the Venture Star team.

He now realized that she had been as much a part of the pressure that had pushed him to become a traitor as his family problems had been. Somehow, he had thought that, once they were in China, she would be forced to depend on him again and would return to his bed. The American saying was that there was "no fool like an old fool," but they needed to coin a new saying that all men were fools when it came to women. At least to women like Selena Del Gato.

Chin picked up his pressure helmet, tucked it under his arm and walked out to wait to board the Venture Star for the last time as her command pilot.

CHAPTER FIFTEEN

Stony Man Farm, Virginia

"They're on the ground," Aaron Kurtzman announced to the crowd in the Computer Room, "and right on target."

"What about that convoy they spotted on the way in?" Hal Brognola asked. All it would take would be for one man to be gazing at the moon when the shadow of a chute crossed it to blow the deal.

"It's just sitting there, not moving, so it doesn't look like they were seen."

"I'll inform the President."

When Brognola left to make his second call of the day to the White House, Katzenelenbogen studied the screen displaying the SR-71's sensor readouts.

The Blackbird was circling the Quinbaki launch complex several miles out at eighty-three thousand feet. With the spy plane keeping watch, the Farm would be able to follow the team's progress to the target and provide early warning. A second SR-71 was standing by at Kadena Air Force Base ready to take over when the first one had to break off to refuel. With aerial refueling, a single Blackbird could have stayed in the sky for the entire mission, but there was no way that a KC-10Q tanker was going to survive for longer than a few minutes in Chinese airspace. Neither would the Blackbird if she had to throttle down to be slow enough to mate up with the tanker.

China

EVEN THOUGH the Stony Man commandos didn't expect to stay in the Gobi Desert very long, they took the time to bury their parachutes, jump harnesses, helmets and oxygen gear. This far behind enemy lines, every measure had to be taken to keep them from being detected. After policing the drop zone, they checked their equipment and got ready to move out.

It was only three miles to the edge of the perimeter around the secret launch facility. If they hadn't been in enemy territory, they could have covered that distance in less than an hour without working up much of a sweat. As it was, they had allotted two hours for the movement-to-contact phase. Once they reached the edge of the defenses, all bets were off on how quickly they would be able to penetrate them. The sensors and radar had mapped out the bunkers and hard defenses, but there was no way to tell where the troops would be posted or patrolling.

Calvin James took the point position with T. J. Hawkins as his slack, with the others following fifty yards behind them. Since it wasn't likely that anyone would be on their back-trail, they took up a wedge formation to get maximum coverage on their flanks. They moved out at the mile-eating, jogging pace known to elite units as the Airborne Shuffle. It was faster than a walk, but not as tiring as a run.

An hour and a half later, they were half a mile out from the perimeter when James signaled a halt. "Vehicle coming," he said over the com link.

The commandos quickly went to ground, taking up a defensive formation in the open sand. McCarter crawled up beside James to check out the situation. Through his night-vision goggles, he saw a small truck with four men in it and a machine gun mounted in the back. It was moving fast enough across their front that it couldn't be looking for them.

"I think it's just a routine patrol," he radioed back.

Once the truck had passed, the seven men moved out again. Now that they had hit the outer edge of the perimeter, they moved in a single file with James on point.

THE SECOND SR-71 Blackbird had replaced the first in a wide orbit over the Quinbaki launch complex. By rotating the overwatch duty between two of the spy planes, they would be able to stay on station for the next several hours. It was a grueling ordeal for the crews and hard on the planes themselves, but it was the only way that surveillance could be kept on the target while the recon satellites were below the horizon. The Chinese weren't stupid enough to do anything they didn't want the world to see while a Keyhole was overhead, and their launch activities would be timed to coincide with the satellite's downtime.

The Blackbird's crew didn't know what was going on below them, but that wasn't unusual for one of their flights. They had been tasked with a coverage mission, and that's what they were doing, covering the target and passing on everything they saw happening around it. In the spy plane's back seat, the RSO kept watch over a series of recon cameras and sensors as they transmitted their real-time digital "take" to satellites for retransmission to the ground stations. It was a fully automated process, but the RSO was ready to break in with a "flash" report if anything critical showed up.

When his wide aperture-radar picked up movement at the edge of his screen, he clicked in the mike to his scram-com satellite radio. "Apex Digger, this is Raven Tango, I have a Flash One report, over."

"Apex Digger," the Blackbird ground-control station answered. "Send your flash, over."

"This is Raven Tango with Flash One information," the RSO sent back. "We have a motorized convoy of nine vehicles bearing two-three-eight, forty-six miles out and moving at an average speed of thirty-eight miles an hour. Their ETA to the center of the target area is a little under an hour. From the size of the vehicles, they could be carrying either troops or cargo. End of Flash One, over."

"Apex Digger, good copy on flash, Raven Tango."

WHEN BOLAN and McCarter heard the Blackbird's flash transmission, they knew they had to pick up the pace even more. There were more than enough troops at the complex already without waiting for reinforcements to arrive. The Blackbird had said that the trucks might be carrying cargo instead, but they couldn't afford to wait around to see.

With the complex as large as it was, the Chinese hadn't put a fence around it. The desert was their fence. For a nation that prided itself on having such a long history, they had forgotten the lessons that history should have taught them. Since they now controlled the desolate western deserts, they didn't expect trouble to come from them. But, as had been proved so often in China's past, the desolation itself was no barrier to determined men.

Even though there was no fence, the Stony Man warriors faced a line of bunkers and prepared fighting positions stretching for hundreds of yards to either side. Interspaced between the bunkers were several surface-to-air missile batteries and their radar vans. How many of the bunkers and trenches were manned remained to be seen, but the roving patrols were the more immediate concern. They needed to pass through the bunker line before the next truck passed and caught them in the open.

Turning up his night-vision goggles to their maximum sensitivity, James swept the fortifications in front of them. The night air was cool enough that the heat signatures of men should show up clearly. Even in enclosed bunkers, their body heat would warm the air and it would pass out through the firing ports.

"It looks like they have only manned every other bunker," he said to McCarter over the com link. "If there aren't any remote sensors out there, I should be able to find a dead zone between them."

"Do it quickly," the Phoenix Force leader replied.

Even a desert wasn't perfectly flat, and James found a small draw leading at an angle past the unmanned bunker inside the perimeter. When a max scan didn't show heat from electronic devices or IR beams covering the route, he clicked in his com link.

"Link up with me," he said. "I've found our way in."

Keeping low to the ground, the commandos followed James up the draw. Though the route had looked clear, he kept scanning for any sensors he might have missed. Even though he knew the Chinese always thought in terms of men rather than devices, he was surprised that they hadn't put out a few sensors of some kind or the other.

Once they were past the bunker line, the layout of the complex was easier to see. They had studied the recon photos, but it never hurt to see the ground in person. Their objective was the mountain that was roughly in the middle of the restricted area, and the fastest way for them to get to it was to cross the air base in the western sector of the complex. Going around either end of it would take too much time and expose them to the roving vehicle patrols.

Hawkins joined James on point, and the two men kept their fingers on the triggers of their silenced MP-5s as they led the way past the buildings and across the open expanses of concrete runways and taxiways. It was slow going, and they kept to the shadows as sentries posted around the hangars walked the line of MiG fighters in their revetments. But apparently none of the guards had been given night-vision equipment.

On their way across the airfield, Jack Grimaldi noticed several Chinese army helicopters parked on the tarmac and made a mental note of their positions. If their bid to recapture the Venture Star turned sour, the survivors might be able to take a chopper out. The fact that they'd more than likely be blasted out of the sky before they could get a mile away wasn't as important as the option of a secondary escape route.

WITH THE BUILDINGS of the airfield behind them, the Stony Man team was able to have an unobstructed view of the base of the mountain, and they saw why the Venture Star hadn't been spotted by the recon satellites. The side of the mountain was opened up, revealing a large, dark opening where a rock face had been seen before. The cave's entrance—because that's what it was—was at least a hundred yards wide and fifty tall. That was more than big enough to allow the spacecraft inside the mountain.

The huge hangar-style doors inside the opening were closed to cut off any light from inside, and they hid the extent of the underground facility from the commandos. But for the Chinese to be able to support a sophisticated vehicle like the Venture Star, the mountain had to be hiding a mini-Cape Canaveral inside.

A set of what looked like narrow-gauge railroad tracks led from the cave entrance for about five hundred yards to a ring of red lights on tall pylons that illuminated a circle a hundred yards in diameter. In the center of that circle was a mobile launch platform, and mounted vertically on it was the Venture Star. In the red light, the spacecraft looked to be covered in dried blood.

"I thought that thing was supposed to be painted white?" McCarter said.

"It was when it left Palmdale," Grimaldi replied. "The Chinese might have slapped a coat of paint on it as camouflage."

"Black's not a good camouflage color in the desert,'' Manning pointed out. ''But I think that paint's why they haven't been able to spot her on radar when she's made her flights to launch the platforms.''

''What do you mean?''

''That black coating could be a radar-defeating stealth covering. That's the hot ticket in aerial warfare right now, and the lab boys have come a long ways in the past couple of years in stealth technology. We have to figure that the Chinese have been working on that, as well.''

''It doesn't matter what damned color the thing is now,'' McCarter said. ''We have to take care of it one way or the other.''

''The crew hatch is open,'' Grimaldi observed. ''I can see a white light inside and the gantry pushed up in place, so they could be getting ready to board the crew. That also means, of course, that she's fueled up and ready to launch. Gentlemen, I think we've found our ride home.''

''Then we'd better get in there quickly,'' Bolan said. ''They know that they have to watch for the recon satellites, so they won't be wasting much time before they launch.''

''That might be easier said than done,'' James said as he scanned the area around the launch site. ''I don't know what they're all doing, but they have a lot of people on the ground between here and there.''

The intervening distance was some six hundred yards dotted with what looked like concrete bunkers, service facilities and fuel tanks for the spacecraft. Even without using the magnification on their night-vision goggles, they could see two dozen men going about their business around the Venture Star. Most of them would be technicians, not armed troops, but even an unarmed man could sound an alert.

The trick was to find a way to get past as many of them as possible before someone spotted them.

WHILE THE OTHER commandos looked for the best way to get through to the launch pad, Manning took out his GPS transmitter and took a reading on the center of the cave entrance. When he had the numbers, he hit the transmission button to send the reading to the satellite that would relay it to the Sea Wolf submarine waiting in the South China Sea. This last piece of critical data would insure that if a nuclear-tipped cruise missile had to be launched to finish the job, it would do it with the first shot. One way or the other, this mission would be a success.

Having secured the last option, he stowed the GPS back into his pack and pulled half a dozen two-pound RDX explosive charges from his backpack and hung them on the front of his assault harness. The explosives represented the second option for the mission—destroying the ship themselves.

These were specially prepared shaped charges with hardened-steel triangular pellets mixed in with the plastique. When they detonated against the skin over the fuel tanks, they were powerful enough to cut through the heat shield and send the red-hot pellets into the liquid-hydrogen tanks. The resulting explosion should completely destroy the craft and everything around it for a two-hundred-yard radius.

The first, and by far most preferable, option was to capture the ship and fly her home because that was the only way they would be going home themselves.

WHEN THE COMMANDOS moved out, James took point again with Hawkins backing him up and the others several yards behind in one group. This close in, James was carrying his silenced Beretta 92 in his hand because the MP-5 was a little too obvious. Hawkins, however, had his silenced subgun with night scope ready to back him up.

The first rule of going any place a person wasn't supposed to be was to act as if he really did belong there. It always worked, particularly at night, and it was working again this time. James wove his way from one building, vehicle and piece of equipment to the next without being challenged.

He was preparing to pass a building with several antennas on top when a door suddenly opened and a soldier stepped out into the light.

Hawkins watched as James went to ground and saw the Chinese soldier catch the movement and turn to look. When the trooper reached back to unsling his AK, Hawkins had him in his scope and he triggered two single shots.

Through the night scope, he saw the shock on the guard's face as the slugs smashed him back against the wall.

A second later, his partner stepped around the corner of the building, and James tagged him with his Beretta. Hawkins quickly dashed up and quietly closed the still-open door. With the way cleared again, he clicked his com link to signal the others forward.

The night was suddenly rent by the wail of a siren.

"Oh, shit," McCarter muttered.

CHAPTER SIXTEEN

Quinbaki Launch Complex, China

The alert sirens caught General Ye relaxing with a bowl of noodle soup and a cup of tea before the launch. As with almost everything else related to his personal life, Ye ate plainly. His only exception to austerity was his sex life, but he would be sleeping alone this night. The foreign she-devil who called herself Moon Daughter would be flying among the stars tonight for the good of the Mother Country.

It took only a few seconds after the alert sounded for Ye to reach his command post. Radio reports from a dozen of his ground-defense units were coming in, but they were confused and contradictory. He couldn't get a clear picture of what was going on, and he didn't know the size of the assault force.

From the first reports, he thought that commandos had come to destroy the spacecraft. On the surface, that made the most sense, but that mission would have been much easier to accomplish with a cruise missile. That kind of attack would, of course, have carried the risk of nuclear retaliation. Beijing had long sought an opportunity to display Chinese nuclear might. But it would be the kind of calculated risk the Yankees might take.

A ground attack, though, made no sense in that it was doomed to failure, and the dead attackers could easily be identified as Americans.

Knowing that Americans didn't like to throw away lives in futile gestures, the thought hit him that commandos might have come to try to recapture the spacecraft and fly it back to the United States. He knew how expensive the Venture Star had been to build, and he knew that its loss was creating a great deal of opposition in the American Congress to spending further funds on space exploration. It was so typical of the capitalists to count the money like petty merchants when national survival was at stake. But he well knew how many times the Americans had thrown away a decisive advantage like Star Wars because it was too expensive.

For the first time in his life, Ye hesitated. If the Yankees stole the spacecraft back, his missile-platform deployment couldn't be completed. But if the ship was accidentally damaged by his forces trying to prevent the Yankees from taking off, his aerospace engineers might not be able to repair it. The attackers had to be stopped without risking any damage to the ship.

"Stop the Yankees at all costs," he snapped. "But no heavy weapons are to be used. Any man who hits the spacecraft will be executed. Acknowledge."

JIMMY CHIN HEARD the gunfire but couldn't believe that anyone could be attacking the launch complex. Ye had bragged about how secure the facility was because it was located in the middle of the impassable Gobi Desert. He had commented that the sand had swallowed up entire invading armies. From what he was hearing, though, someone had escaped becoming the desert's lunch.

"What's happening out there?" he called over to Del Gato in English.

"Yankees are attacking the ship," she called back.

Chin was puzzled for a moment. Yankees? Then he realized that was what the Chinese called Americans. For a moment, his heart swelled with pride. His people were taking a bold step against a treacherous enemy. The fact that he was now one of those enemies escaped his mind for the moment.

Del Gato dropped her helmet and raced down to the arms room. "Where are you going?" Chin called to her.

"I don't have a gun."

Since he didn't, either, he ran after her. He didn't know what he would do with a weapon when he had it, but it seemed to be the right thing to do.

WHEN THE CHINESE SOUNDED the alert, the Stony Man warriors split up into two assault teams. One team would fight its way through to escort Jack Grimaldi to the Venture Star. The other team would provide covering fire while the pilot prepared the ship for launch.

McCarter and Encizo went with Grimaldi, while Bolan deployed the rest of the commandos for a rear-guard action. Bolan's team had the easy assignment. Its job was to stand and prevent the Chinese from keeping Grimaldi from taking off. If they made it inside the ship in time to go with him, that was fine. But if they didn't, that was fine, too, just as long as the Venture Star made it out.

WHEN CHIN AND DEL GATO reached the arms room, they found racks full of the 5.45 mm Chinese versions of the Russian AK-74. He grabbed one of the assault rifles and a chest pack of magazines for it.

"How does this thing work?" Del Gato asked as she pulled one of the rifles from the rack.

Spotting a rack of semiautomatic pistols, he took one of them and slammed a magazine into the butt before handing it to her. "Put that back and take this. It's easier to use."

"Give me some more ammo," she said. "And let's go!"

He handed her a pair of magazines and followed her to the observation post.

BOLAN AND HIS THREE companions were giving a good account of themselves against overwhelming odds. The Chinese had taken a while to react to the threat. But, so far, they hadn't brought any heavy weapons into play, which suited him just fine. In a straight-up gun battle with small arms, the Stony Man team was hard to beat regardless of the odds. Working in unison to move and shoot was their bread and butter, and their experience always gave them the edge. It was only when the opposition brought in things like RPGs and mortars that the situation got dicey.

To keep from being outflanked, the small group was keeping on the move, but they couldn't keep from being crowded back closer to the ship with every volley. That was good if Grimaldi was able to get the launch-sequence program to function in time to take them aboard. But, if he had to go to the automatic emergency-liftoff program, they would be caught up in the inferno of the exhaust plume.

Hawkins saw a Chinese soldier throw a grenade in his direction and ducked, but not quickly enough. When it detonated, he felt a blow behind his left shoulder. Reaching back, he felt blood, but he could still move his arm so he wasn't hit that badly. Seeking out his attacker, he gave him a burst of 9 mm slugs to discourage him from throwing any more bombs.

When Bolan shouted for them to pull back again, he didn't tell anyone about his wound because there was nothing to be done for it beyond applying a field dressing. He would either have it seen to when he flew home with the rest of his teammates, or he would die in the sands of western China.

JIMMY CHIN HAD NEVER FIRED a full-auto assault rifle before, but he had shot the semiauto version of the older AK-47 back in the States. He saw that this weapon had the same kind of safety, a lever on the left side of the receiver, but it had three positions instead of the two found on the semiauto AK. The third position would be for full-automatic fire.

Loading a magazine, he pulled back on the charging handle and flicked the selector switch all the way to full-auto. He was drawing a bead on a small group of black-clad commandos racing for the Venture Star when he realized what he was doing. He was about to shoot at Americans, his own people.

Pulling the rifle down, he took a deep breath before bringing it back up to his shoulder. This time he took aim at a cluster of Chinese troops trying to work around the side of a second group of Americans. He burned through the 30-round magazine in two long bursts before the AK's bolt locked back on an empty chamber.

Dropping the empty magazine from the assault rifle, he took a full one from the magazine carrier and snapped it into place. Stepping back up, he looked for a place to do the most good. Right below him a squad of Chinese was advancing behind a truck, using it for cover. Though they were almost fifty yards away, with their backs to him, they made a perfect target.

Again, he fired long bursts. Right as the magazine went empty, Del Gato saw whom he was shooting at. "You idiot!" she screamed. "What are you doing? You're shooting at our own troops."

"My troops are the ones who are trying to get to the Venture Star," he said calmly as he dropped the empty mag and slammed another full one in place.

For the first time in weeks, Jimmy Chin felt certain that he finally knew what he was doing. It felt good to try to help those brave men who were fighting to right a wrong that he had been a part of.

"Damn you!" she screamed at him. "You're ruining everything."

He almost didn't hear the report of the pistol over the shock of the round hitting him in the back. "Selena!" he screamed as the AK fell from his hands.

She turned her back on him to watch the battle below that would decide her future.

WITH BOLAN'S FIRE covering them, Grimaldi, McCarter and Encizo made their way to the left side of the spaceship almost undetected. The support personnel had scrambled for cover with the first shots, leaving the ship unguarded.

"You two get up there," Encizo yelled from the base of the gantry. "I'll cover you from down here."

The two commandos scrambled up the gantry

and dashed across the walkway to the Venture Star's forward hatch. When Grimaldi scrambled inside, he glanced around the cabin as he made his way to the flight deck.

When the ship had lifted off from Palmdale, it had been configured for a crew of four. There had been no reason for the Chinese to mount additional acceleration couches, so three of the Stony Man commandos were going to have to ride out the liftoff strapped down to the decking with their backs against the rear bulkhead. Sliding into the left-hand command pilot's seat, he started hitting switches before he was even strapped in.

McCarter, himself an experienced pilot, followed Grimaldi to the flight deck and into the copilot's seat. If this went as simply as they had been promised, there wouldn't be anything for him to do until they reached orbit. But if the program didn't work, he would help Grimaldi try to liftoff manually. One way or the other, he was determined to fly home. Dying in China wasn't on his agenda this week.

Plugging in the new computer program was as simple as inserting a cassette in a VCR and punching a button. The program Grimaldi loaded contained an override command that erased anything the Chinese might have programmed and replaced it with the emergency-launch program and initial guidance for a quick trip back to California.

The seconds seemed to drag as the computer digested the new information and sent commands to the ship's systems. When that was done, it automatically ran a systems check to make sure everything had uploaded. When the Ignition Sequence Ready readout came on, they were ready to go.

"Get inside!" Grimaldi shouted over the com link. "We're ready to take off!"

THE COMMANDOS PUT OUT a rain of lead to cover their withdrawal in turn. As each man's magazine went dry, he pulled back, reloaded and fired again to cover the men still exposed. One by one, the commandos reached the gantry and scrambled across the walkway to the crew hatch. From the top of the walkway, Encizo fired to cover them until they could get up.

When Manning reached the gantry, he took two of his explosive charges from his cargo pockets, slapped them on the outer legs of the structure and flicked the fuses over to radio detonation.

"Give me that!" James shouted, and held out his hand for the detonator. "And get your butt up the ladder."

Manning scrambled up and joined Encizo by the hatch as James made it up the gantry.

"Get inside!" James yelled when he reached them.

As they ducked through the hatch to clear it, James went through himself and turned to trigger the small explosive charges on the rear legs of the roll-away gantry. When the legs collapsed, the structure toppled backward into the sand, pulling away from the spacecraft.

"We're clear!" he yelled as he pulled the hatch shut and dogged it against the locks.

Encizo had taken one of the acceleration couches behind Grimaldi and McCarter, and Bolan had the other. James quickly joined Manning and Hawkins against the rear bulkhead, slid into a seated position and held on to a tie-down ring.

"Hang on, guys!" Grimaldi yelled as he activated the ignition sequence.

From that point on, the launch was completely under the control of the onboard computer. The fuel pumps kicked in first, sending liquid oxygen and hydrogen to the nuzzles of the Aerospike engine burn chambers. An instant later, the ignition system flashed, igniting the mixture and bringing the engine temperature to an instant fifteen thousand degrees. The flames bouncing from the blast deflector of the launch pad scattered the Chinese troops. An infantry squad caught in the open was instantly incinerated. The support vehicles and equipment still clustered around the launch pad burst into flames.

Eight seconds after the ship's seven Aerospike engines ignited, the computer signaled them to throttle up to a hundred and ten percent for takeoff. The thundering roar shook the sand and echoed from the hollow mountain where she had been held prisoner. In a burst of light that could be seen for miles, the Venture Star leaped to freedom in space.

The 3.6 G acceleration pressed the Stony Man commandos into their couches. The three men strapped down behind them were brutally pressed into the deck plates. Unable to move without effort, they sat and took the force of three and a half times their weight.

It was a rough ride, but they were on their way home.

THROUGH HIS PAIN, Jimmy Chin heard the roar of the Venture Star's seven Aerospike engines and saw the flash of light from her exhaust plume. It was fitting that she was going home where she belonged. The Americans would strip off the black radar-defeating coating, and once more she would be a gleaming arrow pointing to the stars, leading a peaceful exploration of space. He tried to smile, but it came out as a grimace.

Selena Del Gato had a look of unbelieving horror on her face as the Venture Star disappeared into the night sky on a plume of flame. Her dream of glory had just become a living nightmare. Without the Venture Star, the Chinese had no need for a space force and, therefore, no need for her. Everything she had worked so hard for had turned to sand and was slipping through her fingers.

She spun on Chin and screamed, "You bastard!" She raised the pistol to shoot him again.

Reaching out, Chin found his fallen AK, lifted the barrel and pulled the trigger. The selector switch was set on full-auto and the burst of 5.45 mm slugs stitched her full across the belly.

"Jimmy!" She sounded surprised as she crumpled to the floor.

"I'm sorry," he said, blood bubbling to his lips. "I really am."

CHAPTER SEVENTEEN

Stony Man Farm, Virginia

The sensors on the SR-71 orbiting over western China caught the Venture Star's launch flare, and the data was instantly flashed to the ground retransmission stations. When the screens lit up in the Farm's Computer Room, complete pandemonium broke out.

"Go! Go! Go!" Aaron Kurtzman hammered the desk in front of him with both hands.

Hunt Wethers instantly linked to the NASA satellite telemetry feed that was relaying the telemetry from the spacecraft itself.

"Everything's in the green," he called out over the cheering. "And he's on the preprogrammed flight path. They'll be home in a little under five hours."

"Our man Grimaldi just hit the big-time." Hal Brognola grinned broadly. "He made astronaut on his first time up to the plate."

Barbara Price smiled. "We're not going to be

able to live with Jack now," she said. "His head will be too big to fit into the room."

"The world's first clandestine-operations astronaut," Kurtzman said, laughing. "Maybe we can get our own space shuttle now and can keep it over in the new annex."

"Don't you think the neighbors might notice a launch tower sticking up above the pine trees?"

Kurtzman shrugged. "We could just tell them that it's an irrigation tower."

Brognola glanced at his watch. "I guess I'd better get to Andrews so I can catch my fast-mover ride to Palmdale. I'm going to need to keep a lid on the situation there and lay down some heavy security."

"How are you going to explain the Venture Star's sudden rebirth?" Katzenelenbogen asked. "If you ask me, that's going to raise a lot of questions that aren't going to be real easy to answer."

"To be perfectly honest with you," Brognola replied, "I don't have the slightest idea what I'm going to do. The President is still hashing this over with his advisers, and I haven't been given a decision yet."

He shrugged. "Until I hear something definitive, all I can do is wing it and try to keep things from getting out of hand. That'll start by hustling the ship under cover the minute it lands and imposing a security lock down on the entire Skunk Works."

"Good luck with that program." Katz shook his head. "Even though it's the Skunk Works, they're still a bunch of blabbermouth civilians out there. You might want to lay on a battalion of Rangers to help keep a lid on it.''

''I wish I could,'' Brognola said.

When the red phone connecting the Computer Room to Houston Mission Control Center rang, Brognola snatched it up. ''Brognola here.''

''This is Bill Kruger,'' the NASA director said. ''I'm afraid that we have a little bit of a problem.''

Problem wasn't a word that had brought Brognola much comfort lately, but it seemed to be the theme song of this mission. ''They lifted off and they're safe now, aren't they?''

''They are,'' Kruger admitted. ''As long as Grimaldi lets the computer fly for him, they'll be in a low orbit in twelve minutes and ready to reenter in another three hours. But that's not the problem.''

''What is, then?''

''According to the initial telemetry we're receiving, the Venture Star is carrying a payload and it's heavy, damned heavy.''

Brognola felt a sinking sensation in his gut. ''Do you think it's another one of those launch platforms?''

''I don't see what else it could be.''

''Can they land with it inside?''

''Not safely,'' Kruger stated.

''Shit!''

''The problem,'' the director continued, ''is that with the platform on board, the computer program we gave Grimaldi won't work because the ship will be overweight for the reentry we calculated, and it might not make it."

"Can they dump the damned thing over the side and lighten the ship?"

"Well, from what you told me, the platform's carrying half a dozen nuclear missiles, right?"

"That's what we think," Brognola confirmed.

"Well, if they just jettison the payload, there's a chance that it'll come down somewhere we don't want it to. Even if the missile warheads don't detonate on impact, they could still contaminate a large area of someone's backyard."

"Is there anything we can do?"

"I think we could talk them through a payload launch sequence that would deploy the platform in a stable low orbit, but it would still be operational. I don't know how to disable it from down here so the Chinese can't use it before we can get one of our shuttles up there to recover it. None of your people are cleared for a space walk, and that's what it would take to disarm that thing."

"And you think the Chinese could launch from that low an orbit?"

"They'd have to reprogram it, but yes, we think it could be done."

Kruger thought for a long moment. "You know," he said cautiously, "we might be able to release that thing on an escape trajectory. That would get rid of it permanently. Let me run that by my people and see what they can work out."

"What do you want my people to do?"

"For the time being," Kruger said, "nothing. We're going to have to extend the flight, so they can just float around up there and take in the sights till we can figure this out and work up the flight plan."

"They're going to love that."

"It beats burning up on reentry."

"You've got a point," Brognola conceded.

"Mission Control will talk to them as soon as they reach orbital status and give them the word."

Brognola looked as though he'd just been hit by a truck as he put down the phone. "You can tell the chopper pilot to go back to sleep," he told Price. "And tell the cook I could sure use a cup of coffee."

"My pot is on," Kurtzman spoke up.

Brognola didn't even reply to that. He needed caffeine, but he didn't need to kill the rest of his stomach lining getting it.

Space

THE STONY MAN WARRIORS were still strapped down in back of the Venture Star when Jack Grimaldi took the call from Houston Mission Control.

"Venture Star, this is Houston," the voice in his earphones said. "Congratulations, you're in orbit. Not bad for a rookie. Over."

"The computer gets all the credit, Houston. I was just along for the ride."

"Well, you're going to get to do a little hands-on before this is over. We need to change the game plan a little bit. Over."

This was the last thing Grimaldi wanted to hear. "Let's have it, Houston."

"Well, did you guys happen to see the Chinese put a load into the cargo bay before you took off?"

"They were screwing around with something back there," Grimaldi replied. "Why?"

"We think they loaded another one of those missile-launching platforms, and you're going to have to get rid of it before you can safely come down."

"Wonderful," Grimaldi said. "How long is that going to take?"

"We're not sure, but you're going to need to stay in orbit until we can get this worked out."

"Go sight-seeing, right?"

"Most people would kill to get the view you have up there, Venture Star, me included."

"You're welcome to it." Grimaldi laughed. "All I can see out of this porthole is black with little lights."

"We're going to change that view for you real quick. Do you remember the roll drills you went through in the simulator?"

"Roger."

"Prepare to execute a 180-degree roll to the left on my mark."

"Ready," Grimaldi replied, his hand on the joystick that fired the reaction-control thrusters.

"Three...two...one, execute!"

Grimaldi watched closely as he burned the lower

starboard and upper portside thrusters to roll the ship around her long axis. Halfway through the roll, he applied opposite thrust to kill the movement.

"Very good," Mission Control said. "You did 182 and killed all the residual momentum. Good work."

Grimaldi looked up and saw Earth through the window. It was a beautiful sight, but he was too busy to enjoy it. "What's next?"

"Now have your copilot find the switch marked Cargo Bay Lock."

"Got it," McCarter stated.

"Okay. Now, Copilot, select Unlock. Then select Doors—Open Full."

"Roger." McCarter hit the required switches. "Unlocked and doors open full. The readout indicates that the doors are open."

"Copy," Houston said. "Pilot, turn on your aft monitor and select Cargo Bay."

"Roger."

"There it is, ladies and gentlemen," Grimaldi announced as the screen lit up to show their cargo. "One Red Chinese missile-launch platform, complete with nuclear missiles."

"Venture Star, we see it. Now, select Cargo Bay Interior Monitor Three."

That changed the screen to a view from the end of the bay, showing the rear of the launch platform and the automatic grapples holding it in place.

"Good," Houston said. "We need to study that for a while, so leave it on."

"What do you want us to do in the meantime?"

The controller laughed. "Just relax, Venture Star. Take in the sights, float around the cabin. We'll get back to you as soon as we can."

WHILE MISSION CONTROL was working up a solution to getting rid of their unexpected hitchhiker, the Stony Man commandos were doing what every newcomer to space did. They looked out the windows at Earth, hanging over their heads. The fact that they were all experienced free-fall jumpers made it easier for them to adjust to weightlessness. They automatically knew that up and down didn't mean anything.

Hawkins was particularly mesmerized by what he was seeing. "Man—" he shook his head "—my old granddad isn't even going to believe this."

"I thought you told me he was dead," Calvin James asked.

"He's been dead for years," Hawkins said, "but that doesn't mean that I can't tell him about this."

"Okay."

Rafael Encizo and Mack Bolan shared one of the portholes. "It's a beautiful sight, isn't it, Mack?" Encizo said.

Bolan nodded. It had been said before that from space, national differences couldn't be seen, and he knew that was true. But, seeing it for himself really drove it home. He also knew, though, that as long as men inhabited the planet, they would continue to make their imaginary boundaries and would fight over them.

It was sad, but it was also a reality.

IT WAS ALMOST two hours before Houston Mission Control came back on the air. "Venture Star, this is Mission Control, over."

"Venture Star, go," Grimaldi replied.

"Okay, Venture Star, we have the program worked out, and it shouldn't be too difficult. It'll take two short engine burns, but nothing too fancy."

"That's good, Houston," Grimaldi sent back. "I'm not sure that I'm up to doing anything fancy right as yet."

The controller chuckled. "You're doing fine up there so far."

"It's the 'so far' part that has me worried."

"Don't worry, we'll talk you through this. First, you're going to go into a nose-up position and make a short burn. That will put you in a climb, so to speak, out of your orbit. Once you're on your way up, we'll tell you how to kick that damned thing out of the cargo bay and send it on its way to the sun. Then we'll have you come back down to your planned orbit and set you up to land."

"That sounds good to me," Grimaldi replied. "Just yell when you're ready. We'll be here."

"Copy, Venture Star," Houston said. "Get your passengers strapped down again and prepare for the burn."

On Houston's command, Grimaldi made another short thruster burn to point the Venture Star's nose away from the orbital plane.

"Good position," Control said. "Get ready for the burn."

Though the Venture Star had seven Aerospike engines mounted in the back, only two of the four-hundred-thousand-pound-thrust units were used for orbital maneuvering. On command, Grimaldi hit the firing buttons for engines number one and seven. The thrust jammed the Stony Man warriors back into their seats again, but it lasted for only a minute and a half.

"You're looking good, Venture Star," Mission Control said as Grimaldi cut the thrust. "The burn was right on. Now we need your copilot to unstow the Remote Manipulator Arm control stick. It's behind a panel by his right knee and swings up to lock into position."

"I've got it," McCarter replied as he popped the door open and swung out the joystick. "It looks like a video-game control stick."

"That's the one. It works like the joystick on a fighter—back is up, forward is down and right and left as you would expect."

"I think I can handle that."

"Now, on the same panel as the cargo-bay-door controls, there's a toggle marked Grapple Release. Move that to the Unlock position."

"Roger," McCarter said. "It's unlocked."

"Okay," Houston Control said. "Now comes the

fun part. Put a little rearward pressure on the stick and see what the package does."

With his eyes on the cargo-bay monitor, McCarter eased back on the stick and saw the launch platform stir. "I saw it move," he said.

"Good." The relief was clear in the controller's voice. "We were afraid that the Chinese had screwed around with our hold downs back there."

"Thanks for telling me."

"Didn't want you to have to worry about it unless you had to," Houston came back. "Now, slowly come all the way back on the control."

McCarter eased back and watched as the launch platform slowly rose out of the cargo bay on the end of a long mechanical arm.

"You're doing good," Houston cut in. "Keep going until it stops."

"Okay," McCarter said. "That seems to be it."

The monitor showed the platform barely clearing the tops of the open cargo-bay doors.

"Not quite," the controller said. "On the top of your joystick is what looks like an aircraft's trim tab button, which extends the arm. Roll it all the way forward."

Doing that extended the arm another three yards.

"Now you have it," Control said. "Find the RMA Release switch, toggle that and retract the arm."

"Got it," McCarter said as he watched the arm back away from the launch platform, leaving it suspended in space above the Venture Star.

Following the commands from Mission Control, the remote arm was quickly stowed back inside the cargo bay and the doors closed over it.

''Okay,'' the controller said. ''Pilot, you need to make a nose-pitch-down change and prepare for the return burn.''

The position change and orbital burn went off without a hitch, leaving the Chinese missile-launch platform on its way into the sun. Half an hour later, the Venture Star was back in her planned orbit for reentry.

''Everything looks A-okay from here,'' Houston said. ''Now you just have to wait until you come around far enough to make the deorbit burn.''

''Like I said before,'' Grimaldi radioed. ''We'll be here.''

''Copy, Venture Star. Me, too.''

CHAPTER EIGHTEEN

California

Rosario Blancanales was convinced that Dr. Lin Chu was the main player in the spy ring, and he knew he was taking a calculated risk letting him stay at large. The problem with hauling him in at this stage of the investigation wasn't just that they didn't have proof that he was a spy. That hadn't stopped Stony Man from questioning someone before. The problem was that Lin was too well-known. He wasn't exactly a public figure, but he was one of the top ten aerospace engineers in the nation not working for NASA. Snatching him up wouldn't only alert the Chinese; it might also make people wonder if he was somehow involved with the recent Venture Star disaster. He could, however, keep a close eye on him.

Blancanales had gotten very good results from the INS on the restaurant inquiry, but he didn't want to use them to keep Lin under surveillance. For that, he needed a more experienced team and called upon the nearest U.S. Marshals office. His cover story to them was different than the one he had given the INS. He told them that Lin was suspected of industrial espionage for a foreign power.

He directed a pair of two-man teams to watch Lin's residence around the clock and a third two-man team to track his visitors and movements when he went to the university. They were to watch and note only. They weren't to protect or to apprehend, at least not yet, just to keep watch on him while Blancanales worked the Pacific Rim Exports angle.

The lead on Pacific Rim Exports was proved easy to exploit. Using the reports from the earlier trade commission and the DEA investigations of the company, he got the names of the men in charge. The renegade ex-Cal Tech engineer and possible Chinese agent, Richard Beneudo, wasn't on that list, but that didn't mean that he was clean. All it meant was that he was keeping himself out of the public eye. A phone call, though, was all it took for Blancanales to get a meeting with the firm's "buyers."

WHEN BLANCANALES ARRIVED at the meeting place, a restaurant in a trendy suburb of Newport Beach, his expensive but semiflashy clothes marked him as south Florida. He wasn't as decked out as a Colombian or a Cuban would have been, but no one would mistake him for a gringo. His rental car was a Caddy convertible. His cover required at least that, but it was black, not red.

His role was that of a businessman who didn't

mind bending the customs regulations. He was a buyer and seller of bootleg electronics components when he wasn't running a drug-distribution network. He had money or goods to trade, and he wanted to place a big order. The stipulation was that he wanted to meet the suppliers to satisfy himself that they were dependable. It was a reasonable request, and such meetings usually followed an established protocol.

Blancanales was used to going into a situation alone. As Able Team's front man, it was part of his operational routine. Usually, though, he had Gadgets Schwarz watching over him with some kind of electronic goodie and Carl Lyons waiting in the wings with his finger on the trigger. This time, he was going in completely solo with a story that didn't have much depth, and he would have liked his old partners standing by to bail him out.

He was met at the side door by a three-man security squad. One man stood back to cover him, while the other two checked him for hardware. The pat-down was thoroughly professional and included checking to see if he was wearing a wire. When he came up clean, he was escorted into the restaurant's back banquet room.

Four men were seated at the table—three Hispanics and an Asian. Even though no names were offered, Blancanales recognized one of the Hispanics from the reports as Hector Menendes, a principal of Pacific Rim Exports. The other two looked like locals, but from his clothing, the Asian could have only been offshore.

Blancanales greeted the three Hispanics in Spanish.

"Speak English," Menendes said, "so our guest knows what we say."

"Of course." Blancanales smiled. Not only was English the international language of science and air travel, but it was also the lingua franca of crime, just as U.S. dollars were the preferred currency of illegal transactions.

"How did you learn of us?" Menendes asked.

"In my business, one hears many things," Blancanales said vaguely. "You know how it is."

"No, I don't know," Menendes replied, his dark eyes searching Blancanales's face. "Why don't you tell me?"

Blancanales had been through this part of the initial-meeting playbook many times, as well, but it usually only happened on drug buys. Gangs handling fenced goods usually weren't this paranoid. It made him think that he was on the right track.

"There's a man in Little Havana," he explained, "who has an operation he calls Casa Grande Electronics. If you've ever been to Miami, you've seen his commercials on TV. He's the biggest electronics component dealer in the state. One of my cousins works for him, and he talked me into going into a little sideline business with him."

Blancanales shrugged. "As you know, the only

way a man can make any real money in this country is to go into business for himself.''

''And what business are you in, Mr. Rivera?'' the Chinese asked.

''Well,'' Blancanales said, ''I'm what you call a packager. I contract to the big boys to provide them components at a fixed price. They don't care where I get the products as long as I meet my contract dates. And, as a sideline to that, you might say that I buy and sell whatever I can. Among the things I sell are information and components I happen to come across while fulfilling my contracts. Some of my customers are in interesting lines of work. I understand that your company has an interest in a couple of these areas.''

''And those are?''

''Satellite communications and guidance systems.''

When the Chinese didn't comment, Blancanales continued. ''One thing I happen to have on hand at the moment are zero-grav microswitches, several thousand of them. They were an overrun on a contract for the satellite division of Lowell Technologies, and I managed to pick them up at a good price. These aren't rejects, understand, just overruns because Lowell had to scale back on their work in that area. If you read the papers, you'll remember that they had some problems a while back.''

If having the federal government down on you with everything but the National Guard could be called a problem, Lowell had it. Several of their top management people had taken a major fall, and several others had taken early retirement. Their satellite business had collapsed overnight, and the company had been broken up.

"I remember," the Chinese said.

As well he should, Blancanales thought. One of the reasons Lowell Technologies had taken such a big hit was that they had gotten too close to the Chinese military. Though it hadn't been completely proved, it was believed that they had illegally exported major classified technologies and components to them. In fact, the Chinese missile-launch platforms might well have been carrying illegally exported Lowell components in their bellies.

"What were you asking for these microswitches," the Chinese asked.

"Well," Blancanales said, smiling, "I price my goods two different ways. One is with a dollar price and the other is, let's say, with a value in certain commodities."

"Which are?"

"I prefer China White, but I can deal in Colombian cocaine, as well."

The Chinese stared at him for a long moment. "I think we can work something out."

"Good." Blancanales looked over at Menendes for permission. "I happen to have a selection of my goods in my briefcase."

When the man nodded, Blancanales opened his case and brought out five antistatic packaged microswitches designed to operate under zero-gravity conditions. Modern multiband satellites couldn't operate without these delicate devices. And, as was the case with most space technology, the best were only made in the United States.

"There are the spec sheets for the switches," he said as he handed over a folder of papers, "and the quantities involved for each type of switch. The dollar price for each lot is indicated."

"And the commodity price?"

"That is negotiable."

"I see."

"I'll leave those samples with you," Blancanales said as he stood. Slowly reaching into his shirt pocket, he drew out a card and placed it on the table. "I'll be at this hotel for three days before I have to go back to Florida. I hope we can do business before I leave."

"I will contact you," the Chinese said.

Space

TWO HUNDRED FIFTY MILES above Earth, the crew of the space shuttle *Atlantis* was having a modest celebration. Considering that they had just fought, and won, the first battle among the stars, it wasn't much, just standard-issue space-shuttle ration packs. Nonetheless, a man could work up a bit of an appetite killing orbiting missile platforms.

The galley was on the middeck and, like everything else about living in space, cooking a meal in zero gravity was an adventure. Since this was a special occasion, Cunningham sent Bradley down to do the honors and told him to raid the pantry. The shuttle carried enough food for ten days, and since they were heading straight back to Earth, they could eat the good stuff like the shrimp cocktail and beef-steak and pass on the casseroles and mashed potatoes.

After eating, the crew got ready for the return to Vandenberg. Schwarz at the aft crew station was using the manipulator-arm controls to return the laser to its stowed position in the cargo bay when the shuttle was rocked by a blow.

It knocked him and Carl Lyons loose from their footholds and sent them crashing into the bulkhead. With no gravity to hold them down, they rebounded and hit the other side of the cabin before they could grab on to something.

"We've taken a hit," Cunningham called back from the cockpit.

"What hit us?" Lyons asked.

"There's no way to tell," the pilot said. "It could have been a meteorite, and we took it in the cargo bay."

Cunningham hurried back, and, using the aft crew station video-monitor controls, started to scan the cargo bay for damage. When he found what he was looking for, he went to the window into the bay and double-checked. Whatever it was had torn through the starboard cargo-bay door forward pivot hinge and the forward lock.

The two massive cargo-bay doors weren't

mounted on the shuttle only to open the cargo section to space. They served a dual function. The inner surfaces of the doors were radiators that passed the excess heat from the spacecraft's operation to the cold of deep space so as to maintain a uniform temperature inside. This heat-transfer function was so critical that once a shuttle was in orbit, if the doors couldn't be opened, the mission had to be aborted and the shuttle returned to Earth within eight hours.

By the same token, the massive doors had to be closed tightly and locked down before reentry. If they weren't, when the shuttle hit the atmosphere on reentry at seventeen thousand miles per hour, the airflow would be disturbed and the craft would break up.

"What's the problem?" Schwarz asked when Cunningham turned away from the window.

"Well, Gunner," Cunningham said calmly, "as the old story goes, I have both good news and bad."

"What's the bad news?" Lyons asked.

"I hope you boys have your wills made out, because we're not going home. We can't shut the cargo-bay doors, and we can't make reentry with them open. If we try, we'll go out of control and burn up."

"What's the good news?"

"We get to choose the way we want to die, and not too many people get to do that. We can try reentry anyway and burn up. Or we can stay up here until the oxygen runs out and we go to sleep.''

''Is there any chance of NASA launching a rescue in time?'' Lyons asked.

''None,'' the pilot said with finality. ''The next shuttle launch isn't scheduled for a month and a half, so the *Discovery*'s still in the shop for refitting. Even if they doubled the work crew and went to twenty-four-hour shifts, they still wouldn't be able to reach us in time.''

Cunningham shrugged. ''They'll be able to take our bodies home, though, so I guess that's a plus.''

''I always wanted a fancy funeral,'' Schwarz said.

''You'll get one,'' Cunningham promised. ''We all will. The black horses, the Army's Old Guard and the honor guards all looking good for CNN as they march down Pennsylvania Avenue. Then they'll plant us in Arlington National Cemetery next to JFK.''

''That's great.'' Schwarz smiled. ''It's too bad I won't be able to see it.''

Cunningham started back to the cockpit. ''I need to let Houston know what's happening so they can start planning that funeral.''

Cunningham put his radio call to Mission Control on the intercom so everyone could listen in. This was no time to be keeping secrets. ''Houston, this is *Atlantis.* We have a problem. Let me talk to Kruger.''

The NASA director was on the radio in a flash. ''*Atlantis,* this is Kruger, go.''

"We've taken a hit up here, Bill, probably a meteorite the size of a .50-caliber shell. It tore up the starboard cargo-bay door, and we're not going to be able to close it."

There was a long pause while that information was absorbed. Space debris had always been a primary concern of NASA. They went to great lengths to plot shuttle flight paths through relatively clear space, but there was more than man-made junk flying through space. Most of the material was classified as space dust, and Earth soaked up tons of it every year. But along with the dust, there was tons more space junk and not all of it was big enough to see coming. At tens of thousands of miles per hour, even something the size of a BB could do enormous damage.

"Can you make an EVA to check the damage?"

"We don't have to make an EVA," Cunningham said. "I can see the damage from the aft crew station. There's no way those doors are going to close."

"Are you sure, Greg?" the director asked, hoping against hope.

The astronaut sighed. "I'm sorry, Houston. The entire forward pivot hinge on the starboard side is mangled, and the forward lock took a hit. Even if we can get them closed, there's no way to lock them down. They'll break loose on reentry and that'll be the end of it."

There was a long silence before Kruger said, "Fuck me dead."

"That, too," Cunningham replied.

CHAPTER NINETEEN

Stony Man Farm, Virginia

The minute the Farm monitored the call from the *Atlantis,* Hal Brognola was on the phone to NASA Director Bill Kruger in the Houston Mission Control Center. "What the hell happened?" he snapped. "I thought this sort of thing ended with the *Apollo 13* screwup."

"So did I." Kruger sounded bone weary. "We haven't had an emergency in space since then. The *Challenger* explosion was different because it happened so soon after it lifted off the pad."

"What hit them out there?"

"Right now, we simply don't know," Kruger admitted. "We always hook up with NORAD Sky Watch as part of our regular launch planning to track the latest orbiting space junk so we can avoid running into it. But they can only track the man-made stuff. Space is full of bits and pieces from all over the universe, and lots of it doesn't show up on radar very well because it's rocky, not metallic."

"Is there any doubt about the damage assessment?"

"None," Kruger said bluntly. "With that cargo-bay door damaged, they can't come down. And if they stay up there, they can last maybe a week and a half on the internal air supply and eight more hours in the suits. No matter what we do, we can't get a shuttle up there to rescue them for at least two and a half weeks."

Brognola didn't even need to do the math there. He knew the answer already.

"That's why I fought so hard to keep the Venture Star program on track," Kruger explained. "It has a three-day turnaround and doesn't have to be put together like a kid's model kit before it can be launched again. I know for a fact that we don't have a set of solid-fuel boosters on hand, and it takes almost two weeks to pour the propellant mix in the casings, cure it and inspect it. Then, of course, they have to be transported here and mated up to the airframe. Even if I had a shuttle and the main fuel tank in the assembly building ready to go right now, we'd still have to wait for the damned boosters."

He paused. "I'm sorry, Hal, but that's the way it is."

Brognola wasn't a space fan, but he had seen enough TV coverage of the shuttle launches to know that the director was stating the facts of the case. That he didn't like those facts made no difference.

"Keep me posted," Brognola said.

"I have everyone working on this, checking our figures, and we'll get back to you if we find that anything's changed."

BROGNOLA WASN'T the only one who was looking for a way to bring the *Atlantis*'s crew back to Earth. Yakov Katzenelenbogen wasn't going to give up until they were dead. He walked over to Aaron Kurtzman's workstation and looked over his shoulder. "Show me the *Atlantis*'s orbital map."

He was a land-warfare tactical specialist, but a situation in space didn't have to be insurmountable just because it was taking place so far away. Certain principles of problem solving still applied. He had a team cut off, and he needed to get help to them as soon as possible.

Kurtzman flashed it up on the big screen.

"Now, can you put the Venture Star flight path on top of that?"

When that came up, he saw that their flight paths intersected twice on each orbit. The two spacecraft were at seriously different altitudes, but that could be taken care of one way or the other.

"What do you think about having Grimaldi try to rendezvous with them and make the rescue?"

"Damn," Kurtzman said softly. "Why didn't I think about that?"

His fingers clicked up a new view of the orbital paths showing the difference in altitude. "You know, this just might work."

"No." Brognola had come up behind them and

was looking over their shoulders. "It's too risky. If there was a real astronaut piloting that damned thing, I'd say go for it. But it's all that Jack's going to be able to do just to bring it back to Palmdale in one piece as it is. I can tell you, the President will never go for it."

"Screw him," Katz said. "I'm talking about the only chance Carl and Gadgets have to survive, and that's to say nothing of those three other astronauts. Let's talk to the NASA people and see if they can come up with a simple flight plan that will give Jack a chance to come up alongside the *Atlantis.*"

"But then what?"

"Then the astronauts can suit up and bring our people over to the Venture Star for a ride home."

"Are there enough space suits for our guys?"

"I don't know," Katz admitted. "But NASA can sure as hell tell us real quick. Let me talk to Kruger and see if we can put something together."

Brognola didn't waste any time thinking. If this didn't work, the President might have his head. But he couldn't save his job at the cost of losing Lyons' and Schwarz's lives. "Do it," he said.

Katz was on the phone in a flash. "Director," he said as soon as Kruger came on the line, "my name is Yakov Katzenelenbogen, and I work for Hal Brognola. Call me Katz. I have a couple of questions for you."

Mission Control

BILL KRUGER FELT as if a giant weight had been lifted from his chest. Whoever this Katz guy really was, he had come up with a plan that at least had to be tried. He knew that it would be tricky with a rookie pilot at the controls of the Venture Star. But that spacecraft had state-of-the-art computers that could practically fly the thing by themselves. All the rookie pilot would have to do was set up the program properly, send the readouts to Mission Control and do what he was told.

He glanced over at the orbit plot and realized that he had to make a move in less than fifteen minutes to prevent the Venture Star from breaking orbit and landing as programmed. That, though, was the easy part.

"VENTURE STAR, this is Houston. Bill Kruger speaking. I need to talk to the pilot."

"You've got him, Houston."

"Look, there's been a development with the *Atlantis* mission, and we need you to remain in orbit a little longer. We're going to uplink a new program for your nav computer and wanted to warn you first."

"What happened?"

"*Atlantis* took a hit and can't make reentry without burning up. Everyone's okay so far, but we don't have anything on-line to send up to get them. We're going to try to get you into position to rendezvous with them and take the crew on board."

"Oh, Jesus," Grimaldi said softly. "Are you

sure I'm up to that, Houston? I'm really not Buck Rogers or Luke Skywalker. I just found the space suit at a garage sale."

"That's okay." Kruger chuckled. "This plan came from some guy named Katz, and he told me to tell you that he thinks you can do it."

Grimaldi laughed. "Man, that makes me feel a lot better to know that Katz has confidence in me. If he had his ass up here with me, I might take that a lot more seriously. But," he hurried to add, "I'm game. Just tell me what to do."

"I'm turning you over to FIDO and he'll talk you through the changes to your flight plan."

"A dog?"

Kruger laughed. "No, the Flight Dynamics Officer. He and GDO will walk you through this."

"Great, a pooch and an Italian guy are going to save the day."

"Actually," Kruger said, laughing, "GDO *is* Italian. We call him Guido the GDO."

"Let's get on with it before I laugh so hard I fall out of my damned chair."

"Venture Star, this is Guido the GDO. The first thing I need you to do is to set your nav computer to accept a program upload. I'm sending you a program that'll make it easier for you to go through this maneuver."

"Roger. At least I know where that computer is."

"First, I want you to..."

THE PLAN TO HAVE the Venture Star rescue the stranded astronauts lightened the mood in the Computer Room. It was a dangerous plan, but it was a plan and, no matter how risky, trying it was better than waiting for the men to die.

"I hate to pour cold water on this party," Hunt Wethers announced, "but I've been working with the NASA data on the environmental systems of the Venture Star. I need to confirm my calculations with Houston, of course, but it looks that even if the linkup goes okay, we may still have a problem before we can get them back down."

"What kind of problem?" Brognola asked.

"Well, it's the same problem the crew of the *Apollo 13* ran into on their mission—oxygen, or a lack thereof. The Venture Star is designed to supply three people for a certain number of hours, and we already have seven men on board. Had they made the landing as was first scheduled, the problem wouldn't have come up. There would have been enough air for all of them. Now, though, the flight has been extended to dump that Chinese launch platform and we're talking about extending it again to several more orbits, then bringing five more people on board. My calculations show that there might not be enough oxygen for them to survive the reentry."

Brognola wasn't in any mood to hear talk like that right now. He had his ass hung out on this plan, and it had to work as advertised or they'd all be lucky to be sent to the Sahara Desert to inventory sand dunes. And that was to say nothing of the men who would die in space. In one blow, Stony Man would simply cease to exist.

"Find a way to make it work, Hunt," he ordered. "I'm not about to go through all of this just to have everyone die in space. That is simply not going to happen. As I think someone said during that *Apollo 13* mess—'failure is not an option.'"

Wethers wasn't a chemist who could tell the Stony Man warriors how to make oxygen in their kitchen sink, but he did know how to talk to the people who were.

"I'll get on it," he replied.

"And do it quickly before I have to report this to the President," Brognola snapped. "I'm expecting this to work, because sooner or later, I'm going to have to talk to him about what we're doing."

"We all want it to work, Hal." Katz stepped between the two men. "And we do need to check this out completely. But even if Hunt is right, I strongly feel that we need to keep this between us and NASA for the time being. We spend too much time talking to the President when there's not a damned thing he can do to change any of this. We have the best people NASA has working on it and if they can't solve the problem, no one on Capitol Hill can. We'll tell the guys, of course, but that's it. If it does go bad on them, they don't need to have to listen to the President blather on about how sorry he is that they're all going to die in space."

"I agree with Katz," Barbara Price said. "Cut

him out of the loop completely until this is a done deal no matter which way it goes down.''

Brognola was a battle-hardened survivor of the bureaucratic cover-your-ass game, but he knew that Katz and Price were making the right call this time. If the rescue worked, no damage was done. If it failed, at least the men would have died without having to listen to a politician second-guessing their efforts.

''Okay,'' he said. ''We'll keep this tight and I'll tell Kruger to do the same.''

Space

''I JUST GOT A CALL from Mission Control,'' Cunningham told the two Able Team astronauts. ''They want us to hang on for a couple more orbits while they try to work something out.''

''I thought that this was a done deal,'' Lyons said bluntly. ''We got shot up and we can't go home.''

''It is,'' the pilot confirmed. ''But I think it might be a good idea to follow their advice on this.''

''I thought you guys always followed Mission Control's orders?''

''Normally, yes,'' Cunningham replied. ''But we have what we like to call the last-wishes protocol on these missions. In other words, if we're going to die up here, they give us the chance to do it our way.''

''That's nice of them,'' Schwarz said.

"Considering the situation," Cunningham stated, "it's the least they can do."

"As far as I'm concerned," Lyons growled, "the least they can do is get a goddamned tow truck up here."

"Unfortunately, the tow truck's called the space shuttle *Endeavor,* and she's in the shop right now waiting a pair of engines. They can't get her launched for at least two weeks, probably three."

"That figures."

"There's one thing I have to know," Cunningham said, changing the subject. "That Rivera guy isn't a real Air Force general, is he?"

Schwarz grinned. "About as much as we're real astronauts. He's one of us, and we're civilians."

Cunningham frowned. "Who the hell are you guys, then? I thought you two were government scientists."

Schwarz looked over to Lyons. "Should I tell them, Ironman?"

"Why not?" Lyons shrugged. "They have a right to know who they're dying with."

"Well," Schwarz started out, "we call ourselves Able Team, and we do work for the government, sort of. We take care of things for the President."

"What kind of things?"

"Things that he doesn't want anyone to know about."

"Wet work?" the pilot asked.

"Sometimes."

"I thought the CIA or the Special Ops Command took care of things like that."

"Well, the problem with those agencies is that Congress and the media know about them, and they can be checked up on fairly easily. Since me and my partners don't exist on paper, we don't ever have to answer questions from anyone but the President."

Cunningham shook his head. "I thought that kind of thing only happened in TV shows and technothriller novels."

"Nope." Schwarz grinned. "We're the real deal, and that's why we're up here. We could do the job on those targets, and the Man knows that no one would ever learn about it from us. You guys can't talk because you're wearing the blue suit and we don't exist, so he's covered."

"Pretty sneaky."

"Isn't it."

"Do you guys get hazardous-duty pay?"

Lyons looked Cunningham right in the eyes. "Colonel, everything we do is hazardous."

CHAPTER TWENTY

Stony Man Farm, Virginia

Aaron Kurtzman was monitoring the radio chatter as Mission Control walked Jack Grimaldi through the course-correction rocket burns he had to make to bring the Venture Star to a higher orbit to rendezvous with *Atlantis.* In hopes of repairing the shuttle at a later date and bringing it back to Earth, the rescue would be attempted in a relatively low orbit. Once Grimaldi had the Venture Star on station, Colonel Cunningham would bring his crippled craft down to a 180-mile orbit and meet up with it.

In terms of space flight, it was a relatively simple maneuver and, so far, Grimaldi had been performing like a real pro. But, the fickle finger of fate was no respecter of professionalism. Every time he fired up the machine's engines, there was a chance of something going wrong. Grimaldi had proved to be one of Lady Luck's favorite sons and hopefully she wouldn't abandon him now.

With David McCarter doing the copilot chores in the Venture Star's right-hand seat, Grimaldi counted down to the initial burn that would break them out of their trajectory and send the ship up to a higher orbit. The Stony Man team was strapped down again so the acceleration wouldn't throw them around the cabin. The three strapped down to the floor, Manning, James and Hawkins, had added a little padding to try to protect them from the deck plates. But it was going to be a rough ride.

"Three...two...one...ignition!"

ONCE THE VENTURE STAR was safely parked in her rendezvous orbit, Bill Kruger got back to Hal Brognola to bring him up to date on the rescue plan. There were a couple of things he had purposefully delayed mentioning until it looked as if the plan was a definite go. For one, since there were five men on the *Atlantis* and only three space suits, the transfer was going to have to be made using an emergency system called rescue balls.

"These things have never been used before, right?" Brognola asked after Kruger described them to him.

"We've tested them in vacuum chambers on the ground, and they worked well. They're claustrophobic as hell, but they work. But I have to admit that we've never had to use them in space yet."

"How long does the air in them last?"

"The POS—Personal Oxygen System—the man wears inside the ball has two hours' worth. But we can put an extra lithium hydroxide CO_2 scrubber canister in with them, which should stretch it to another thirty minutes.''

''And how long will it take the Venture Star to come down after the transfer has been made?''

''That's the rub,'' Kruger admitted. ''We're still looking at a little over three hours.''

''So that puts Schwarz and Lyons running out of air a half an hour before landing?''

''So far it does, yes.''

''What do you mean, 'so far'?''

''Well, the boys in environmental services and the Flight Control Center are working on a fix.''

''Tell them to work fast.''

''They are,'' Kruger said. ''Believe me, they are.''

Space

COLONEL GREG CUNNINGHAM floated back to Able Team's stations with a gleeful look on his face. ''Are either of you two guys claustrophobic?''

''Why?'' Carl Lyons asked.

''Well, someone came up with a plan to get us out of here in one piece.''

''I'll be damned,'' Schwarz said softly.

He'd been looking out the port at Earth, below him, trying to come to grips with the fact that he was never going to walk on dirt again. Dying in a gunfight was one thing, and he'd been prepared to accept that end for years. In fact, he expected that some day he'd screw up or the law of averages would catch up with him and he'd take a round some place critical.

While he could accept dying in a firefight, floating in space looking down on Earth and knowing that death was coming slowly as the air ran out or quickly in a fiery reentry was something else entirely. He'd been watching the astronauts go about their duties and wondering what was going through their minds. This was their turf, and death in space was one of the hazards that went with their job. Nonetheless, they seemed to be taking it pretty calmly.

"Okay," he said. "I'll bite. What's the plan?"

"Well, your partners got out of China with the Venture Star intact, and they're hanging in orbit below us right now. We're going to drop down low enough to make a rendezvous with them, pull up alongside and transfer over for the ride back home."

"Outstanding." Schwarz grinned.

"What's the catch?" Lyons asked. He'd been watching the colonel's face and knew that it wasn't as simple as he was making it out to be. It never was, and that went double for anything that took place in space.

"The problem is that there are only three space suits on board. In the hurry to get the laser mounted so we could launch, no one thought about emergencies."

"Can't the three of you go over first and then one of you come back with two empty suits?"

"If these were diving suits," Cunningham said, "we could. But we can't do that with the EVA suits, as we call them. Each one of them is tailored to fit one man and only that man. If you tried to wear it, you'd probably die because it wouldn't work properly."

"This is a 'good news, bad news' thing, right?" Schwarz said. "The good news is that a cab's coming to get us, but the bad news is that we're going to have to miss the ride because we're not dressed properly?"

"Not really," Cunningham replied. The nice thing about working with these guys, whoever they really were, was that they were pros. They could take the punches and come out swinging. "That's why I asked if either of you suffer from claustrophobia. We have a backup emergency-rescue system on board."

"I can see this one coming," Schwarz said. "You're going to stuff us in a can and seal the lid."

"Good guess, but it's not quite that bad."

Schwarz turned to his partner. "I like this 'not quite' part of it, Ironman, don't you? I feel like I'm listening to a goddamned politician tell me that raising my taxes is going to be good for me."

The copilot came up from the lower deck with a white bag in his hand that looked like a deflated giant beach ball with a zipper running halfway around it.

"That's a rescue ball," Cunningham said, "and you'll be transferred inside of it."

"That looks a little too much like a body bag for my tastes," Lyons stated, looking at the thirty-inch sphere.

"It's the bag that's going to keep your body from exploding in the vacuum of space," Cunningham said. "So I guess you can call it that."

"Have these ever been used?" Lyons asked.

"Only in vacuum-chamber tests," the pilot admitted. "But they worked well there."

"This is getting better and better," Schwarz said. "First we tested lasers in space, and now we're human guinea pigs for the space program. I always wanted to donate my body to science, but I expected to be dead first."

He reached out to feel the thick fabric. "There's no window in it."

"That's why I asked you guys about claustrophobia."

"And no night-light, right?"

Cunningham understood Schwarz's and Lyons' apprehensions about the rescue balls, but he was getting weary of playing the straight man for their jokes. "Look, guys, if I could give one of you my EVA suit, I'd do it and use the ball myself. But I can't. This is it."

"Let's get this thing on the road," Lyons growled. "We don't want to keep our man Jack waiting. He gets real impatient and might fly home without us."

"We have to wait for two hours while we make the rendezvous," Cunningham said. "And, during that time, we all have to go through a nitrogen purge.''

''Like a deep dive,'' Lyons said.

''Exactly. We can get the bends up here, too.''

''At least that's something I understand. I've been behind the power curve ever since we started this program, so it's nice to run into something I'm familiar with.''

''You guys are doing okay,'' Cunningham said. ''This hasn't been what you'd want to call an average mission. You've had a lot thrown at you all at once, and you've done well. Most of the people I work with, even the pilots, would be out of their fucking minds right about now.''

Schwarz looked at him. ''We are out of our minds,'' he said. ''We just don't like to share it.''

Cunningham grinned. ''That I understand.''

''VENTURE STAR, this is Houston, over.''

''This is Venture Star,'' Grimaldi answered. ''Go ahead.''

''The *Atlantis* has completed her deorbiting burn, and she should be on station in a little over an hour.''

''Is there anything we need to do till then?''

''Nothing,'' the controller said. ''We decided to let them meet you more than halfway. They'll be doing all of the necessary maneuvering, and all you need to do is stand by and wait for them to come on board.''

''I think we can do that,'' Grimaldi said. ''By

the way, where would we expect to find rations and water in this thing? Particularly water. We had to dump all our gear when we got on board.''

''We don't know what the Chinese might have put in, but at least the survival packs should still be there. They'll have water and emergency rations for three meals for four crewmen. That should hold you until you get back.''

While they were waiting for the *Atlantis,* Grimaldi and McCarter were making themselves as familiar with the controls and systems of the Venture Star as they could. The launch and insertion into their initial orbit had been mostly automatic, and the little nose-up maneuver they had done to get rid of the Chinese platform had been almost idiot proof. But the easy stuff was over. The reentry maneuvers and landing were going to need a pilot and copilot at the controls who knew what they were doing.

While Grimaldi and McCarter played with their spaceship, the rest of the team went into time out. After a quick meal of survival rations, some of them watched Earth, while others learned to sleep floating in zero gravity.

Hawkins was starting to feel real uncomfortable from the fragment in his back and asked Calvin James to take a look at it.

''You didn't tell me you'd been hit,'' James said. The ex-SEAL was Phoenix Force's medic, and he prided himself on keeping his teammates patched up.

"It wasn't bothering me much before this."

"Let me take a look."

Since getting out of his jacket in zero gravity was more than either of them was up to, James simply cut open the shoulder of the jacket. "It's not too bad," he said. "But I can't get the frag out."

"No sweat. Just slap a pad on it to cushion it a little."

CHAPTER TWENTY-ONE

Space

The *Atlantis*'s orbital-maneuvering burn took almost two hours to complete. First Colonel Greg Cunningham had to bring his ship down to the Venture Star's lower altitude, then he had to change both speed and direction to match the smaller craft. When it was over, both vehicles were flying in formation a hundred yards apart with their open cargo-bay doors facing each other.

"Okay, gentlemen," Cunningham announced as he got out of his seat and floated back to Gadgets Schwarz and Carl Lyons. "It's time for us to get into our respective traveling clothes for the trip home."

As the first part of the operation, the copilot and flight engineer both got into their EVA suits, and Boomer Boyd cycled out through the air lock into the cargo bay.

Like the astronauts who would make the space walk in their EVA suits, the Able Team partners had been breathing pure oxygen from walk-around packs for the past two hours to purge the nitrogen from their bloodstreams. They were both wearing thermal undersuits to keep them warm for their trip through the cold of space, as well as a close-fitting communications helmet nicknamed a Snoopy Helmet because it looked like something out of the Red Baron's days.

"Okay," Cunningham told Schwarz and Lyons. "It's your turn."

"Let's do it," Schwarz said as he unbuckled himself.

He went into the bag first, assuming a weightless seated position in midair so Cunningham and Bradley could open the fabric ball and pull it over him like a body bag. After making sure that his oxygen mask was working, they zipped the bag closed and sealed the seam.

"Gadgets, this is Cunningham. How do you hear me?"

Schwarz clicked on the throat mike on his Snoopy Helmet. "I hear you loud and clear. How about me?"

"You're loud and clear," the pilot replied. "I'm taking you off the ship's oxygen supply now so I can move you into the air lock. Boomer's waiting to take you out the other side and tie you down to the MMU—the manned maneuvering unit—for the transfer."

"Let's do it."

Cunningham grabbed the ball and shoved it into the inside of the air lock and closed the door behind him. Schwarz could feel the air pressure change in the ball as the air lock purged. Suddenly, the fabric strained from the internal air pressure and became as taut as an overinflated basketball.

Shortly after that, he heard the outer door open and felt himself being pulled out into the cargo bay and jostled around. But, with no window, he could only guess at what was happening outside.

"You're strapped down to the MMU now," the flight engineer said. "It'll take a few minutes for Flash to hook you up to it, so hang tight."

"I'm not going anywhere."

A few minutes later, he was moved around again as Bradley hooked up his EVA suit to the MMU. "Are you ready to go?" the copilot asked Schwarz.

"Let's do it."

He felt a tiny push as the MMU's thrusters fired for a few seconds then weightlessness returned. "Is that all?" he asked.

"It doesn't take much," the astronaut answered. "There will be a couple more short burns when we arrive."

"If that's all there is, I'm taking a nap. Wake me up when we get there."

THE STONY MAN WARRIORS were taking turns at the portholes of the Venture Star watching the transfer. The *Atlantis* hung motionless less than a hundred yards above their ship, and it took a conscious effort for them to keep from expecting it to fall on them.

"Here they come!" Gary Manning called out when he saw the *Atlantis* astronaut come out of the shadow.

The astronaut was wearing the manned maneuvering unit that made short flights possible in the vacuum of space. It looked like a combination of a huge white backpack and a lawn chair. Small rocket thrusters controlled by hand grips provided the force to propel them. Strapped on the back of the MMU was the white rescue ball with Schwarz inside.

As they approached the Venture Star, the astronaut fired a retro burst to check his movement. That brought him to a stand-still almost exactly over the Venture Star's open cargo-bay doors. Another burst from the MMU thrusters slowly pushed him down into the open bay.

Grimaldi had the aft monitor switched on to show the interior of the cargo bay. With the doors open, the sun lit it up almost too brightly to look at with the naked eye. The astronaut had his face-shield glare filter down, and the video camera automatically compensated for changing light levels.

After docking the MMU so it wouldn't float away, the astronaut disengaged himself from it, went around to the back and released the rescue ball. Using the bay's built-in cargo tethers, he secured the ball against the rear bulkhead and returned to the MMU.

"Gadgets," Bolan radioed, "can you hear me?"

"I got you loud and clear, Striker."

"Welcome aboard. We can see them going back over for the Ironman right now."

"When do we get the hell out of here?"

"Jack's waiting for Houston to give us the final program. Then, as soon as you're all on board, we're out of here."

"Tell Jack to get his finger out," Schwarz growled. "It's dark in this damned thing."

Bolan laughed. "I guess the dome light isn't working."

"Neither is the heater," Schwarz said. "I should have worn my own long johns. The ones they loaned me don't work for shit."

"Mission Control says that as soon as we can close the cargo-bay doors, it should warm up. They've told Jack how to transfer heat back to you."

"I hope so," Schwarz said. "The wall I'm tied up to is sucking the heat right out of me. It's giving a whole new meaning to freezing your ass off."

Bolan laughed. "Just hang on, Gadgets. We'll get you out of here."

"I'm not going anywhere."

AFTER LYONS WAS transferred over, Flash Bradley went back to the *Atlantis* for Boomer Boyd, then made a last flight to pick up Greg Cunningham. As the command pilot of the ill-fated mission, he had elected to be the last man to leave the shuttle. He had shut down all unnecessary systems, leaving just enough of them running to keep the ship from freezing solid. Hopefully, if all went well, he would be able to come back in a few weeks and salvage his command.

First, though, they had to get home.

"We're all strapped down back here," Cunningham called up to Grimaldi. "You can close the doors now and tell Houston to get you set up for reentry."

"Roger."

Stony Man Farm, Virginia

HAL BROGNOLA HAD BEEN following the transfer closely and had been in communication with Houston every minute. After everything that had happened, it all came down to this last, desperate gamble.

"There's been another change," he told Aaron Kurtzman. "Kruger's boys have decided to bring the Venture Star down at Area 51 rather than have Jack try to land her back at the Skunk Works. For one thing, Groom Lake has a much longer runway and there's less chance of collateral damage if something goes wrong."

Barbara Price knew that was NASA-speak for what would happen if Grimaldi crashed. Area 51 was in exactly the middle of nowhere, and no civilians would die if the Venture Star made a big hole in the ground.

"Also," Brognola continued, "we have a real security problem here that still has to be dealt with, and Area 51 is better equipped to handle it. The President isn't exactly sure yet how he wants to deal with the return of the spacecraft. Since the crew isn't coming home with it, if he announces that we have it back, a lot of awkward questions will be asked. And no matter how they're answered, the space program is going to look bad."

Price could hardly believe what she was hearing. "You mean that he's going to continue this charade about it blowing up in space?"

"Think about it," Brognola replied. "What other real choice does he have? We've gone through a national funeral for three hero astronauts. We have congressional hearings on the future of space flight going on right now. We've got engineers on the hot seat, and NASA has already suspended the APU manufacturer because of the phony radio call about the fire in the Venture Star. People are losing their jobs and reputations over this, but the deception has to continue."

"Why, Hal?"

Brognola took a deep breath. "Because it will be much worse if it doesn't."

"I want to hear this one."

"There are a number of reasons," he said. "For one, we're at war with China right now every bit as much as we ever were with the old Soviet Union during the cold war. People forget that over the past fifty years, we've lost more lives to Chinese gunfire than we ever did to the Russians. Just because they have McDonald's in Beijing now doesn't mean that they're any less our most deadly enemy."

She had to acknowledge the truth of that. The reality of the Chinese regime was too often forgotten in the rush to try to make them out to be a kinder and gentler dictatorship. Regardless of their welcoming Western business now, they were unlikely to change.

"Secondly," Brognola continued, "if the world learns that we can't even guard our space shuttles, we'll be opening ourselves up to copycat attempts and not just hijackings, either. We'll be seeing suicide-bomb attempts, car bombs and everything else in the terrorist handbook launched against our space facilities. I think the only reason that the shuttle program has gone as smoothly as it has is that NASA has been seen as being completely bulletproof.

"Also, don't forget the American pastime of shooting ourselves in the foot. The blame fixing for the Venture Star fiasco is bad now, but it would be a hundred times worse if the facts were known about what really happened. And, of course, that's to say nothing of having to explain how we managed to get the Venture Star back. Or why the *Atlantis*'s crew needed rescuing."

"What about the missing astronauts?"

"You mean those national heroes who were posthumously awarded the Congressional Medal of Freedom and who were symbolically interred in Arlington National Cemetery? Those astronauts?

They're dead and they'll remain dead. If, for any reason, they should appear undead, that condition won't continue very long."

He softened his voice. "Barbara, we have no choice. We really don't."

"I still don't have to like it."

Space

"VENTURE STAR, Houston." The voice in Jack Grimaldi's earphones was different than the one he had been listening to for most of the mission. "We have decided to divert your landing to Area 51. Over."

"Copy, Houston," Grimaldi replied. "Are you guys trying to start another UFO scare?"

"Negative, Venture Star." The controller chuckled. "We just wanted to get you guys a longer runway to come down on, and they have the longest in the world. Not that we doubt your ability to land that thing, but you know how it is."

"That's affirmative, Houston," Grimaldi replied. "We're overweight, and I might need all the pavement under me I can get. This thing doesn't have the biggest wings in the world."

"First, though, we're going to talk you through a deorbiting burn to start you on your way. There's nothing to it, but you have to do a 180 so you're flying rear end first before we do the burn."

"I've flown that way before," Grimaldi said, "and I wasn't even in a spaceship."

The controller chuckled. "You realize, of course,

that we're recording all of this com-link chatter, and you're likely to hear it as part of a stand-up act some day. Comics in space."

"Remind me to give you my agent's phone number. He does all my bookings."

By now, Grimaldi had a deft touch with the reaction-control thrusters, and he got the Venture Star turned properly on the first try.

"You're right in the groove," Houston said. "Get ready to do a two-and-a-half-minute deorbiting burn on my mark."

"I'm ready."

"Three...two...one, fire!"

Again the passengers and crew felt the acceleration give them a sense of weight, but it didn't last long. As soon as the engines shut down, they were weightless again.

"Is that it?" Grimaldi asked.

"Roger, Venture Star," Houston confirmed. "That's it. You lost only a little over two hundred miles per hour speed, but it broke you out of orbit, and you're coming down now whether you want to or not."

"How long will it take?"

"About half an hour. First, though, we need to get you pointed in the right direction again, so you'll need to do another end over end."

"No sweat."

As soon as Grimaldi repositioned his craft, Houston came back on the air. "As you come down, you will enter a communications blackout lasting about twelve minutes, starting at about 310,000 feet. Don't panic if you don't hear from me during that time. You'll come out of it at 180,000 feet and that's when you'll start actually flying that thing. I'll get back to you then and start talking you down."

Grimaldi was flying "hands off" for this part of the descent. The onboard computer was handling the angle of reentry, but he was keeping a close eye on the eight ball anyway. No pilot liked to trust his craft to a machine, least of all a machine he wasn't all that comfortable with.

Mission Control Houston didn't have to tell Grimaldi when the Venture Star hit the outer edges of the atmosphere. The vibration started as a faint shudder, but it quickly built to bone-rattling strength.

"Hang on, guys," he called over the intercom. "We're in it, and we're going down."

Stony Man Farm, Virginia

THE COMPUTER ROOM WAS packed for the finale of what had become much more than anyone had ever intended. What they knew that Grimaldi and the men in the Venture Star didn't was that the only way NASA had been able to work out to save oxygen was to bring them down faster than usual. The hope was that they could shave off half an hour, twenty-eight minutes to be exact, and save the men in the rescue balls.

It was risky, but then the entire mission had been a risk that no sane man would have ever taken. But, so far, the gods of luck and war had been with them and hopefully would guide them the rest of the way down.

CHAPTER TWENTY-TWO

Space

In the Venture Star's cargo bay, Gadgets Schwarz and Carl Lyons felt the building deceleration as their rescue balls lurched against the restraints. It was like being inside of a basketball at full dribble at an NBA playoff game. No one had designed the balls to withstand this kind of punishment, and there was no way for him to hang on inside.

The three *Atlantis* astronauts in the bay weren't faring that much better in their space suits. The EVA suits also hadn't been designed to be worn under these circumstances. In fact, for them to operate as they had been designed, they had to be worn in zero-gravity conditions. With the deceleration forces slamming them around, too, the suits' joints were bruising the astronauts.

AS THE VENTURE STAR fell into thicker air, the faint whine turned into a continuous, thundering roar. The spacecraft shuddered as it was rocked by air turned as thick as concrete by their Mach 17 speed. The small porthole in front of Grimaldi looked like a window into a blast furnace. The heat of their reentry was turning the air into superheated plasma hotter than the exhaust of a rocket engine.

Although he couldn't see it, Grimaldi knew that the ship's nose and leading edges were glowing white hot with their hypersonic passage. Most of the heat was being soaked up by the heat-shield tiles. But even with the air conditioner turned up full, the temperature in the cabin soared. Since none of the ship's impromptu crew or passengers were wearing the usual air-conditioned flight suits, the heat was quickly becoming uncomfortable.

As quickly as it had appeared, the blast-furnace plume of superheated air disappeared from Grimaldi's window. Now he saw the blue sky of Earth in front of him. They were back in the atmosphere and had slowed enough that they wouldn't burn up.

"Damn," Hawkins said, wiping at the sweat pouring into his eyes. "Now I know how a slab of ribs feels on a barbecue. I was just about ready to put a fork in me."

"You guys okay back there?" Grimaldi called back to the men in the cargo hold.

"We're okay in the suits," Cunningham replied, "and we're checking on your guys in the rescue balls right now."

"Get back to me as soon as you can."

"Roger."

"Venture Star, this is Houston. Come in, please."

"This is Venture Star. Go ahead."

"Venture Star, you're looking pretty good. How is everyone on board?"

"The suits in the back are checking on the two guys in the body bags. I'll let you know as soon as I find out their status."

"Houston, roger," the controller answered. "We need to get you set up to start making the scheduled deceleration maneuvers."

Grimaldi was back on the radio instantly. "I need to find out about the guys in the cargo bay before I start throwing this thing around in the sky too much. Over."

"Understand." The controller kept calm. "But be advised that you don't have much time to start the deceleration maneuvers. You're still coming in at Mach 15, and if you don't lose most of that speed before you get too much lower, you're going to make a real big hole in the ground."

"Roger, copy."

"Jack," Cunningham called from the cargo bay, "Schwarz's ball broke loose, and he got battered around a bit. We have him tied back down, and you're go for deceleration maneuvering."

"Is he hurt?"

"I don't know," Cunningham said bluntly. "He's alive, but his com link's out, and I can't unzip the bag to check him out. We need to be on the ground to do that."

"Houston, Venture Star. We need to put this

thing down as quickly as we can. One of the guys in back is hurt.''

''Houston, roger.''

This was where Grimaldi was going to get to do some old-fashioned stick-and-rudder work. The deceleration maneuvers were a series of S turns called roll reversals designed to bleed off more of the ship's speed by turning the flat bottom of the ship against the airflow.

''Give me your indicated airspeed,'' Houston requested.

Grimaldi glanced at the instrument readout and saw a staggering number—8323 miles per hour. There was a long pause after he read the numbers to MCC.

''That's a little too hot,'' Mission Control replied. ''To help bring that down, I want you to deploy your speed brake to one hundred percent now.''

Grimaldi hit the switch and watched the readout as it deployed. Instantly, the ship started to shudder as the vanes bit into the air like dams. ''Speed brake deployed. Airspeed dropping.''

''Roger, that matches our telemetry. You are go for the first roll reversal. Turn on my command—three...two...one...execute!''

On command, Grimaldi banked the Venture Star to the right, watching the eight ball to make sure that he didn't overcontrol. The maneuver put the ship's belly forward against the flow of air like a speeding jet ski turning sideways. The buffeting grew even harder as the air slammed against the flat surface. Even though the ship's controls were all fly-by-wire, the control stick shuddered in his hand. At the count, he banked back, rolling in the other direction before leveling out again.

"You're looking good so far," Houston said. "Take a heading of one-six-zero and prepare for the second roll reversal."

"Roger one-six-zero," Grimaldi replied as he fed in a bit of rudder to correct his course.

"Three...two...one...execute!"

This time, the pilot put the spacecraft into a left-banking turn. Again, only the Venture Star's high speed kept it from falling out of the sky as it skidded sideways, reducing speed. At the end of the count, he reversed direction and leveled off again.

"What's your airspeed now?" Mission Control asked.

"Much better," Grimaldi sent back. "We're down to only Mach 3.3."

"That's in the groove. One more S turn and you'll be set up for your final approach."

"Roger."

"Three...two...one...execute!"

WITH HIS RADIO knocked out, Schwarz had only the vaguest idea of what Grimaldi was doing. For whatever reason, it felt as if the pilot were throwing the ship around in the sky from side to side in wide sweeping turns. Considering that they were being talked down by Mission Control, there had to be a reason for it, but Schwarz didn't have a clue. All he knew was that it was slamming the hell out of him.

The other thing he did know was that it was getting damned hard to breathe. He was already on his standby CO_2 scrubber, but it didn't seem to be helping much. He forced himself to remain calm and breathe slowly. But the lack of oxygen had him panting as his body cried out for fresh air.

To make things even worse, it was hot in the cargo bay, too hot for comfort. It was like being in a very small sauna minus the steam and with the heat turned all the way up. He wasn't sure what was going to get him first, the heat or the lack of oxygen. The next time he flew in one of these things, he was going to insist on sitting up front with the first-class passengers. These cheap seats in economy class just weren't cutting it.

AS GRIMALDI CAME OUT of the last deceleration maneuver, he made the final turn that would bring him on course for the runway at Area 51. Once he was inbound, he heard a new voice in his earphones. "Venture Star, this is Chase One. I'm off your starboard wing and you're looking good. Chase Two is above you, and we'll make sure that you don't get in trouble on final approach."

"Roger, Chase One," Grimaldi replied. "Be advised that I need all the help I can get."

Chase One chuckled. "Roger, Venture Star. We

understand your situation and we'll do our best. We haven't lost a space shuttle on landing yet."

The final approach to Groom Lake was straight over the desert, and it went quickly. The long runway and buildings of Area 51 soon came into sight. All he had to do was aim for the end of the pavement.

"Mission Control," Grimaldi radioed as he watched his altimeter wind down like a falling rock, "I'm down to two thousand feet. Shouldn't I be extending my landing gear right about now?"

"We're going to hold off a little bit on that," Control sent back. "Since you don't have much time in lifting bodies, we want to lose a little more speed so you don't start buffeting when the gear doors hit the air. You're still in the groove and doing fine."

"Roger."

Grimaldi had to do as he was told, but he could now distinguish individual figures on the ground waiting to see if he splashed the Venture Star all over the concrete. If he didn't get his wheels down pretty soon, they'd get their wish.

"Venture Star, this is Chase One. I'm off your nose now and I'll guide you in to touchdown. On my count, drop your gear and go into your flare out."

"Roger."

McCarter's fingers rested on the landing-gear release switches and watched the long runway of Area 51 get closer and closer through his window.

Dropping the gear any time now would be fine with him.

"Ready on the gear," the chase pilot radioed. "Three...two...one...deploy gear and flare out!"

McCarter hit the switches and heard the gear doors open in the belly of the ship.

At the same time, Grimaldi had pulled the nose of the ship up in a ten-degree flare and watched the altimeter slow its unwinding as the air cushioned the lifting body. Even so, it was still falling out of the sky and the impact of the wheels hitting the tarmac took him by surprise.

"Your main gear's in contact," Chase One radioed. "Keep your stick centered and put your nose down real gently."

Grimaldi eased the stick forward, but he couldn't feel the nose wheel make contact with the tarmac.

"More, more," the chase pilot radioed.

Pressing harder, Grimaldi felt the last bump.

"You're down all the way!" Chase One called out. "Pop the chute and get on the brakes."

McCarter pulled the drag-chute release while Grimaldi toed the top of the rudder pedals to activate the brakes. He pressed as hard as he could, but it didn't seem to be making much difference. It was only when McCarter joined in with his own set of brake pedals that the ship started to slow.

Though he was thankful to be back on the ground, Jack Grimaldi also knew that the day would come when he would regret that the flight of the Venture Star hadn't lasted longer. No matter what else he ever did in life, this would remain the high point.

Rosario Blancanales had joined Hal Brognola in the control tower when the Venture Star was only a couple hundred feet off the ground. "You're almost too late," Brognola said.

"I got hung up at the damned terminal," Blancanales explained.

There were no roads leading to Groom Lake, and anyone attempting to drive to Area 51 overland simply wasn't going to make it. Those who had legitimate business at the classified facility were flown in from Las Vegas on what were code-named Janet flights. A terminal operated by the Air Force controlled these flights, and, even though Blancanales had been given a top-priority clearance, someone had decided to question it. A phone call to the Farm sorted it out, but he had barely gotten on the last flight out.

Watching the landing had nearly given him a heart attack. The Venture Star had come in nose high with all the grace of a falling brick. Lifting body craft flew well at high speeds in the thin air of the upper atmosphere. But in denser air, they became clumsy, particularly at landing speeds. The ship had small wings on either side, but they were for aerodynamic control, not lift. If Grimaldi had screwed up his landing, he couldn't have been able to take a "wave off" to go around and try it again. That flying doorstop was coming down one way or the other. Blancanales had sucked in his breath when he'd seen her coming down without landing gear.

At what looked like the last possible moment, the spacecraft's landing gear had come down and locked into position. Mere seconds later, the main gear had touched down on the runway. As soon as the Venture Star's drag chute popped open, the two F-15 chase planes banked away and, hitting their afterburners, cleared the area.

Blancanales let out the breath he had been holding.

The ship had been designed to land on any eight-thousand-foot runway, but it looked as though she had come a little too hot and was eating up more asphalt than that. The rescue vehicles headed after her, sirens screaming, down the sides of the tarmac.

No sooner had the spacecraft rolled to a halt than the half dozen trailing vehicles converged on it. Two of them were full-sized ambulances with aerospace medics on board. A fire tanker started spraying a fine mist of water on the forward section of the ship by the entry hatch. A second tanker sprayed the top of the ship. The Venture Star's skin was still hot from the fiery reentry and the water flashed to steam, obscuring the view.

When the steam cleared, a portable access ladder was wheeled up to the spacecraft, and two men in protective suits clambered up to open the crew hatch. As soon as the hatch was opened, the men shoved a three-foot-diameter flexible plastic duct into the opening.

"It's a cool-air force feed," Kruger explained. "That's the fastest way to get the oxygen levels inside back up and the temperature down. That thing is still too hot to touch with a bare hand, and the air is too hot, as well."

"How about the guys in the cargo bay?" Blancanales asked.

"That's coming up right now." Kruger pointed toward the team dressed in full heat-resistant suits who had just climbed on the curved top deck of the ship. "They'll get the cargo-bay doors open in a flash."

As he spoke, the doors started to open. As soon as they were opened a few feet, another of the air ducts was put in place to force cool, breathable air into the cargo bay. Two of the men in the protective suits jumped inside the cargo bay to start getting the men out of the rescue balls and space suits.

"How are they?" Blancanales asked again.

"They're taking them out now." Kruger sidestepped the question.

Even with the faster than usual reentry, the oxygen-consumption numbers had been close and there was still a chance that they'd be taking bodies out of the rescue balls. And, if that was the case, he didn't particularly want to be in the same control tower with their partner Blancanales.

CHAPTER TWENTY-THREE

Groom Lake, Nevada

Hermann Schwarz woke to a blast of cold air in his face. He coughed and shuddered as he sucked it deep into his lungs. Plain old air had never felt so good. Two men wearing some kind of protective gear were lifting him out of the rescue ball while two more were standing by with a stretcher. He wanted to walk out on his own two feet, but found that he was too weak to stand alone.

"Give me a couple seconds, guys," he rasped to his two helpers. The bottled air and heat had turned his throat to sandpaper.

"If you'll get on the stretcher, sir," one of the suits said, "we'll have you out of here in no time."

Looking over, he saw that Carl Lyons was also being helped onto a stretcher and fitted with a medical oxygen mask. If the Ironman was letting himself be carried out, he could go that way, too.

"Let's do it," he said.

After being crouched in the ball for so long,

stretching out flat felt real good, almost as good as the cool air.

BILL KRUGER LOOKED at Hal Brognola and Rosario Blancanales with a big grin on his face. "Your two men in the rescue balls are okay. They're heat stressed and oxygen starved, but the medics say they'll recover. They're being taken to the sick bay for observation and a checkup."

He listened again to his earphone. "One of your other guys in the cabin has some kind of a wound, and he's being taken to the emergency room. The ER has been alerted."

"Who is it?"

"Hawkins."

"Tell the others to meet me there," Brognola said as he headed for the stairs. Blancanales quickly followed.

WHEN BROGNOLA WALKED into the base hospital's emergency room, he found Hawkins sitting on an ER table having a two-inch-long gash in his left shoulder sutured. It looked nasty, but Brognola knew that it wasn't as bad as it looked. If it were serious, he'd be in a surgical suite.

"Forget to duck?" he asked the ex-Ranger.

"Shit." Hawkins pointed to the inch-long, bloody steel shard in the stainless-steel bowl beside the table. "This is no big deal, Hal. If it hadn't been for Grimaldi throwing us around up there, I'd be okay. I kept getting slammed into the wall, and that drove it in deeper."

"The fragment was driven deep into his rib cage," the doctor explained. "But it only did soft-tissue damage. There's no skeletal involvement. He'll need to be on light duty for at least three weeks and will need to be reexamined before being returned to full-duty status."

The doctor had no idea how a crewman on a spacecraft had acquired a fragment wound such as this, but he knew better than to try to satisfy his curiosity. Alien UFOs weren't the only things at Area 51 that one didn't want to ask about. Those who were addicted to asking questions didn't last long at Groom Lake, and he'd been there a long time.

While Hawkins was being treated, a team of doctors started looking over the rest of the Venture Star's passengers and crew. The Stony Man team was quickly checked over and released. Schwarz, Lyons and the three *Atlantis* astronauts were given a little more thorough check because they were sporting assorted bruises from being slammed around in the cargo bay. Beyond that, though, they were also fit and were released immediately.

Stony Man Farm, Virginia

BARBARA PRICE and Aaron Kurtzman didn't have a video link to Area 51 to watch the Venture Star come home. There were certain things that not even

Stony Man could do. Instead, they had been in communication with Hal Brognola, who had given them a blow-by-blow of the ship's descent. When they got word that everyone was okay, the sudden release of tension was almost painful.

"Damn, I feel like I went ten rounds with Godzilla," Kurtzman said. "I'm glad that's finally over."

"It's not over till it's over, Aaron." Price's voice was low but firm.

"I thought Hal said that he wanted us to let this thing drop," Kurtzman said cautiously.

"What he said," Price said, "is that the American people wouldn't be allowed to learn what really happened to the Venture Star and her crew. He also said that the Chinese would be severely warned about trying anything like that again, etcetera."

"It's the old political wrist-slap routine with no teeth in it. Those Beijing bastards will smile the way they always do, and the minute our backs are turned, they'll give us the finger again."

She shuddered. "God, I hate that Washington cover-your-ass crap. Dedicated men are being raked over the coals by political hacks and losing their careers for something they had nothing to do with. It's the typical congressional response. When something goes wrong, find a scapegoat, beat him to death and get reelected."

Fire seemed to spit from her eyes. "Dammit, Aaron, it's just not right."

Kurtzman knew better than to smile at her. He

didn't feel like being fitted for dentures. For someone who had gone through as much as she had, her sense of fairness in a world that had completely forgotten the concept was refreshing. One could say that it was quaintly naive, but Barbara Price was anything but naive. She did, however, have a well-developed sense of justice. And, unlike most Americans, in her line of work justice was something she could make happen. She had good friends in the business.

"It sounds to me like you're working up to something," he ventured to say.

"I'd like to," she admitted, "but I'm fresh out of ideas on this one."

"How about taking out their spy network?" he suggested. "Now that we have our muscle back, why don't we unleash them on Dr. Lin and everyone associated with him? Make a clean sweep of it. I know that won't put an end to Chinese technological espionage, but it'll stop them in their tracks for a while at least. It will take them time to get new people up and running again."

"You want to help me put something together?"

"From what Rosario said, that will mean conducting an operation in Mexico," he replied. "And the last time I checked, they were supposed to be on our side."

"It won't be the first time we've gone south and stomped on our neighbors, Aaron."

"Just checking."

"Start putting something together, so I can see if Katz wants to get in on this."

"Did I hear my name being taken in vain?" Yakov Katzenelenbogen walked into the Computer Room.

"As soon as Aaron compiles everything we've been able to get on Dr. Lin and his pals, you and I are going to work up a strike to take him out."

Katz paused. "Hal didn't say anything about that before he left."

"The hell with Hal," she snapped.

Katz grinned. "I like the way you think, lady."

"I thought you might."

"You want me to call Striker?" he asked.

"No," she said, smiling, "I'll do that."

Both men knew that Mack Bolan wasn't the kind of man to let a woman, any woman, drag him around by the lapels. But they also knew that Price and Bolan had an understanding that went beyond the purely operational. Best of all, though, both of them felt the same way about justice.

Groom Lake, Nevada

WHEN THEIR DEBRIEFING concluded late that afternoon, the Stony Man team and the three NASA astronauts got together in the base officers' club for an impromptu postmission celebration. Though the astronauts would never work with the Stony Man warriors again, they had shared the danger for a short time and that made them comrades-in-arms.

A dinner buffet had been laid on, and the bar was open.

Colonel Greg Cunningham walked up to Mack Bolan with a drink in his hand. "I get the feeling that you're the guy who's really in charge around here."

Bolan smiled and extended his hand. "Mike Belasko," he said without answering the question.

The astronaut introduced himself and shook hands. "Well, are you?"

Bolan took a long swallow of his beer. "Not really," he said. "I just work with these guys sometimes."

"Just like they sometimes work for the government."

Bolan smiled thinly. "You might say that."

"Okay." Cunningham grinned. "I've been through the plausible-deniability drill before. I know the score. Anyway, I'd like to thank you for getting the Venture Star back. We'd still be up there in the *Atlantis* if you hadn't."

"It was a joint effort," Bolan said truthfully. "We all work as a team."

"What is your team going to do about the assholes who were behind the hijacking? I admit that I'm just a plain old stick-and-rudder guy myself, but from where I sit, I can't see letting them get away with shit like that. They might try something like that again, and you guys might not be able to put it right next time."

Bolan kept a straight face. "That part of it will be handled by someone else."

The astronaut took a long drag on his drink. "You know, Kurt Miller, the command pilot of the Venture Star, was an old friend of mine. We flew fighters together during the Gulf War, and I know damned well that he didn't have anything to do with that hijacking. Since he didn't come back with you, I have to assume that he's dead."

"To be honest with you," Bolan said, "we don't know what happened to him or the others. We were too busy trying to get the ship back to find out."

"I understand," Cunningham said. "I was just hoping that somehow, someone would get a little payback for him. He was a good man."

Bolan locked eyes with him. "I feel very confident that the people who were behind this incident will be taken care of."

"Thanks."

"No problem."

Cunningham held his hand out again. "It was nice talking to you, Belasko. But, if you'll excuse me, I need to break off and find that flyboy buddy of yours. The guys and I decided to award him an honorary set of astronaut wings. I don't know who in the hell he is, either, but I can tell you he's one hell of a flyer."

"That he is," Bolan said.

The Executioner watched Cunningham walk away and wished he could have brought the astronaut into his confidence. He and his crew had proved to be good men, and they had brought Carl Lyons and Gadgets Schwarz back alive, so he owed them. The debt would be paid, and he hoped that Cunningham would hear about it through the grapevine.

At the other end of the room, Jack Grimaldi was standing at attention while two of the *Atlantis* astronauts poured champagne over his head and his Phoenix Force and Able Team buddies howled with laughter. On the left breast of his shirt were the gleaming silver wings of an American astronaut. He would never get to wear them for real, but in this line of work, public recognition didn't count for much. The recognition of your brothers-in-arms was all that mattered.

Pasadena, California

DR. LIN CHU WAS STARTLED when he heard the knock on the door of his small house in Pasadena. He rarely had visitors and wasn't expecting anyone that evening. Flicking on his house security monitor covering the front door, he was puzzled when he saw that his visitor was Carlos Montoya.

Montoya was the Cuban leader of a group the Beijing bureau used to smuggle high-tech equipment out of the United States into Mexico for transportation to China. For him to have risked coming to California meant that something had gone seriously wrong. What it could have been, Lin had no idea. That had been the main difficulty he had faced as a deep-cover agent—he'd never had a direct communications link to Beijing. His instructions from them and his reports to them had always been transmitted by third parties.

"What has happened?" Lin asked as he opened the door and motioned for the Cuban to enter.

"I have no idea," Montoya replied. "I was just told to get you and take you south with me immediately."

Lin had been expecting to leave for some time now, but this wasn't the way his extraction had been set up. He was to have driven alone to San Diego and to have made contact with Montoya's people there before going on to Mexico.

"This is not the procedure I was told to follow. I do not understand."

Montoya shrugged. "I do not, either, but you must leave with me now."

"I will get my things."

"My orders are that you are to bring nothing."

"Can I bring a change of clothing?"

The Cuban shrugged. "Only that."

Lin didn't look back after closing the door to his small house and locking it behind him. He had hoped that he would be able to take a few things with him when he left, but he wasn't a man who cared much for the material world. Everything of importance that he would need in China had already been sent either in hard copy or on computer disks. The most important thing he would be taking back to the Mother Country was, of course, his years of experience with American science and engineering, and he carried that in his head. That alone was worth more than anything else he owned.

A nondescript van was parked on the street with a driver at the wheel, and Lin was given a seat in the back.

"We are going to cross at Tijuana," the Cuban said as they pulled away from the curb. "I have a helicopter waiting there to fly us to the villa at Cabo San Lucus."

"When is the pickup?" Lin asked. It had been a long time since he had been in China, and he was of two minds about going home. On the one hand, he was sure to be richly rewarded upon his return. His efforts had put the Chinese space program on a firm footing, and that was to say nothing about his role in the Venture Star incident. He had no idea what the reward would be for the man who had delivered that advanced machine to the Mother Country.

"I do not know yet," the Cuban replied. "I was only told to recover you immediately."

Lin was content to wait. He had waited all these years, and a few more days wouldn't matter.

CHAPTER TWENTY-FOUR

Pasadena, California

In accordance with their instructions, the two federal marshals that Justice Department Special Agent "Juan Rivera" had posted to keep an eye on Dr. Lin Chu followed him when he left his house. They followed the van as it got onto I-15 and traveled south to the Mexican border crossing point at San Ysidro, California. They were forced to stop there because they didn't have authority to pursue Lin into Mexico. They did, however, go up to the window of the Border Patrol booth in the lane the van had used to get the particulars on the vehicle and its passengers.

Returning to their car, they wrote out a report and placed a call to the twenty-four-hour number Rosario Blancanales had given them. That done, they drove back to their unit, satisfied at having racked up another job well-done. Exactly what the job had been all about, they didn't have a clue, but they'd done it to the letter as requested.

Stony Man Farm, Virginia

BARBARA PRICE WASN'T surprised when she got the call from the marshals that Lin had slipped across the border. Considering everything that had gone down over the past few days, she wondered why it had taken him so long to get out of the country. This did, however, put the finger on him fair and square. If he were clean, he'd still be at the Pasadena campus lecturing graduate students about the wonders of engineering. As the saying went, "the guilty flee when no man pursues."

That he had gone to Mexico instead of going north to hide in the vast Asian population of Vancouver, B.C., was a bit of a surprise. But with the leads Blancanales had developed on his possible involvement with Carlos Montoya and Pacific Rim Exports, it made sense. It also made her plan to send a message to Beijing much easier, and the Stony Man warriors wouldn't have to split their forces. They could all take their R and R together in Mexico.

Now that she had an area of operation to concentrate on, she stepped up the planning phase. Since Akira Tokaido had been working with Blancanales on the Lin surveillance, Price had him continue to be the contact point for the wrap-up. The teams usually kept in touch with the Farm when they were on stand-down, so it wouldn't be unusual for him to be in contact with them.

She also put him on the preliminary recon of the

suspected strike zone. Fortunately, that was easy to do because of the spy satellites that had been permanently parked over Latin America to watch over the drug trade. One of them, a DEA bird, was in position to pick up most of Baja California and the waters around it.

She wasn't going to go to great efforts to hide what she was doing from Hal Brognola, but she wasn't advertising it, either. If he did find out what was going on, she'd handle it then. Right now, she had to get their preliminary information drawn together so she could discuss it with Bolan. She knew him well, and she was confident that he'd sign on for this off-the-book mission. His career as the Executioner had consisted of bringing justice to people who richly reserved it.

There might be more payback than justice in what she wanted to deal out, but payback also had its uses, and it was justice's little brother.

Groom Lake, Nevada

MACK BOLAN WAS a little surprised when he answered the phone in his Groom Lake quarters later that night and found Barbara Price on the other end of the line.

After passing pleasantries and getting the status on everyone, Price jumped into it. "Mack," she said, "Aaron, Katz and I are working up a little operation to finish up this affair, and I wanted to sound you out before we went too far with it."

Bolan knew that the President had told Brognola to let the matter drop now that the Venture Star had been recovered. While that didn't sit very well with the Executioner, Brognola had been pretty emphatic about it. Bolan had, however, added Lin to a mental file he kept of people he would remember if the opportunity ever presented itself. And it looked as though the opportunity was being created.

"Just a guess," he said, "but Hal isn't in on this, is he?"

"No, he's not," she said. "And at this point in time, I don't think he needs to be, either. As far as I'm concerned, he's been doing a little too much flagpole kissing lately and just isn't looking at the big picture.

"Mack, some real good people are being torn apart because of this incident, and they weren't responsible in any way for it having happened. Under the President's guidelines, there's nothing we can do about that, but I think that we can at least send the Beijing boys a message. If we take out the network that set this up, and take it out hard, they might be a little more cautious before trying something like this again."

That was how he saw the situation and thought it was well worth doing. "Okay," he said. "I'm in. What do you have in mind?"

"Well," she said, "since Phoenix and Able are due for a little R and R, I thought you guys might want to take some time off down in sunny Mexico. I understand that lower Baja is real nice this time of year. I've even arranged for Rosario to borrow a sixty-five-foot yacht from the DEA capable of landing a light helicopter on the fantail so you can do a little fishing."

"Fishing by gunship," he said. "That should be lots of fun."

"You'll be going after some pretty big fish, and you might need the firepower. We just got word that Dr. Lin slipped across the border accompanied by someone who might be Carlos Montoya."

"The Mexican Mafia Montoya?" he asked.

"The very same. If I remember correctly, he's been in your book for some time now."

"That he has. How does he fit into this?"

"Rosario thinks that he's been running contraband high-tech gear for Beijing. Probably in exchange for China White."

"That makes it even more interesting."

"I thought you'd feel that way."

Mexico

THE VILLA ON THE CLIFF at the tip of Baja California overlooking the Pacific screamed money, and in this case, it was drug money. Unlike many drug palaces, though, this one had been built in good taste instead of looking like a gaudy bordello. From the ocean side, it blended into the rocks as if it had grown there instead of being built by the hands of man. Only the expanse of glass and the breakwater for the boat moorage gave it away. The landward side had the usual patios, garages, driveways and outbuildings, but even they had been done in good taste.

Dr. Lin Chu was impressed with Montoya's villa. He had been to meetings with the Cuban in Mexico, but never had he been invited to this sanctuary. This, too, was something he would never see again once he returned to China. And he now knew that he would be returning, but not in triumph as he had thought. Shortly after arriving at the villa, Montoya had given him a message explaining why he had been pulled out of California so abruptly.

Lin was still shocked to learn that the Yankees had somehow managed to destroy the orbiting missile-launch platforms and to steal the Venture Star back from the secret space complex. Part of his shock was that it was all so unexpected. There had been absolutely nothing in the news to indicate that any of this had happened.

Usually, the Americans telegraphed their clandestine operations to the point that anyone with a TV set knew what was being planned. This time, though, there had been no prime-time presidential blustering and threatening, no "unnamed Pentagon sources" leaking information and no senators from the Foreign Relations Committee on the weekend newsmagazine shows talking tough about the Chinese regime. This had been more like the American operations of the early cold war years before America lost her guts and surrendered to the concept of government-by-the-media.

However it had been done, everything Lin had worked so hard to accomplish had been brought down almost overnight. He still didn't believe that the Yankees had been able to steal the Venture Star from Quinbaki. Of all of the secret military installations in the Mother Country, it should have been the most inviolate. But even worse was the destruction of the deep-space missile platforms.

The orbiting platforms had been his main contribution to China's space program. The idea had originated in a concept paper that had come from one of the Rockwell think tanks as the ultimate strategic deterrence, nukes in space. The idea had been kicked around for a while at the highest levels of the American government, but no one had wanted to put his name to such a political hot potato, and the project had been shelved. But not before the system had been completely designed and blueprinted in hopes that it might be revived someday.

When Lin learned of this classified study, it intrigued him. It took a long time before he was able to take it any further than that, but when one of his agents got him a copy of the classified plan, he instantly saw that it was completely workable. Better than that, it was also well within the technical abilities of the fledgling Chinese aerospace industry.

The platforms had originally been designed to launch four advanced MIRV missiles, each carrying four 50-kiloton warheads. Since China didn't have the technology to build the multiple independent reentry vehicle warheads the plans called for, they were modified to carry six single 75-kiloton warheads. It had been intended that the platforms would be put in orbit with the CZ-4 Great Leader launch vehicles then being developed at the Xichang Satellite Launch Center. But the CZ-4 program had run into difficulties beyond the ability of Chinese engineers to overcome, and the missile-platform idea had been shelved again.

The concept had stayed in the back of his mind until he learned that one of his top agents had been accepted into the Venture Star program. The selection of Selena Del Gato to be part of the Venture Star program had been completely unexpected—frosting on the cake, as Americans said. There was no way he could have planned something like that. But when it happened anyway, he quickly took advantage of that good fortune and put together the plan to hijack the ship.

He saw the operation as a way to do two great things at once to advance China's space program. Hijacking the Venture Star would give the Mother Country the most advanced spacecraft on Earth, and that ship could be used to put his missile platforms in orbit. Beijing had immediately approved the plan, and it had been carried out flawlessly. In one blow, the United States would have gone from being the premier space power to a subject nation.

Even though Lin probably knew Americans as well as any Asian-born Chinese could, he had seriously underestimated them this time. He had often cautioned his superiors in Beijing not to do that very thing, but he had failed to follow his own advice. Never in his wildest dreams had he expected the Yankees to mount a commando raid deep into the Gobi Desert. Even if he had, he didn't know what he could have done to prevent it.

General Ye was the one who would bear the brunt of this failure at his facility. Even so, Lin was aware that his activities would come into question, as well. He was confident, though, that he wouldn't be disciplined. He had performed his tasks diligently, and the evidence of how well he had performed them was in the storage sheds behind Montoya's villa.

Several tons of high-tech material were stored there waiting shipment to the Mother Country. Much of it had come from Montoya's Pacific Rim Exports operation, but that wasn't the only source Lin had arranged for the goods China needed but couldn't purchase. A dozen other smaller sources also fed the pipeline he had created.

Nonetheless, the fact that General Shan, the head of the Technical Intelligence Bureau, was coming to interrogate him was unnerving. He had never met the shadowy figure, but he had heard much about him. Shan was a legend in post-Maoist China. An engineer himself, he had survived the bloody purges of the Cultural Revolution in the sixties when China's educated classes had been brutalized in the name of stamping out the remaining pockets of reactionary thought. It might have been a politically correct policy, but it had ravaged China's industries.

Lin himself had been in Hong Kong during that time and had escaped the fate of so many engineering and science students in China. That Shan had survived in the middle of the bloodbath said much for the strength of his mind.

Even so, Lin was confident that he would be able to explain to Shan what had happened and turn the interview his way. After all, he was the man who had made the missile-platform program possible in more ways than one.

Stony Man Farm, Virginia

WHEN HAL BROGNOLA GOT BACK to Stony Man Farm, he didn't have to be a mind reader to know that something was going on that he hadn't been informed about. While the tension wasn't as high as it had been during the *Atlantis* rescue, the Stony Man crew wasn't on stand-down status.

There was always an edge to everything that went on at the Farm, even when they were doing nothing more useful than counting fuel tanks in Romanian oil refineries. This, though, had the unmistakable smell of a mission. On top of that, everyone seemed to be looking over their shoulders when he was around. The phone conversations that abruptly halted when he walked into the room and the blanked computer screens were a dead giveaway that Price and Katzenelenbogen were up to something. He also didn't have to be a mind reader to know that whatever they were putting together was associated with the Venture Star mission, a cleanup of the many loose ends, as it were.

He had to admit that he, too, had been outraged when the President had prohibited any kind of retaliatory measures being taken against China. There wasn't to be even a formal diplomatic protest about the affair. The message would be given outside of normal channels and would be couched delicately so as not to disturb fragile Chinese-American relations. He and Price often went head-to-head over things like this, but that didn't mean that he didn't agree with her a vast majority of the time. All it meant was that he was under much greater constraints than she was.

The only way Stony Man could operate the way it did was by walking a fine line between the outlaw world of anything-goes-as-long-as-it-gets-the-results and being subject to political control. Spending as much time in D.C. as he did made Brognola a convenient target every time that line was infringed. Also, when the Man looked him straight in the eye and said something would or wouldn't happen, he had no choice but to agree.

If Price and Katz were cooking up something, he really didn't want to know about it. Whatever happened, he had to be able to tell the truth if he was questioned by the Man and said that he didn't know anything. If something came out in the end, he'd be open to criticism for not knowing what his people were doing, but he could easily field that. What the men of Phoenix Force and Able Team did on their time off wasn't his concern. And if they did it in a foreign country, so much the better.

To clear the field so the operators could operate and the players could play, he decided to make himself scarce. It would be easier for them to keep from missing something and making a mistake if they didn't have to try to hide everything from him. Plus, this might be a good time for him to take a little R and R himself. He didn't know what he'd do with time off, but it might be a nice change.

CHAPTER TWENTY-FIVE

California

Rosario Blancanales flew out of Area 51 on the first Janet flight to Las Vegas early the next morning. From there, he caught a Southwest shuttle flight to San Diego, arriving well before noon. Going downtown, he rented several rooms with an adjoining conference suite in an ocean-side resort hotel and started to set up a command post. By the time Bolan and the rest of the team started to arrive that afternoon, he was ready to go and was in communication with Barbara Price and the crew at the Farm.

After the men got settled down in their rooms and cleaned up, they met in the conference room for a buffet and open bar. For the first couple of hours, they wound down, releasing the tension of the past several days. Being pros, though, they could do that by simply sharing a meal and a couple of drinks, camaraderie and a few laughs. Getting drunk and stupid was for amateurs.

"What's all this bullshit about our being on stand-down, Mack?" Rafael Encizo swept his arms to encompass the spread on the table and the loaded bar. "Hal doesn't pay for this stuff unless we're on the job."

Bolan grinned. Leave it to Encizo to pick up on that. Stony Man had almost unlimited operational resources, but it was perks like this that always got shortchanged. "Let's just say that someone is trying to show their appreciation for a job well-done."

"Come on, Mack," McCarter called out. "We're not newbies. We know better than that. What's the drill?"

"Well, let's say that there's a feeling in certain quarters that the book is still open on the Venture Star incident."

"I thought that Hal would be taking care of what needs to be done through his political channels," McCarter said.

"That's what we've come to expect to happen," Bolan agreed. "But it looks like we're in another political catch-22 again. Since we were successful, the Man wants to let this thing fade away without taking any positive measures to make sure that it doesn't happen again."

His eyes swept past each of the commandos. "I don't think I need to take a poll to know what your thoughts are about that."

Though no one in the room sounded off to confirm his assessment, the grim faces gave him his answer.

"As also might be expected," Bolan added, "Barbara had been working up a little something on the side. She's concerned that a lot of innocent people in the aerospace business and NASA are taking a heavy hit over something that wasn't their doing. Since this whole thing has been put under a White House seal, they can't defend themselves because they don't know what really happened."

"That's just part of working for the bloody government, isn't it?" McCarter offered.

"It is," Bolan agreed. "And I know we've all seen it more times than we like to remember. But I have another concern beyond that. We got real lucky on this mission, but it might not work out that way the next time it happens. Since the government isn't going to send the Chinese a message, I think we need to."

"What do you have in mind, Mack?" Encizo asked. Of all the Stony Man warriors, he was the one who had the least faith in government, any government, doing what was necessary.

Bolan smiled at his old comrade. "I was thinking of taking out the operation they ran against us to snatch the Venture Star."

"What's the plan?"

"Well, while we were away, Barbara and Akira worked with Rosario to try to get a lock on how this whole thing came about. They started by working the backgrounds of the two Chinese-American astronauts and came up with something completely unexpected."

He turned to Blancanales. "You want to brief us on that, Pol?"

Blancanales poured himself another drink before starting. "After a couple of false starts, we came up with a Chinese-born, ex–Hong Kong immigrant who ended up in the aerospace-engineering department at Cal Tech in Pasadena. Among other things, of course, this gave him access to a lot of engineering students who were moving on to NASA and the aerospace industry after graduation. We feel that he was using this personal contact to recruit agents. One of his protégées was Selena Del Gato, the mission specialist on the Venture Star."

"That's sweet," McCarter said. "I thought that kind of academic hanky-panky was out of favor nowadays."

"We can't confirm that aspect of it, but we do know that she was sleeping with the ship's copilot, Jimmy Chin, during their training period."

"The lady gets around."

"Dragon Lady is more like it," Blancanales said. "The word is that prior to her getting her hooks into Chin, she'd been shacked up with his predecessor before he bought it in a car crash. The crash, we feel, was designed to take him out because he didn't want to go along with her piracy scheme."

"Too bad we didn't run into her at Quinbaki," Hawkins said.

"I'm afraid that's one that got away," Bolan said. "But that happens sometimes."

"Anyway," Blancanales continued, "everything that we turned up kept going back to this Dr. Lin and the possibility that he was the ringleader of a technical-espionage network. I had him under surveillance, but he was picked up and driven across the Mexican border last night while we were at Area 51."

"What do we have left to work, then?" Encizo asked.

"Right before you guys came down, Barbara found another link to Lin through an ex-student of his who got caught in an industrial-espionage rap. We traced him to an operation in Newport Beach called Pacific Rim Exports that deals electronic gear to Asia and Latin America."

"That's a good way to be in the technology-smuggling business," Encizo said.

"That's what we thought and, better yet, we think the company's linked to Carlos Montoya, a Cuban businessman living in Mexico who dabbles in drugs and industrial espionage as sidelines."

Bolan took over from there. "Montoya's name has come up before as a major player with the Mexican Mafia, but no one's been able to put a lock on him yet. The DEA's had him on their list, but he's never made the top ten. If he is, in fact, working with the Chinese, as far as I'm concerned, he's just moved up to the top of my list."

It was no news to the Stony Man warriors that those who got themselves on Mack Bolan's personal list had reason to be concerned about their health and welfare.

"It's also known," he continued, "that Montoya has a coastal villa close to Cabo San Lucus in Baja and that could be where Lin is hiding out now. At least it's worth taking a look at. Barbara made a deal with the DEA to provide us with a yacht and a gunship so we can go down there and find out."

His blue eyes swept the room. "This is all off-the-books, of course, so I thought I'd ask for volunteers."

McCarter raised his glass and was immediately joined by everyone else. Off-the-books or not, if Bolan was leading they would follow.

"I sure as hell owe somebody for my new stitches," Hawkins said. "I'm in."

"Okay, then," Bolan said. "I'll tell Barbara we're a go and we'll hold on to these rooms until we're ready to move out. The cover documents for Mexico should catch up with us tomorrow and once they're here, we'll launch."

"In the meantime—" he turned to Blancanales "—you and I will sign off on the boat and the heavy hardware from the DEA tomorrow."

"David," he said to McCarter, "while we're doing that, I'd like you, Carl and Gadgets to recon Pacific Rim Exports. We'll be calling on them before we leave to try to confirm the Montoya connection."

"My pleasure."

IN THE NEWPORT BEACH offices of Pacific Rim Exports, Hector Menendes was a bit puzzled. He didn't at all understand what was behind the message he had just received from Carlos Montoya, but the message itself was plain enough. The company was to shut its doors and go out of business at the end of the week. In a month, the operation would open up again in San Diego under a new name. The contents of the warehouse were to be left behind except for the material that was destined for China. That was to be immediately transported to Cabo San Lucus. The rest was to be abandoned.

Further, all of his pending business transactions were to be put on hold, except for the deal concerning the zero-gravity microswitches that had been offered by the man from Florida. That transaction would be completed immediately and the switches shipped to Cabo San Lucus with the rest.

Taking out the card he had been given, Menendes phoned the hotel and left a voice message for Señor Juan Rivera in room 317, inviting him to call at his earliest convenience.

THE PHONE CALL Blancanales received from Pacific Rim Exports made the team's job a bit easier. Now he had an invitation to be on hand while the boys raided the place. Moving against Pacific Rim Exports before they went south made sense in a number of ways. For one, taking it out would cut the Chinese pipeline of contraband material for a while at least. They weren't naive enough, though, to think it would put an end to it. There would always be someone willing to take the risks to handle this clandestine trade.

Secondly, examining the company's files might

give the federal authorities an idea of how much material had been smuggled to China and exactly what it had been. Technical intelligence worked both ways, and knowing what the enemy was interested in buying was a good clue to what they were trying to work on.

Thirdly, they needed a confirmation on Carlos Montoya's whereabouts and his involvement in this affair. The man had been accused of masterminding a number of criminal enterprises, but he'd never been brought to justice because he was good at covering his tracks. If they could talk to the right people at Pacific Rim Exports, they might be able to confirm Montoya's involvement and call him to account for it.

AT THE END of the block from Pacific Rim Exports, Gadgets Schwarz and Gary Manning were wearing what could easily pass for phone-company uniforms. Their white rental van wasn't marked, but the way phone companies changed names nowadays, it wasn't any wonder that it was hard to keep up. Their pole-climbing gear and tool belts sure looked legitimate and it appeared that they knew what they were doing at the top of the phone pole.

"Gadgets," Lyons's voice said over Schwarz's earphone, "we're ready to move in."

"Copy," Schwarz replied. "Give me a second."

The first to go was the security system at Pacific Rim Exports. Security companies liked to sell the idea that hardwiring your security system to your phone lines made them more secure from tampering. That worked with petty thieves and smash-and-grab burglaries, but not with people who knew what they were doing.

"Okay," he said. "You're free to go."

"Roger, we're entering now."

"Pol," Schwarz called over the com link, "you're up next. Stand by."

"Roger, I'm one minute out and waiting."

Pacific Rim Exports was located in the warehouse and industrial area of Newport Beach, but the Stony Man warriors were all packing silenced weapons. Since this was an unauthorized operation, they didn't want to have to deal with the local authorities if someone reported hearing a firefight. The company's warehouse sat behind the office building and was surrounded by a chain-link fence topped with three rolls of razor wire. Considering what part of town it was in, the wire wasn't an uncommon precaution. Three rolls, though, was a bit excessive and indicated that something was stored there that was worth stealing.

Since the primary mission was to gather information, the plan was to go in without inflicting too much damage. If, however, the opposition decided to get stupid, it was no big loss. The hoods were expecting to pay for Blancanales's goods with heroin, and none of the Stony Man warriors had much use for drug dealers.

With the security alarms turned off, James and Lyons cut through the chain-link fence and were on the grounds in a little under a minute. "We're in," Lyons radioed to Schwarz. "Cue Pol."

"I'm rolling, Ironman," Blancanales replied. "ETA one mike."

HECTOR MENENDES usually didn't like making that kind of transaction at the office. But Montoya's instructions had been specific—get it over with quickly and get the material headed south without delay. The van was waiting in the back to take the microswitches to the trucking company to be included in the last load headed south.

Since quite a bit of product would be changing hands in payment today, he had brought extra guards with him. Rivera looked innocent enough and his story seemed to check out, but Menendes hadn't gotten where he was by trusting anyone and certainly not another player, no matter how small-time he was.

When Blancanales arrived, he was patted down at the door before he was escorted into Menendes's office. Menendes greeted him by offering him a chair.

"My principals have instructed me to complete our deal," he said. "Do you have the goods with you?"

Blancanales nodded. "In the trunk of my car."

"What do you want for them?"

"Well," he replied, "I was thinking that I'd like to get their retail price in China White of at least ninety-five percent purity at wholesale value. I have

208 of the switches, and the retail for the package is 186 grand."

That was a little steeper price than Menendes usually liked to pay, but he knew the Chinese wanted the goods and they wouldn't quibble over a few thousand. And, since he got ten percent over and above the agreed price as his commission, he had no complaints.

"I can do that." He smiled. "One of my men will go out with you and check the contents and help you bring them inside."

"No problem," Blancanales said. His com link had been open, and he knew Schwarz and Manning would be waiting to take out the guard.

WHEN BLANCANALES LEFT the building, he held the door open for the hood to come out. But when the guard saw Manning aiming a silenced Beretta at him, he reflexively went for his own piece. His hand never reached the butt of his pistol before Manning drilled him through the heart, twice.

Schwarz stepped past him through the open door and took out his partner with another double tap.

"What the hell's going on out there?" Menendes asked as he heard the body fall to the floor.

"Check it out," he snapped to his guards as he jerked open the top drawer of his desk and reached for the pistol inside.

Before the two thugs could clear the office door, Manning and Schwarz were in the doorway, their silenced Berettas blazing.

Menendes was standing up when he took a round in his gun arm. One of his guards fell into him, slamming him back against a bookshelf and opening a cut on the side of his head.

"Clear in the office," Schwarz called out.

"We're clear back here!" Encizo answered.

CHAPTER TWENTY-SIX

Pacific Rim Exports

When Rosario Blancanales stepped over the bodies of the guards, he was relieved to see that Hector Menendes was alive. They had all been trying to look out for him in the melee, but a firefight played no favorites, even when the attackers were trying. Menendes had lucked out, though; he was still breathing. None of his hirelings were.

"Calvin," Blancanales called out, "I need a medic in here."

"On the way."

James entered the room, pulling the small med kit from his assault harness. The pressure cut on the man's head was bloody but not serious. The bullet wound on the outside of his right arm was also a flesh wound. When James stepped back, Menendes was bandaged and alert.

The first thing he saw was that Blancanales was part of the gang that had invaded his business. "You bastard," he hissed in Spanish through gritted teeth. "My boss is going to kill you for this."

Blancanales smiled. "Not if I kill him first. And, like you said before, please speak English. My friends need to know what we're saying."

When Menendes started cursing them all in Spanish, Lyons walked up to him and stuck the barrel of his Colt Python in his mouth and thumbed back the hammer. "He said English, amigo. Nod your head if you understand."

Menendes nodded as best he could with the barrel in his mouth.

"Good." Lyons recovered his pistol. "Now that I have your attention, I have a couple of questions I want you to answer. Number one, where is Carlos Montoya and, number two, where did he take Dr. Lin?"

"Please, *señor,*" Menendes said. "I do not know about things like that. I work for Señor Montoya, yes, but I do not know anything about his personal affairs. And I do not know who this Dr. Lin is that you ask about."

"If you know nothing—" Lyons shrugged and brought his Python back up "—you are of no use to me. Adios."

"Wait!" the man screamed.

"Why?" Lyons looked astounded at the question. "If you don't know anything, that's okay with me. I really don't care one way or the other, you know what I mean? But you were disrespectful to me, man, and that pissed me off. So I'm going to waste you and find someone else to talk to who can tell me what I want to hear."

"Please, *señor,*" Menendes pleaded as he looked into the merciless blue eyes of the gringo and saw death. "I can tell you about Montoya and the Chinese."

"Oh," Lyons said, smiling as he lowered his gun. "That's different then, amigo. You get to live."

Menendes quickly recounted going to Pasadena with Montoya to retrieve Lin and drive him to Tijuana, Mexico, where a helicopter was waiting. "From there, *señor,* I do not know where they went."

"Does Montoya use a chopper to go to his villa in Baja?"

"Sometimes," Menendes admitted.

"What do you want me to do with this guy?" Lyons jerked a thumb in Menendes's direction.

Blancanales thought for a moment. Normally, he'd turn him over to the authorities as a drug bust, but that wasn't going to work this time. They didn't need anyone asking questions about what had gone on here. Turning him loose, though, could cause problems, too.

"My friend here still wants to kill you," Blancanales told the hood. "Personally, I don't give a rat's ass one way or the other, but if you want to try to talk him out of it, go ahead. If you can convince him that you're going to leave California and never come back, he might let you go."

He shrugged. "If you can't, amigo, I'm afraid it's *vaya con Dios* for you."

Menendes turned to Lyons and started to talk as fast as he could about how he had wanted to go live with his brother in Texas for years now. The brother had a successful Tex-Mex restaurant in El Paso, and he missed being close to his family. He swore on his mother's life and the Holy Mother that he would never return to California for any reason.

Lyons listened to this impassioned plea with a completely neutral expression on his face. He was waiting for this guy to tell him that he was going to enter a monastery and take a vow of eternal silence.

While Lyons and Blancanales had been interrogating their prisoner, Schwarz and Manning had been busy dismantling the office's computers and files. The computer disks, drives and the contents of the file cabinets were dumped in boxes and quickly carried out to the team's rental van. They'd be sorted out back at the hotel and forwarded to the Farm.

"What do you want me to do with this junk?" James indicated the bags of Chinese heroin scattered around the office. The street value was enough for a man to retire on comfortably.

"Leave it here," Blancanales said. "After we've cleared the area, I'm going to give the DEA a call to come get it and the bodies, as well."

"And—" he turned to Menendes "—I still might leave you here, too, amigo."

"I think we can let him go," Lyons said. "Hector here has promised that he is going to give up this life of crime and become a good man.''

"I swear,'' Menendes said, tears forming in the corners of his eyes.

Blancanales jerked a thumb at the door. "Goodbye.''

Menendes wasted no time making himself scarce.

Stony Man Farm, Virginia

BARBARA PRICE WAS all smiles when she got the call from Bolan about the Pacific Rim Exports raid. The results showed that the commandos hadn't suffered all that much from their misadventures in space. It had been a trademark Stony Man operation, quick in, inflict maximum damage, grab what they had come for and disappear.

The bulk of the information from the Pacific Rim Exports files would have to wait to be gone through, but the important thing was that they had confirmed Carlos Montoya's involvement in Dr. Lin's disappearance. They didn't get a positive location for the fugitive, but the smart money was on his being at the villa, and that put the second phase of the cleanup operation right on track.

Now that the target had been confirmed, Price had Akira Tokaido give Montoya's Baja villa the full, close-in recon treatment. Anything in the vicinity was to be tracked and logged. It didn't take long for the satellite to pick up some interesting activities in the area.

For one thing, there were two small freighters lingering around the tip of Baja on the Pacific side. One of them was of Liberian registry, but the other one was out of Hong Kong. Now that Hong Kong had gone back to the Red Chinese, their merchant fleet could no longer be considered friendly.

Even more interesting were the trucks that had been spotted pulling into the villa compound and off-loading cargo. They were long-distance haulers and, while the satellite's camera angle wasn't good enough to read the license plates, most of them bore American or northern Mexican transportation company logos on the sides of their trailers. They weren't local delivery vans bringing cases of champagne and caviar to Montoya's latest social gathering.

The presence of the trucks and the Hong Kong freighter in the same area painted a picture that fitted right in with the rest of the information they had gathered. It wouldn't be making a leap of faith to conclude that the trucks were delivering technological contraband that was going to be loaded onto the freighter. And part of that contraband would be one Dr. Lin Chu.

California

THE STONY MAN WARRIORS arrived at the San Diego moorage early the next morning to pick up their boat for the trip south. "One thing I'll say about Barbara," T. J. Hawkins said when he saw the yacht. "The woman sure knows how to arrange a first-class ride. I'm almost going to enjoy this little vacation."

Since Hawkins was still recovering from the shrapnel wound he had picked up at Quinbaki, he had drawn the short straw for the wrap-up operation. That meant that he would be at the helm of the yacht Rosario Blancanales had requisitioned from the San Diego office of the DEA. The boat had been confiscated in a drug bust, and the drug agency had been more than willing to loan it to a Justice Department special agent. They had also been willing to let him borrow some heavy firepower, no questions asked, and provide the customs clearance for the operation.

It was a real good example of federal interdepartmental cooperation, and it had been accomplished without having to get Hal Brognola involved. Blancanales's cover story invoking national security insured that it would stay that way. The phone numbers he had given the DEA, involving several cutouts, all rang at Stony Man Farm, not the Justice Department.

"I love the name," Calvin James said, pointing to the gold letters spelling out *Risky Business* on the boat's stern. "You'd think a drug dealer would know better than to advertise like that."

"There's a lot of real dumb bastards in that particular business."

"And we're going after one more of them."

The additional weapons and ammunition Blancanales and Bolan had signed for were already stored belowdecks, and the boat was fully provisioned for a week's sail. All they had to do was take her out and set a course south to Baja.

"Since you're going to be the captain for this trip," James told Hawkins, "I guess I'd better show you which end of this thing is the front and how to make it go."

"What are you talking about, man?" Hawkins replied indignantly. "I know all about boats. My granddad had the best little catfish boat you ever saw, and it had a real good little twelve-horse motor on the back."

"Come here," James said. "I'm going to show you a real boat motor, one that you don't have to hang over the side of the boat."

"I thought there was something funny about the back of this boat. I didn't see a motor."

"The back of the boat is called the stern."

Hawkins shrugged. "Whatever."

THE YACHT WAS twenty-five miles out to sea when the radio in the wheelhouse came alive. "Phoenix," Grimaldi's voice came over the speaker, "this is Flyboy. I'm inbound, ETA zero-five. Clear the deck and prepare to receive aircraft, over."

"Roger, Flyboy," Hawkins answered. "You're clear to land."

A few minutes later, a black Hughes 500 came in at wave-top level. At the last minute, the pilot pulled up sharply and flared out to kill his forward speed. A second later, the small chopper had her skids on the deck and the pilot killed the turbine.

Grimaldi stepped out of the cockpit, grinning as he pulled the Nomex gloves from his hands. "Hi, guys. How do you like my new ride?"

"The bird's okay," McCarter said. "But your flying sure as hell hasn't gotten any better. You must think that you're still behind the wheel of the Venture Star."

"That was a fun ride, but I'll take a gunship any day. You just can't throw a space shuttle around the way you can a chopper."

"Speaking of guns, where are yours?"

"They're stowed in the back where the seats usually go. I didn't want to draw too much attention to myself back at the airfield by mounting them there. There were a lot of civilians hanging around."

McCarter glanced at the matte-black machine completely devoid of markings except for a small U.S. registration number in red on the tail boom.

"You' re right," he said. "No one would notice you in that thing as long as the guns are hidden. You probably started another wave of black-helicopter, government-conspiracy call-ins to talk shows all over southern California."

"That's okay." The pilot grinned. "Just as long as they don't mistake me for an alien. I'm a hundred percent, red-blooded American born and bred."

McCarter shook his head. "You could only be

an American, lad. The way you fly, only Uncle Sam would claim you."

Turning to face the bridge, Grimaldi rendered a snappy salute. "Request permission to come aboard."

"Permission granted," Hawkins replied.

Stony Man Farm, Virginia

AKIRA TOKAIDO WAS maintaining his surveillance of Montoya's villa while the Stony Man warriors made their way down the coast. Aaron Kurtzman was spelling him at it so they could keep up around-the-clock coverage.

When Barbara Price walked into the Computer Room, Tokaido was on duty again. "How does it look today?" she asked.

"I still have that one ship holding offshore."

"The Hong Kong registry?"

"That's the one. I looked it up in Lloyds and it's called the *Spring Rain*. The other one turned out to be legit and it went on its way."

"Tag that ship," she said. "If it starts to come closer to shore, I want to know immediately."

"I already have it marked."

"What about those trucks we've been seeing?" she asked.

Tokaido switched screens to show the color-coded truck markers with the date-time group showing when they had first been spotted. "There haven't been any more since that morning, so that might be the end of it.''

The wrap-up wasn't only aimed at eliminating Lin and Montoya, but was also designed to destroy the shipment of high-tech contraband Lin was believed to be taking back to China with him. Every one of the trucks that had showed up at the villa over the past two days had off-loaded cargo into the outbuildings on the compound.

Katzenelenbogen had also been following both the recon and the progress of the *Risky Business* as she sailed south. While Tokaido had been watching the trucks and the freighter, he had been trying to count the people at the villa. From what he had been able to see, there were at least ten men on the grounds at all times, day and night. That was many more than would be needed for any kind of legitimate work around the place during the day, and the men on the night shift had to be purely security. But that many men meant that there was something there that Montoya felt was worth guarding.

''What do you think?'' Price asked him.

''Well,'' he said, ''the *Risky Business* is on station and they're ready to launch on command. I think we've seen enough, and we'd better do it now before something gets in the way or the target disappears. We have all the information we need to make the strike, and there's no point in putting it off.''

He grinned broadly. ''We also need to get this wrapped up before Hal comes back.''

"You know," she said, frowning, "if I didn't know any better, I'd think that he took off specifically to give us the time to do this."

"He is a sneaky bastard," Katz agreed. "And I wouldn't put it past him to do something like that to us. Which is all the more reason that we need to have them launch as soon as they can. We don't want him coming back unannounced and catching us with our fingers in the cookie jar."

"Or on the trigger."

She turned to Tokaido. "Give them the update," she said. "And tell Striker it's his call. He's clear to go whenever he wants."

CHAPTER TWENTY-SEVEN

Stony Man Farm, Virginia

After talking it over with Katzenelenbogen, Bolan had opted to make a predawn insertion. With Grimaldi flying air cover for them, a daylight raid made more sense. So, while the *Risky Business* stayed well offshore that night, the Stony Man crew kept watch over the target.

"The *Spring Rain*'s coming closer to shore," Tokaido called to Katz, "and she's got her lights off."

Day or night, lights or not, the DEA satellite Tokaido was using to keep watch sent almost the same images. Night-vision technology had gotten to the point that the dark was no longer cover.

"Let's see it," Katz said.

When Tokaido transferred the screen, Katz saw that the freighter had maneuvered to within a thousand yards of the shore line and had lowered her anchor. Dropping the hook like that meant only one thing—she was going to load or off-load cargo and or personnel. From the trucks that had driven into

Montoya's place over the past few days, Katz was opting for a cargo transfer.

"Keep an eye on her and tell me how many loads she's taking on."

"Do you want me to pass this on to Striker?"

"Give him a heads-up and tell him we'll be keeping an eye on them. If the ship heads out to sea before dawn, we may need to board her."

Mexico

THE CURRENTS around the tip of Baja California where the Pacific Ocean and the Gulf of California met could be tricky. It made for good fishing, but small boats needed an expert hand at the wheel or the tiller. That spelled good business for the resorts and the fishing-boat captains of Cabo. At the turn of the tides, however, the waters calmed enough for even personal watercraft to play in the waves.

It was during one of those predawn calms that the *Risky Business* pulled in close to the shore with her lights out and anchored in a little cove south of Cabo San Lucus. The black Zodiac inflatable boat with the muffled motor was quickly put over the side. Able Team loaded their heavy weapons and ammunition into the boat, and James took them in to shore. As soon as the boat had been pulled back on board, Hawkins started his engines, cast off and went back out to sea, heading east this time.

When they were below the horizon, he steered north, sailing back past Montoya's villa. Half an hour later, he turned into the shore again. This time Grimaldi piloted the Zodiac inflatable boat to take Phoenix Force into the beach. When he came back, Hawkins took his boat back out far enough to be hull down over the horizon again.

Now that the teams had disembarked, Hawkins was feeling a little lonely. He still had Jack Grimaldi for company, but he would have much rather been with his comrades. After being dropped on the coastline five miles north of Montoya's villa, the Phoenix Force warriors had moved in to good observation positions and were sitting tight while the rest of the operation came together. Since Able Team had drawn the more difficult opening move, the timing was dependent upon their progress.

After Able Team had landed outside of Cabo San Lucus, Blancanales had gone into town to rent a four-wheel-drive rig and had driven it back to the cape to pick up his teammates and their heavy weapons. From there, they had driven up into the hills as far as the four-wheel-drive vehicle would go. When they could drive no farther, the mortar, RPG and the ammunition would have to be put into position overlooking the villa. Once the mortar was in place, the fun could begin.

ON THE FANTAIL of the yacht, Jack Grimaldi was making a full systems check after mounting the weapons packages on his helicopter. He was very familiar with both the chopper and the armament systems, but it never hurt to double-check everything. For this mission, he had opted for a single 7.62 mm minigun and four of the seven round 2.75-inch rocket pods. That gave him the best mix of high explosive and automatic-weapons fire without overburdening the small bird. Even so, with twelve thousand rounds of 7.62 mm ammo on board, he was going to be heavy until he started using it.

When Grimaldi finished and went up to the bridge, Hawkins glanced to the chopper sitting in the aft deck. "That's a bit of a comedown after flying the Venture Star, isn't it?"

"Not really." Grimaldi grinned. "It was great to put a few spacecraft hours in the old logbook, but I prefer to fly a little closer to the ground. You don't have to worry about running out of oxygen in a chopper. Plus, except for that laser lashup on the *Atlantis,* space shuttles don't carry guns. Half of the fun of flying is the shooting."

Hawkins laughed. "It would be."

CARL LYONS SWEPT the expanse of rock one more time before signaling for Gadgets Schwarz and Rosario Blancanales to move out again. The three Able Team commandos were wearing desert-camouflage uniforms, and they blended in perfectly with the rocks of the arid terrain they were traveling through. Baja could be a tropical paradise as long as you hugged the coastline tightly, but once you got inland, it was rocky and barren.

"The next time, you get to carry the damned artillery," Schwarz grunted as he shifted the weight of the 81 mm mortar tube. Able Team usually didn't go in for heavy weapons, but since the assault needed to look like a military operation, the 81 mm was called for.

Rather than drag around the heavy base plate and tripod that was used to support and sight an 81 mm tube, Lyons had taken a shortcut. They had brought only the tube itself and would fire it by jamming the ball end of the barrel into the ground and holding on to it with a pair of asbestos gunner's gloves. Accuracy was a bit dicey firing it that way, but a good gunner could sight it by eye. Also, all ten of the 81 mm HE rounds they had brought had been precut to charge one, so the recoil wouldn't punish the guy holding the tube. It was an old guerrilla-warfare solution to lightweight, mobile, heavy firepower that had been proved on many battlefields.

Firing the rounds at charge one would cut the range considerably, but they wouldn't have to go for distance or even accuracy this time, just volume and effect. When the mortar rounds started to fall, no one was going to want to stick around to see how accurate they were. For accurate shooting, they had the RPG-7 rocket launcher Blancanales was packing.

When the Mexican *Federales* got around to surveying what was left of Montoya's villa, it would look as if it had been hit by a large force, much larger than the Stony Man team.

WHILE ABLE TEAM WAS moving the heavy weapons into position, Mack Bolan and David McCarter lay in the scrub brush overlooking the villa on the cliffs. After the China operation, they were both glad to be taking on something a little less rigorous than the Chinese army. They had a full Stony Man operation going, satellite overwatch, fire support and an extraction plan. Even so, the prestrike personal recon was still important.

"The man's got a lot of security down there for a summer house," McCarter said. "I count almost two dozen men."

"It's not too much for a drug runner," Bolan replied. "But I haven't seen any heavy weapons. Have you?"

"None. And only a few prepared positions. This should be a piece of cake."

"You know better than to think like that," Bolan admonished. "If he has a couple of fifties stashed in the shrubbery, it could make things difficult for us."

"That's what we have Jack on hand for," McCarter said. "He's good at taking out the heavy stuff."

"We don't want to have to call on him until the grand finale. If he uses up all his ordnance in fire support, we'll have to blow that place ourselves, and I don't want to stick around that long. The Mexicans might not be all that great at rapid response, but I'd rather not chance it."

"Gary won't mind, though." McCarter grinned.

"And Carl might have some mortar ammunition left over, as well."

Stony Man Farm, Virginia

ALONG WITH THE DAYLIGHT optical recon from on high, Akira Tokaido was monitoring the satellite's air-traffic radar and he picked up a track outside of the normal flight patterns. "I think I've got a chopper inbound to Cabo San Lucus," he told Katzenelenbogen. "And it's not on the flight path to the airport."

Katz looked at the radar plot and saw that the chopper seemed to be heading for the villa. "Better call and tell them to take cover."

Mexico

WITH KATZ'S WARNING, Bolan and the Stony Man warriors were well under cover when the red-and-white Aérospatiale chopper passed overhead and landed on the grounds behind Montoya's villa.

"It looks like our man Montoya is having an Oriental guest," McCarter said, watching the chopper unload through his field glasses.

"If Lin is down there, that would fit," Bolan said. "And my guess is that he's from the mainland."

"That means we have two people we don't want to kill. I know someone's going to want to talk to him, too."

"No one's talking to anyone this time," Bolan said. "This is pure message-sending payback time."

AS SOON AS THEY WALKED into the villa, Carlos Montoya led his guest into the scenic living room overlooking the pounding surf below. "As we say here, General, my house is your house. Is there anything I can get for you, or would you like to rest before we begin? I know it was a long flight."

General Shan, the Technical Intelligence Bureau chief, glanced around the room. "I am rested now, thank you," he said in British-accented English. "I was able to sleep much of the way from Hong Kong. Before we start, though, I would like to see Dr. Lin."

"I will get him."

The general's face was expressionless and his eyes deep and piercing when Lin introduced himself.

"It is going to be strange for me to be back in the Mother Country," Lin started out a bit nervously. "I have lived away for so long that it seems like a dream to me. I think it will take me a while to get used to it again."

"You will not be going back to the Mother Country right away," Shan said bluntly.

Lin couldn't believe what he was hearing. "You don't want me to stay in America, do you?"

"No, Lin. As you well know, that would be foolish. You are to be attached to our embassy in Mexico City where you are to continue the work you were doing in California. Montoya will continue to be your conduit for moving the needed technical material out of the United States."

"But that will be almost as dangerous as being in California, General. The Yankees are known for crossing the border and kidnapping people they want to prosecute. If they learn that I am there, I will be in danger every minute I remain in Mexico."

"You will be well guarded," Shan said. "In fact, for your protection, you will not be allowed to leave the embassy grounds."

Lin's stomach tightened. He wasn't being given a new assignment for the bureau; he was being sent to prison. It would be a plush prison in a foreign country, but it would be a prison nonetheless. "How long can I expect to be there, General?"

Shan looked at him. "As long as it is necessary for you to be there."

Lin knew that he had just been given a life sentence.

"You will run your network from Mexico City and continue to provide information and equipment for the Mother Country. This setback has disrupted our plans, and we must make up for it. Your network is still intact, though, and you will continue to work through it as you did before."

Calling the loss of the Venture Star from one of the more secure facilities in China and the destruction of the missile platforms a setback was a joke.

It was a disaster, but Lin knew that he wasn't in any way responsible for it. If he was being sent to a virtual prison in Mexico City, he wondered what was happening to the others who were directly responsible for this debacle. They were probably already in their graves along with all of their families.

"It will be more difficult to do my work from Mexico," Lin tried to explain. "Part of my success in California was that I had access to the best aerospace-engineering firms in the world because of my position at the university. That is gone now, and I am certain that the Yankee security agencies will be contacting everyone I ever worked with to tell them to be on guard against any further contact with me. Without that network to call upon, it will not be as easy as it was before."

"Your operation will change, that is true, but you still have your handpicked agents like Del Gato who are working on the inside. In the past, you have indicated that they are completely loyal to you. Is there any reason to believe that will have changed?"

"No," Lin said. "I believe that most of them will continue their activities."

"They had better," Shan said. "Your future depends upon them doing that."

"When do I leave?" Lin asked.

"I will be staying here until this shipment is loaded, and you will go back when I do. Until then, enjoy yourself while you can. Mexico City does not have air this clean."

Nor did it have graceful seabirds wheeling through a serene blue sky and the soothing sound of the waves crashing on the beach, Lin thought. He had just been sentenced to hell on Earth.

"IRONMAN," BOLAN'S VOICE said over Lyons's earphone, "this is Striker. We're in place. Any time you're ready, go for it."

"Give me another three," Lyons called back.

CHAPTER TWENTY-EIGHT

In the Villa

When General Shan dismissed Dr. Lin Chu to go back to his room, he and Carlos Montoya started to go over the invoices of the equipment waiting to be loaded into the Hong Kong freighter waiting offshore. With the Venture Star back in American hands, the hopes of Chinese space power had crumbled. For the Mother Country to become a great space power, her engineers would have to start to work on the stalled CZ-4 Great Leader launch-vehicle program again.

If that massive rocket could be made reliable, new missile platforms could be put into orbit again and the game would go on. But before the CZ-4s would be reliable, the engineers were going to have to incorporate a great deal of "borrowed" American technology into the design. Hopefully, the material stored in the outbuildings around the villa would help meet those needs.

The general was reading through the thick list

when an explosion sounded outside. "What was that?"

"I do not know." Montoya frowned. "My guards are not doing anything with explosives today."

The Cuban turned to his bank of security monitors and punched a button. "Report!" he snapped in Spanish.

Before anyone could answer, one of the video screens went blank, then another blacked out.

"Report!" he roared.

Another thunderous explosion of a detonating mortar round answered him.

"You told me that this place was secure," Shan shouted. "You know I cannot afford to be caught in your country."

Snatching up a handheld radio, Montoya ran for the arms room, barking orders.

Looking out the window that faced inland, Shan saw another mortar round impact beside one of Montoya's vehicles. The explosion blew it up off its wheels and set it on fire. The Cuban might not know what was going on, but Shan did. He had spent his early years as an infantry officer of the People's Liberation Army, and he remembered what mortar fire sounded like.

The hollow chunk of the round leaving the tube and the flat crack of the detonation were unmistakable. The compound was being hit by a strike force, and the attackers had to be Americans.

Montoya paid enough bribe money to the Mexican authorities on both the national and local levels to be left completely alone to conduct his business in peace. It wasn't bribery as much as it was simply the way things were done in Mexico. Obviously, though, he hadn't paid enough to keep someone from talking about him to the Yankees.

Shan felt, though, that the attack coinciding with his visit to Baja had to be just that, a coincidence. Montoya knew better than to even think about betraying him. But while the Yankees might have come after Dr. Lin, the spy was nothing compared to the prize he would make if he was captured. That couldn't be allowed to happen.

CARL LYONS WAS as happy as a kid with a new toy and a rather destructive new toy at that. With his first three 81 mm HE rounds, he had bagged a four-wheel-drive vehicle, two guards and had landed a round in the middle of a large garage. He was looking around for another good target when he heard the chatter of AK fire aimed in his direction.

Schwarz was helping him crew the mortar, leaving Blancanales alone as their security man. "Where the hell are they?" Lyons called over to him.

"I've got half a dozen men about three hundred yards a little to the left of the garage coming up the hill."

"I've got them." Lyons corrected the aim of the mortar tube. "Hang it," he told his loader.

Schwarz stuffed the mortar round into the muzzle

of the tube, tail fins first, but held it halfway out rather than letting it fall. It was called hanging a round.

"Fire!" Lyons said.

On command, Schwarz released the round and it fell down the barrel. The mortar coughed and another 9-pound HE round was on its way. This one impacted twelve yards in front of the guards, spraying them with red-hot, razor-sharp shrapnel.

Seeing that he had almost the correct range, Lyons inclined the tube a bit forward and ordered Schwarz to fire two more rounds. With each shot, Lyons tilted the tube first to the right, and then to the left to spread the fall of the bombs to either side.

When the smoke cleared, the survivors were fleeing back toward the villa, and Lyons went back to dropping his remaining rounds on the outbuildings.

CURSING FATE and the Cuban's lack of security, General Shan was headed for the elevator that led to the boat docks when Lin ran down the hall to the living room. "What is happening, General?"

Shan looked disgusted. "My guess is that your Yankee friends have come to take you back. You must be more important to them than I thought."

Lin was stunned. The only reason the Americans would want him back was to put him on trial. "But how did they learn that I was here?"

Shan didn't bother to answer the man. Back in Beijing, he had argued for Lin's immediate termination, but he had been overruled by the regime. They had felt that the spy could be of further use to the fledgling space program. It was no longer the days of the Cultural Revolution, but Shan still didn't question the orders of his superiors. This situation, however, hadn't been figured into their decision, so he would act in what he felt was the best interest of the Mother Country.

"What is going to happen?" Lin was approaching a state of panic. He was an engineer and he had never fired a weapon in his life, to say nothing of fighting a war.

"I have no idea," Shan said. "That is in the hands of the gods and our Cuban friends."

Shan decided that not only could he not allow himself to be captured alive, but he couldn't allow the Yankees to get their hands on Lin, either. The setback they had just suffered at Quinbaki was bad enough, but if the Americans interrogated the spy, he would reveal the extent of the Technical Intelligence Bureau's operations and set them back twenty years.

He had been grudgingly willing to send Lin to exile in the embassy as he had been instructed, but this attack changed everything.

There was an arms rack by the door that contained several 9 mm Heckler & Koch MP-5 submachine guns and some kind of semiauto pistols. Walking over, he took one of the MP-5s and several magazines for it. Quickly examining the pistols, he chose a Beretta 92, also in 9 mm. Slamming a loaded magazine into the butt of the Beretta, he racked back on the slide to chamber a round.

"What are you doing?" Lin asked.

"I am going back to the Mother Country now," Shan said.

"But what about me?"

"You, Lin Chu," Shan said as he brought up the Beretta in one smooth movement and triggered a single shot, "are going to stay here."

The 9 mm slug took Lin right in the middle of the forehead. His eyes bulged and he pitched over backward.

Shan stepped over Lin's body without giving it a glance and headed for the elevator. If he could get to the freighter, he would be safe. If Montoya should somehow win this battle, he would come back for the rest of the stockpiled equipment. If not, he would cut his losses and return to China with what had already been transferred.

UNDER THE COVERING FIRE of Lyons's 81 mm mortar, the Stony Man commandos had moved to the edge of the compound. Advancing into the face of oncoming mortar fire was always a tricky affair, particularly a handheld mortar. But by keeping Lyons informed of where they were, they should be able to keep out of the line of fire.

When they took up positions to wait out the last of the mortar fire, Manning unlimbered his Winchester sniper's rife and started to look for targets. If they worked this right, all they'd have to face when they got in among the buildings was a cleanup operation. That was preferable to doing a building-to-building rat hunt.

"Striker," Carl Lyons called over the com link, "that's the last of the 81 mm rounds. I think we softened them up for you."

"Roger. Good work," Bolan replied. "Just keep that RPG ready in case we run into any hard points."

"We've got our side and the road out well covered. They won't be coming through this end."

OUTSIDE THE VILLA, Carlos Montoya found himself a man fighting a losing battle. Along with his two dozen armed security guards, every man in his employ had armed himself to try to repel the intruders. Hernando Grizo, his second-in-command, was doing a good job of organizing them, but there was little they could do as long as the mortar rounds were falling.

Grizo and half a dozen men were firing up the hill toward the mortar crew and preparing to take it out. The gunners spotted them and shifted their fire. The first explosion took out Grizo, and the next two shots scattered the rest of his men, leaving another one on the ground.

Seeing Grizo fall, Montoya realized that this was even more serious than he had thought. When a shot from behind took out one of his men, it brought home the point that there were at least two groups of attackers moving in on them. He was a leader, but he wasn't a front-line battle commander. He was the leader because he was smarter than the men he led, and he knew that he was outclassed.

His mind made up, Montoya radioed for his chopper pilot to join him at the landing pad and pulled back, taking the closest two men with him as guards.

WHEN GENERAL SHAN MADE his way to the lower-level boathouse, he saw that there were half a dozen cargo handlers from the *Spring Rain* standing around anxiously. Since the freighter's crewmen were PLA naval arm personnel, they were armed, but no one had told them what to do.

"Take your weapons and help our Cuban friends fight off the Yankees," he ordered them. "I am going out to the ship to get reinforcements."

Now that they had been commanded, the Chinese sailors ran for the stairs that led to the surface, leaving Shan alone to make his escape.

Montoya had several powerboats tied up, one of them an eighteen-foot speedboat with a 220-horse outboard motor. Stepping on board, he turned the ignition key partway and watched the fuel gauge come up to the full mark. With a full tank, he could get to almost any place up and down the coast for two hundred miles. He fired up the powerful outboard and cast off the lines.

With the big V-8 engine bubbling, he reversed the craft out of the moorage.

LYONS'S MORTAR ATTACK had also been the signal for Jack Grimaldi to take to the air in his minigunship. The black chopper, now hung with the rocket pods and the centerline minigun mount, rose off the *Risky Business*'s fantail and turned toward the shore. He dropped down to wave-top level and racked the throttle to 110 percent as he bore in on the *Spring Rain*.

When he saw that the Chinese freighter had pulled up her anchor and was heading in closer to shore, he clicked on his mike. "Striker," he radioed, "this is Flyboy. It looks like our freighter is coming in closer, as if they want to get involved. If she's packing heavy weapons, she might ruin our whole day. I'm going to try to change their minds."

"Roger," Bolan replied. "We don't need to deal with offshore bombardment."

Since he was coming in so low, the Chinese didn't spot Grimaldi until he pulled up to flash over the top of the ship's masts. He saw the startled looks on the faces of the sailors as they dived for cover and saw the officers shouting orders from the bridge.

In the bow of the freighter, sailors whipped back canvas covers to reveal twin machine cannon mounts. He didn't stick around long enough to firmly ID them, but they looked like the standard Communist Bloc 37 mm antiaircraft guns.

The 2.75-inch rockets in his pods were more antipersonnel and soft-skin vehicle rounds rather than something one would choose to attack a ship. But the freighter shouldn't be packing any armor on her belt line. It was just a tramp freighter with a couple of guns welded to the deck, not a WWII Q-ship. The hull plates would be far less than an inch thick, and they would be cold rolled steel, not armor plate. The two rockets could punch through them without much effort.

Stomping down on the right rudder pedal and slamming the cyclic over against the stop, Grimaldi racked the chopper in a tight banked turn and came in on an attack run. With the chopper's skids barely clearing the water, he started triggering the rockets in pairs.

Trailing dirty white smoke, the first two were low, hitting the water a glancing blow before exploding. Raising his aim point, he fired another brace. These two hit a foot above the waterline and blew jagged holes in the hull plates, but they were too far up for water to pour in.

The 37 mm gun crew had finally gotten his number. The glowing orange tracer shells were walking their way across the water toward him. It was time to do some of that fancy flying he liked to brag about.

Hauling up on the collective to pull maximum pitch to the spinning rotor blades, Grimaldi pulled the nimble Hughes into a zoom climb before laying it on its left side in a snap turn. As he flashed past the bridge, he triggered the minigun pod, spraying the superstructure with 7.62 mm slugs at a rate of twelve hundred rounds per minute.

The link belts for his minigun were the standard one tracer, two AP and three ball military mix, and he saw the sparks as the AP rounds punched through the bridge's skin. As he flashed overhead, he saw blood splattered on the bridge windows.

Once he had cleared the ship, he dropped back down to wave top level, trying to keep the bulk of the freighter between him and the autocannon. A thousand yards out, he snapped the speeding chopper into a pedal turn and came around to do it again.

This time he came in from the ship's starboard rear quarter. Lining up the waterline in his sights, he triggered another pair of rockets. These two hit in exactly the right place and blew holes in the hull at the waterline. As far as damage went, these weren't big holes, but they were big enough to let water in, which should be enough. No captain was going to risk further damage.

Raising his nose, he hosed down the 37 mm gun position with the minigun and followed it up with a single rocket. It hit in front of the gun, but the warhead's shrapnel splashed far enough to take out the gun crew.

CHAPTER TWENTY-NINE

Off the Coast of Mexico

General Shan screamed in rage as he watched the small gunship chopper savage the ship he had expected to escape on. The crew of the *Spring Rain* were from the People's Liberation Army Naval Arm, and they were supposed to be well trained. The vessel was also equipped with antiaircraft guns. But the cannonfire wasn't having any effect on the nimble machine. As he watched, the gunship dived in again, rockets streaking from her pods. Two explosions rocked the ship at her waterline. The fools!

As he turned the speedboat away, he saw an oceangoing yacht on the horizon several miles farther out. He didn't know if the boat had anything to do with this attack, but maybe it could serve as his escape out of a rapidly deteriorating situation. He had to reach international waters before the Mexican officials arrived. Under no circumstances could he allow himself to be captured.

Turning the speedboat's wheel hard over, he

slammed the throttle all the way forward and steered directly for the yacht.

GRIMALDI ZOOMED LOW over the wave tops again, putting two more rockets into the waterline of the freighter before pulling up to strafe the wheelhouse again. He was turning to make one last pass when he got a call on the com link.

"Jack," Bolan said, "Montoya's taking off in his chopper and we're not in position to take him under fire. I didn't see if the Chinese got on board, too, but I need you to take it out."

"I'm on him, Sarge," Grimaldi said.

He hauled back on the cyclic control and pulled maximum pitch to go into a zoom climb. When he reached one thousand feet, he saw a white-and-red French helicopter rise up over the cape before turning and dropping behind the cover of the sea cliffs. It was flying south and had a ten-mile head start on him.

Twisting the throttle up against the stop, he fine tuned the pitch to the rotor to get maximum rpm out of the screaming turbine. When he saw that Montoya's chopper was still pulling away from him, he reached out to trigger the release for the rocket pods. He had only two rockets left anyway, and the drag was slowing him down.

Glancing at the ammo counter for the minigun, he saw that he had only a little over eight hundred rounds left in the magazine. At twelve hundred rounds per minute, that didn't give him much firing time—about forty seconds. But unless the enemy chopper was armored like a gunship, a good five-second burst should be enough to take care of it.

HAWKINS FELT about as useless as tits on a boar hog on the *Risky Business* while a battle was raging both on shore and at sea. There was little he could do but watch the fight and listen to the com-link chatter over the radio. To make it worse, he didn't have anything heavier than his H & K subgun on board, so he had to keep out of range of the Chinese ship's machine cannon. He knew the kind of damage 37 mm HE rounds would do to their ride home.

He had been so busy watching Grimaldi work over the hapless freighter that he hadn't noticed the speedboat when it had pulled out of the basin below the villa. It was only when it turned away from the *Spring Rain* and headed for him that he spotted it against the waves.

When he did, he keyed his mike. "Jack," he said, "I've got a speedboat coming right toward me at full throttle. I think it escaped from the villa, and I know I can't outrun it. If there's more than a couple of guys in it, I'm going to have my hands full. Over."

"Roger," Grimaldi called back. "Try to hang on for a bit, T.J. I'm tied up right now, but I'll get back to you as soon as I can."

"Don't take too long."

Setting the *Risky Business* on a course parallel to the shore line, Hawkins engaged the boat's autopilot and reached for his H&K. It was time to prepare to repel boarders. Ducking into a stateroom, he looked around to see if someone had left some extra firepower behind. Maybe a loose grenade or two. It was too bad that they'd only brought one RPG with them.

CARLOS MONTOYA'S departure didn't mean much one way or the other to the gunmen he left behind. The Cuban was their paymaster, not their battle leader, so they didn't miss his example. But with him gone and several of their number dead or wounded, including their leader, the surviving gunmen knew the name of the game. They couldn't surrender to whoever was attacking them because they weren't true mercenaries who followed a code. They were all drug gang gunmen with prices on their heads, and they had been in the business long enough to know that no mercy would be shown to them. They had no choice but to fight or die.

Pressed on both sides now, the remaining gunmen retreated to the villa to sell their lives as dearly as they could. As they entered the building, they met the half dozen Chinese sailors Shan had sent up to help them defend the villa. With the losses from the mortar attack, the sailors were welcome even if they didn't know any Spanish. They didn't need to be able to speak the language to pull a trigger. The Chinese didn't seem to know how serious the situation was, either, but since there was no way to explain it to them, that, too, didn't matter.

"THEY'RE PULLING BACK to the main house, Striker," Lyons called to Bolan.

"Can you stop them?"

"Not from up here."

"Damn. Now we're going to have to go in and dig them out."

Leaving the mortar tube behind, the three Able Team commandos grabbed the RPG launcher and headed down the hill to join their Phoenix Force comrades. This was the part of the operation they hadn't wanted to undertake, but battles had a way of taking their own direction.

WHEN GENERAL SHAN GOT close enough to the yacht, he saw only one man in the wheelhouse and no one on the deck. When he saw that the fantail of the boat was big enough to land a small helicopter, everything clicked into place. He had found where the mystery gunship had come from and how the Yankees had been transported to Baja. He was a bit surprised to see that this wasn't a more massive operation, but was little more than a commando raid. It struck him, though, that the attack on Quinbaki had been a commando raid, too. It could be that the two were connected.

Regardless, the yacht was now his objective, and he had to capture it.

AS SOON AS the rocket pods fell away from Grimaldi's speeding chopper, the airspeed indicator inched up and he slowly started to draw closer to Montoya's aircraft. Even so, with the head start it had, it was going to be a long chase. The little Hughes 500 was fast for her size, but the Aérospatiale was much more powerful and, even though it was heavier, that extra power translated into speed.

He had pulled to within a mile or so of the fleeing chopper when it suddenly whipped around and turned back into him. With a closing rate of almost four hundred miles per hour, they were nose to nose in a flash.

Even though the Aérospatiale wasn't wearing weapons mounts, her doors were slid back and men were leaning out firing assault rifles. Grimaldi abruptly chopped his pitch, and the Hughes fell out of the sky as the rotors lost lift. The enemy fire flashed over his head.

Pulling pitch, he stomped down on the right pedal and let the rotor's torque snap his tail around so he was lined up with the enemy aircraft. He triggered a short burst, but the pilot had been expecting that move and neatly sideslipped as he racked his machine around into another attack run.

Whoever was piloting that thing was good, but Grimaldi had flown gunships against the best pilots in the world, and this guy just wasn't in that category. That didn't mean, though, that he could afford to be sloppy. More good pilots had died from being sloppy than from bad luck.

Jack Grimaldi went to war. It was as if the chopper had become an extension of his body. His hands and feet worked the controls almost without his even having to tell them what to do, sending the little Hughes dancing around the sky.

He was at a disadvantage in this fight because his minigun mount was fixed to fire forward. It had to be pointed directly at what he wanted to hit. Since the Aérospatiale had door gunners on each side, they could bring fire on him from almost any quarter and could keep him under fire even when he was flying away from them.

There was one thing, though, he could do with his Hughes rigid-rotor system that the Aérospatiale couldn't—he could fly upside down for a short period of time. He could roll his gunship like a fixed-wing airplane and he could do an inside loop.

When the door gunner's fire made him break off his next pass, he flew past the Aérospatiale before racking his machine into a vertical climb. When he had gained several hundred feet, he pulled the Hughes over onto her back and for an instant was flying upside down. Pulling through the inside loop, he came down above Montoya's chopper and a little to the rear, with it fixed in his gunsight.

Triggering the minigun, he walked his fire from midtail boom forward through the rotor disk and into the turbine cowling. The 7.62 mm slugs chewed deep into the enemy chopper. Bits of metal tore off in the slipstream, and a gout of black smoke shot out of the exhaust as the howling turbine ate armor-piercing rounds and destroyed itself. A second later, flame enveloped the turbine housing as the JP-2 fuel caught on fire from the tracer rounds.

When Grimaldi came out of his loop, the Aérospatiale was falling from the sky trailing smoke and flame. The transmission had declutched, though, and the ship was autorotating enough that it didn't plunge nose first into the ocean. A few yards above the wave tops, the pilot pulled pitch and managed to set his machine in the water right side up. He hit hard, but the chopper floated. Grimaldi saw at least two figures inside struggling to get free before it sank.

Since this operation was intended to send a message, Grimaldi swooped over the floating wreckage and used the last of his minigun ammunition to send that message. Even though no one would survive to pass the word on, if the bullet-riddled bodies were recovered, they would show that it was hazardous to one's health to operate against the United States. The Chinese might pay well, but they couldn't protect a person from the long arm of Uncle Sam.

After his gun pass, Grimaldi climbed into the sky and headed back for the villa.

"T.J," he called, "I'm bingo ammo, but I'm on the way back.

"T.J," he repeated when there was no answer. "Come in, T.J."

Reaching out, he switched channels to the Stony

Man com link frequency. "Sarge, I'm on the way back, but I can't raise T.J."

"We haven't heard from him, either," McCarter stated. "You'd better check it out."

"I'm on the way."

THE OPEN GROUND in front of the rear of Montoya's villa had been turned into a killing field. The drug lord's gunmen had barricaded the doors and were using the second-story windows to their advantage. Attacking a building always favored the defenders, and they were going to make the attackers pay a heavy price to gain entrance. There was no way the Stony Man warriors were going to cross that ground without suffering casualties.

Gary Manning had held back on the hillside so that he was a little above the level of the second-story windows. That gave him a good angle of fire into the second story, and he was taking advantage of it. Though it was dim inside the house, the light-gathering scope on the Winchester took that advantage away from the gunmen who were thinking to hide in the dark.

Manning caught sight of a figure moving against the rear wall of the right corner of a second-story room. The man thought he was safe, but thanks to the scope, Manning put a bullet into him and he went down. His next shot was through the big picture window over the entranceway, and it also struck home.

While Manning was keeping their heads down,

Blancanales decided to make himself useful, as well. Unslinging his RPG-7 rocket launcher, he loaded an antitank rocket in the front and thumbed back the firing hammer. Sighting in on the center of the massive wooden door that led onto the patio, he pulled the trigger.

He was so close to the target that after the prop charge kicked the rocket out of the launcher, the rocket motor had barely ignited before the warhead hit the door and detonated. The RPG rockets had been designed to punch holes in tank armor, and even though the mahogany door was four inches thick, it came apart as if it were made of cardboard.

He sent the next rocket through the wall right below one of the second-story windows. The gunman who had been using that window disappeared along with a hundred pounds of masonry and the windowframe, complete with glass.

When he dropped back down to reload, Manning took up his long-range fire again. Under the barrage of RPG rockets and sniper fire, the gunman knew it was simply a matter of time. Even hiding behind thick walls, they were clearly outgunned. Rather than cowering in the villa waiting to die, they decided to die like men. Gathering the remaining Chinese sailors with them, they stormed out, their weapons blazing.

The Stony Man team was ready to take the charge, and it was over in just a few seconds. Most of the gunmen hadn't made even ten steps, but they all would have said that they had died on their feet like men.

"What a fucking waste," Encizo said in Spanish.

EVEN THOUGH SHAN BELIEVED that there was only one man on the yacht, he wasn't about to take any chances. He had his MP-5 ready as he chopped his throttle and pulled the speedboat alongside of the yacht's transom. Pulling himself up with one hand, he scrambled onto the deck. No one was in sight, but he saw an inflatable boat in the water. No one was in the boat, either, but the outboard motor on the back was running at an idle.

It looked as though the man he had seen on the bridge had tried to abandon his boat. Apparently, though, something had happened and he had gone over the side. If that was the case, the man's fate was of no importance to him. But he would search the yacht anyway.

After clearing the top deck, Shan went up to the bridge and saw that the boat was on autopilot. He left it that way until he could complete his search. The door leading to the staterooms was closed, and he crouched beside the sill when he opened it. Peering down, he saw that the companionway was empty. Holding the MP-5 in one hand and the pistol in the other, he started down into the dimly lit cabin.

He was so intent on looking for his opponent that he didn't see the OD nylon cord lying across one of the steps. Hawkins hadn't found an extra grenade, but he had found a roll of parachute cord.

When Shan was halfway down, Hawkins snapped the cord tight, catching the general's foot. When he pitched forward, Hawkins put a short burst into his back.

"Never try to sneak up on a Ranger," he said.

"YOU GUYS CAN COME BACK anytime you want now," Hawkins called. "I got rid of the hitchhiker."

"Roger," McCarter called back. "We're about done here, as well."

CHAPTER THIRTY

Stony Man Farm, Virginia

Hal Brognola was all smiles when he stepped out of the chopper at the Stony Man landing pad that morning. For once, he looked fresh and unharried. How long that would last was anyone's guess, but it was nice to see for a change.

"You're looking rather chipper today," Barbara Price greeted her boss. With the Cabo San Lucus operation concluded, he had returned just in time for things to go back to normal around the Farm.

"Things are all in the green for a change. I think the Man misplaced my extension number again."

"If you'd quit changing the number," she joked, "he'd have an easier time reaching you."

"Bite your tongue."

He took his briefcase from the chopper and headed for the farmhouse. "Did you happen to catch the CNN report on the shootout at that drug lord's villa down in Baja yesterday?" he asked. "It was the top-of-the-hour story."

Price kept a poker face. "Yeah, I saw it late last

night. It only goes to show you that those drug gangs will do anything to eliminate their competition."

That was the interpretation the news agency had given the story, two rival drug gangs shooting it out in an escalated turf war.

"There was also an interesting report from the Mexican coast guard in that same area, too," he said. "I don't think it made the news, but I saw it on the NSC intel summary this morning. It seems that one of their patrol boats picked up some Chinese sailors in a life raft off the cape. It took some time before they could get an interpreter flown in from Mexico City so they could get their story."

"And what was it?"

"Well," he said, "they claimed that they had been attacked by some kind of helicopter gunship that strafed and rocketed their ship. No one really believed that, but they were close enough to the tip of Baja so it could be that whoever attacked the villa thought they were running drugs, too."

Price smiled. "I guess you have to watch what neighbourhoods you go into down there."

"Particularly if you show up in the middle of a firefight."

"Particularly then."

"Anyway," Brognola said, "has Striker checked in with you lately?"

"The last thing I heard, he and the guys were fishing their way down to Puerto Vallarta."

"That's great." Brognola smiled. "Let them relax without bugging them, but make sure that they get that fancy boat back to the DEA when they're finished, will you? I don't want to have to pay for it."

She looked at him, a smile tugging at the corners of her mouth. "Sure thing, Hal."

California

COLONEL GREG CUNNINGHAM and the other two *Atlantis* astronauts were in permission training at Vandenberg Air Force Base for another classified mission in space. This time they were going up on the *Endeavour* to try to salvage their old shuttle. In a series of space walks, they would remove the damaged cargo-bay doors and fit new ones in their place before trying to fly it home. Even damaged, a space shuttle was simply too valuable to abandon.

If it was at all possible to repair the *Atlantis,* it would be returned to Earth intact. If it couldn't be salvaged, though, it would be sent crashing into the Pacific Ocean. One way or the other, it was coming back to Earth.

Not only was the concern to recover a valuable space shuttle, but there also was the Brilliant Pebbles laser mounted in her cargo bay. It had proved to be a weapon of great potential, and the Alamagordo Weapons Development Center wanted it back at all costs. The President had instituted a new Black Project to make a series of laser weapons and get them ready for use in space immediately. If one enemy could mount a strike from orbit, another one could get the same idea, and America had to be defended.

As with the original *Atlantis* mission, this flight was also wrapped in deep security. Again, no announcements were being made, and Bill Kruger had kept the same team on who had launched the earlier flight. The Delta Force security was still in place, although most of the gunships had returned to their bases.

"Did you see the *L.A. Times* yesterday?" Major Flash Bradley asked Cunningham at their lunch break.

"No, why?"

"Well," Bradley said, grinning. "It seems that there was some kind of major dustup at some drug lord's villa on the tip of Baja California. No one is accepting responsibility as yet, but when the Mexican authorities showed up to count the bodies, they found a Chinese-American aerospace-engineering professor from Cal Tech among the dead. No one knows what he was doing down there, and particularly what he was doing with an ex-Cuban suspected of being in the drug business."

"Interesting. It might be that our buddies were at work again."

Belasko had told him that retribution would be taken, and it looked as if the man had been as good as his word. Somehow, he also saw the commando as having delivered it in person rather than by proxy. It would fit with his persona. It was nice to know that in the America of the late nineties, those kind of men still existed.

"I know what they told us," Major Boomer Boyd said, shaking his head, "but that story was straight out of some paperback spy thriller. I'd still like to know who they really were."

"I guess we'll never know, will we?"

He did know, however, that his old wingman, Kurt Miller, had been avenged. He also knew that it would be a long time before anyone ever thought about hijacking an American space shuttle again.

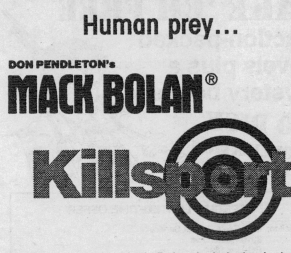